The Abyssinian Boy

Also by DADA books

I am memory
by Jumoke Verissimo

"In this her first collection of poems, Jumoke Verissimo, remakes language beyond mere lyricism to uncover the roots of pain and the passion that will heal it. She addresses communal hurt as a personal fate that awaits an assured balm....This poet will travel."

- ODIA OFEIMUN (Poet and critic, author *The Poet Lied*)

Coming soon from DADA books

A fistful of tales
by Ayodele Arigbabu

"Ayo's muscular, playful language is assured, versatile, and stuffed to the gills with energy and joie-de-vivre...'A Fistful of Tales' is a small collection but it packs a mighty punch... ...Ayodele Arigbabu is a writer to watch."

- LIZ JENSEN (Author, *The Paper Eater*)

Praise for *The Abyssinian Boy*

"Unique style... very interesting imagery"
-**Clare Dudman**, author of *Edge of Danger* and *Wegener's Jigsaw*

" A young writer with immense imagination and vision... an
authentic narrative that will grip the reader. He has not only dared
to dream, but also focused inexorably on the complexities of modern
family and its history in an uncompromising, fast changing world"
- **Uche Peter Umez**, author of *Sam and the Wallet*

"Onyeka has written an ambitious novel which blurs not only
geographical lines but other lines too. It reminds us (or ought to) that
what unites us, our humanity, is much more than those that seek to
divide us"
-**Chika Unigwe**, author of *The Phoenix*

"The Abyssinian Boy not only treats a universal theme; even the
characterisation of the novel is universal. Excellent!"
-**Lanre Ari'Ajia**, author of *Women at Crossroads*

"Onyeka Nwelue is an interesting new voice. For one so young, he
shows rare insights into the lives and sensibilities of people faced
with racial intergration; a concern as relevant today as ever before"
- **Jude Dibia**, author of *Walking with Shadows* and *Unbridled*

The characters in Mr. Nwelue's delightful world move between
concepts and continents with a gentle humor, compassion and
sensibility that will readily appeal to all citizens of the global village
at large.
- **Arun Krishnan**, Author, *The Loudest Firecracker*

The Abyssinian Boy

Onyeka Nwelue

LAGOS, NIGERIA.

Published in Nigeria in 2009 by DADA books
an imprint of Design And Dream Arts Enterprises
3/5 Ogun Abewela Street, P.O. Box 130 Ipaja, Lagos, Nigeria.
City Office: 1st Floor, 95 Bode Thomas Street, Surulere, Lagos, Nigeria.
Tel: 234-01-7451990
Mobile: 234-803-3000-499
e-mail: dreamarts.designagency@gmail.com

Cover Photograph by Sima Dubey
Author's Photograph by Vanson Studio, New Delhi
Cover Design by Ayodele Arigbabu
Typeset by Caleb Prints & Packaging, Palmgrove, Lagos.
Printed by Laminated calendars Ltd., Somolu, Lagos.

ISBN: 978-978-088-217-4

for

Honourable Sam C. Nwelue

and

Mrs Katherine Ona Nwelue

my Creators, for their love and for believing that I would make it

CJ, *for believing in me and this story*
Jaffey, *for the laptop, without which*
I wouldn't have written this story
NK, *for encouraging me boldly to write this story*
Eby, *for listening to me while I read this story*
Ify, *for wanting to steal this story*

For being my siblings, for loving me so much I couldn't imagine

CONTENTS

PART ONE

PART TWO

a story is like the surface of water

ARUNDHATI ROY

PART ONE

29th October, Twenty Hundred and Six

India

1

A Tree Was Once an Embryo

NO FAMILY in Delhi, or the whole of India celebrated Diwali more sweetly than the Rajagopalan family. The festival brought the Rajagopalan spirits together. So, on this good Diwali morning, Rajaswamy Rajagopalan enjoyed the breezy wind that blew around the wildflower sprinkled New Delhi as he drove through the city.

The skies were clear, somehow blue, but not blue *enough* to be cloudy. The streets were so neat, as though cleaned by no human hand; roadside kiosks stood tall beneath tall trees, which as the wind blew, would bend, as if prostrating, and wave their branches, smile and wave and smile. Temple bells were rung and in front of the many ashrams, beggars sat cross-legged, some on their haunches, with their steel alm-plates set before them, chanting *anything* but preferably Sanskrit verses, begging. Girls in saris and salwars leaned by the rickety railings of high-rise houses, on the balcony, giggling and chuckling and shooing themselves. Some of them, when they laughed, would close their mouths with their hands and laugh, especially when a foreigner passed, *especially*, when a black man walked past. They would giggle and point at him, and they laughed again. They thought it was a deep-laughter.

Paan shops were suffused with bearded men in dirty-looking clothes, thinking about Diwali, as though Diwali was the next-big-thing that had happened to Bollywood. A chaiwallah stepped across the street, passed the metro railway line, carrying a rack of glasses, filled with salted milk; the smoke rising up into the air and never forming rings. He went from one stall to the other, handing a glass to the man in brown singlet, who was smoking bidi and collecting a coin, for his glass of tea. The man in brown-singlet-who-was-smoking-bidi sat on a heap of clothes, before the large vegetables, smiled up at white tourists as they passed him and he would say, 'Oh saabji, come buy my vegetable. I make very cheap price for you'. But he felt disappointed when the white sahib didn't want of any of his vegetables. But oh yes, if white sahib want my picture, my vegetable he must buy, the vegetablewallah said to himself, feeling exasperated.

Looking around him, Rajaswamy remained perturbed with the slum called Pahar Ganj. Once, with political motives, he had written in one of the daily newspapers requesting the government to close up the slum. From here and there, Indians attacked him, firing letters at the newspaper company, demanding that Rajaswamy be moved out of India. For over two weeks, letters kept pouring in at the newspaper offices. Sensation-seeking TV journalists went into the slum and spoke to people about the 'controversy.' A young handicapped boy, with crutches, lambasted 'who-ever-that-person was.' He made the journalist understand that if it weren't for one American woman he met in Pahar Ganj, he'd still be crawling on his legs. A beautiful dark woman, with beautiful black hair, sporting a long black skirt and white long-sleeved shirt said that if Pahar Ganj was to be closed, she would not be able to get white tourists to sign the book she had with her, which she always carried around, claiming she ran an orphanage home. If you signed, you gave money. That was the rule and the rule you must follow. Some businessmen in Pahar Ganj - who couldn't read or write English - paid those who could, to write that Rajaswamy wasn't proud of India. But inside him, he believed India was his heartbeat.

Before heading towards Connaught Place, Rajaswamy had gone to the Sri Ramakrishna Temple in Main Bazaar near R.K Ashram Marg metro station. His mother, Swathi, had asked him to go to the swami for blessings. As he was about to go, he asked his wife, Eunice, to join him along with their son, David, but Eunice smiled and said, 'Remember- what you want me to do now is why my mother hates me.' He made his 'what-is-it-eyes' and she continued, 'I don't go to such places. I only went once because I loved you. And still love you, babe.' She kissed him lightly on his cheeks, dragged her son into the study, and screamed at him: 'Go and read, David!'

Rajaswamy was filled with many thoughts as he drove through Main Bazaar towards the New Delhi Railway station. Yes, the day was Diwali; he needed to go to McDonald's in Connaught Place with his family or Little Venice. On the last Diwali, he went secretly to Piccadelhi with his wife and son. Now, there was nowhere else to go. He smiled. Of course, he couldn't stoop so low by taking his family to all the local restaurants in Pahar Ganj. Only people with little money do that. Now as he drove, he could feel the anger of Pahar Ganj, spreading out its wings against him, for writing against it. He knew that if his picture had been published in the newspaper along with the article, he would surely have been recognized everywhere he went. And Pahar Ganj people would kill him. But how could they, when they didn't even know him? He smiled at the thought and almost braked his car when he saw about four heavily bearded men. *These are Jews,* he concluded. 'Hitler took them for granted,' he said aloud, but only for his ears. Just before Ajay Guest House, after Hare Krishna's, he stopped in front of a music-bookshop on the right, opposite a local restaurant and asked the old man - who he knew was the seller - to give him the discs of some Hindi films.

'Oh Saabji,' the old man said in English. 'We sell no films.'

'What do you sell?'

'Only music books we sell,' he replied. He meant music and books.

Rajaswamy sighed and accelerated his Maruti Suzuki into the slightly rowdy street. He drove past the New Delhi Railway Station, turned on the far right and sped through the road that ran towards Connaught Place. As soon as he looked at the smiling faces of the porters at the station, he remembered the time the Rice Ceremony of his son was performed- that is, a night before that, his wife had told him about the dream she had. The dream, she said, was about an albino dwarf who had walked up to her as she sat under the mango tree in the garden, reading Salman Rushdie's *Midnight's Children.* Then, she continued, the dwarf told her that he had come for the Rice Ceremony.

'And who are you?' she had asked quizzically.

'The man who owns your son,' he had answered.

'You are insane,' she had shouted and woke up dripping wet, as though she had been swimming in a river.

Rajaswamy was now walking past Palika Bazaar, when he glimpsed a room filled with exotic clothes. He went in and bought shirts, trousers and boxer shorts for his son and Vimala, his sister and her son, Raghu. As a rich and peaceful family, the Rajagopalan spirits had learnt to buy things in surplus, so no one could complain of being neglected. They did things the right way, but they could be quite hot-tempered.

Once, when Rajaswamy was in the study typing an article on his computer, Vimala entered, stood behind him, started to read what he was typing and then said: 'You are wrong.' And he asked, 'What's that?'

'The Narmada River is not to the south of the Vindhya hills,' she said.

'So where?' he asked, still looking at the computer while he had stopped typing.

'On the west, you know.'

The argument was rife, really. Rajaswamy stuck to his knowledge saying that the river was to the south of the Vindya Hills and Vimala said it wasn't. This went on until he got up and pushed her out of the study, closing the door on her face. Incidentally, she fell down the staircase and became unconscious. Raghu, her son, saw her blood-splattered face and screamed in tears. Quickly as possible, because if he didn't do it, the next place he'd find himself would be in the court being sentenced to death, by his father's friend, Justice Pramod Nair, Rajaswamy carried her, put her in the car and drove straight to Apollo Hospital.   .

After the doctors had attended to her, Rajaswamy sat on a chair near her bed and whispered to her: 'Sorry, dear. It would never happen again.' And he kept to his word. It never happened again.

Rajaswamy was driving home and his eyes shot towards the dirty guesthouses in Main Bazaar. In front of Hotel Vishal, near

Medicos Opticians, he saw a black boy and a white boy hanging rucksacks on their backs and the white boy was holding a guitar. He loved that. Once, when he was delivering a paper at Hindu College under the Delhi University over his book, *Regenerating the Polemics of Inter-Racial Marriage*, which he had wanted Penguin Books to publish, but got rejected, he'd said that the 'immersion of the whites, the blacks and the Indians is a way to quell labels.' He ended his paper this way: 'The time when Adolph Hitler destroyed the Jews because he wasn't a part of them has gone. Nelson Mandela and his fellow blacks have regained their position moderately and generally in the once apartheid-ridden South Africa. and by extension, that's if it wants to overshadow the US, India must make its economy swell by integrating with people of different colour to mash out the most powerful economy in the world.'

A huge Sikh boy at the first row of the lecture hall joined the other students as they applauded him wholeheartedly. Rajaswamy stood there motionless, watching the handsome Sikh boy. But my son doesn't like you, he told himself.

After the lecture, students flooded him with questions. A slender beautiful bespectacled girl, asked him: 'Sir, from your bio-data, we have come to know that you are married to a black Nigerian woman?'

'Yes,' he said and nodded politely, with his sparkling glasses perched on the tip of his nose.

'Was it love that led you to marry her?' the girl continued. 'Or just a way for you to research your book?'

'Both,' he said and briskly walked away.

As he left, he heard someone say that he wouldn't marry a black no matter what the condition may be. He turned and found that it was that Sikh boy. He walked ahead with the Principal of the college. That's why my son doesn't like you, he said to himself.

Like legs leaving long letters, Eunice got a copy of *Delhi Times* the next day and the headline was: POLEMICIST CONFESSES HE MARRIED BLACK WOMAN TO RESEARCH FOR HIS BESTSELLER. She read the story and it read that 'the Essayist Rajaswamy Rajagopalan had traveled to Nigeria and married a black Nigerian woman just to write his best-selling book...' When she finished reading it, she slumped into one of the couches in the sitting room. She didn't find the article real, because it was in India that Rajaswamy met her. And they fell in love. But to a certain point, it could be true, she said, that he married her to write a bestseller. So, she quietly took her bag, left a note on the fridge and took a black-yellow-coloured taxi to see Helen, her Liberian friend who lived at Nizamuddin East.

Helen's full name was Helen Patricks. She had lived in India for very long with her young son, Sunny. She came to India as a student, promising herself to return to her Monrovia-based parents with a good certificate. But her dream was thwarted one night, when as she had gone to buy some pills after a hectic lecture and was returning to where she lived with her Mizoram-born Indian friend, she was confronted by two policemen. They dragged her to a nearby bush and the senior officer raped her, while the junior officer held her mouth and trapped her hands.

Weeks after, she became pregnant. She had to drop out of the University. Then, she was studying in Bangalore and when she found how heavily round-bellied she was, she decided to relocate to Delhi. Months later, she gave birth behind an ashram, helped by some cheerful dalit women. She called her Mizoram friend over the phone and she took the next available train to

Delhi, after a shopping spree. Her Mizoram friend was the one who rented her a house at Krishna Menon Marg, but she was later pushed out with her son by the police and landlord because they were told by the other tenants that she housed some African boys 'who sold drugs.' So she moved to Nizammudin East.

One day, as she bent making chapatti on a stone, while her baby was gurgling in his crib in the room, she saw a shadow. When she turned, she was stunned to see a slightly moustached tall handsome man. She rose fearfully and her hands shook.

'Don't shiver,' he told her. 'I came for good. Please... would you find it in your heart to forgive me?' And he was saying this in English.

'Sorry,' she pleaded, backing away. 'We haven't met. I don't know you.'

'We have,' he said, persistently. 'You may not know me.'

A bit relieved, Helen said, 'So, who are you?'

And he told her that he was the police officer who had raped her. In deep tears, he confessed that since after that incident, he hadn't been able to rest and that he had been searching for her, till his young officers investigated, came back and told him that she was always seen with 'that Chinese-looking Indian girl.' He said he had come to see his son. Helen asked him how he knew about the sex of the child and where she was living. He said that her Mizoram friend gave him her address. She sobbed uncontrollably. From that moment, the police officer- Chandra by name, promised to raise Helen's son.

It was as she sat with Eunice in the verandah of her house, while they sipped from their coffee cups that she recalled this. Eunice never knew this part of her life.

'There's nothing greater than the love between two lovers with different skin colours,' Helen said to herself. 'Chandra loves me and I love him too.' She turned to Eunice and said:

'Rajaswamy loves you, honey.'

Eunice was silent.

'Yes, he loves you,' Helen continued. 'Go back and fix up the strings, honey.'

Eunice, like in a trance, placed the cup on the stool in front of her, carried her bag and walked away without saying another word to Helen.

She sat serene in the backseat of a taxi and only spoke when the driver asked: 'You from West Indies, madam?'

'No,' she replied, her voice so low and soft.

'Ah, you from Kenya,' he assumed.

'No,' she said.

The driver frowned and said: 'You from South Africa?'

'No, South India,' she replied wisely. 'Tamil Nadu.'

'You Hindu vegetarian or Christian?'

She didn't answer.

'Ah, you eat shicken,' the driver mumbled, deeply engrossed with the road, with his fat stomach almost touching the steering wheel. 'Shicken not good for your body. You eat fried rice? Ah, vegetable fried rice good for your body. Shicken make you ill. Mutton not good. You try chapatti.'

Eunice ignored him completely because she knew he was drunk as soon as she entered the car and he had said that to take her to Panchkuia Road was five hundred rupees. She just entered without bargaining the price with him.

Finally, she got home and told Rajaswamy: 'I don't like that article on you.' And he had replied planting kisses all over her face, 'Don't mind the Indians. They like fairy tales. You know how many copies of Harry Potter these pop-corn-headed Indians have bought?' She said no and they kissed deeply.

Rajaswamy drove past Main Bazaar, turned on the left, went a bit further, then turned on the right of that mosque on Panchkuia Road and when he got to the traffic control opposite Delhi Heart and Lung Institute, he turned on the right and gently drove into Rani Jhansi Road. He passed the Gopalakrishna's compound and after it, he saw the American couple the Fraziers as they sat on the terrace of their house sipping from their teacups. Mrs Frazier held a cigarette in her left hand. They waved as they saw him, and Mrs Frazier screamed at the top of her voice: 'Happy Diwali.' Rajaswamy didn't answer. He just drove towards his home. These Americans, he had muttered, think that Indians are mad like them. Rajaswamy begrudged those Americans. He had many reasons to:

a)   *It was their son, Picard that taught David and Raghu to call anybody a bitch.*
        But the most annoying was that:
b)   *These Americans had once claimed that America was the Garden of Eden.*
        And had said:
c)   *That if they were to be part of the American Immigration.*
        This annoyed Rajaswamy the more
d)   *That they would never allow the Indians into it.*

        Something like that could have happened to Vimala when she had applied for a tourist visa to attend a conference in Arizona. After being interviewed by one of the Entry Clearance officers, she came home howling like a dog: 'These Americans are crazy.' Swathi, her mother wanted to know why she had said that and she said: 'Can you imagine that when I got to the entry clearance office, they asked me if I would return to India at all. What makes them think that their country is better than mine?'

Rajaswamy asked her if she was finally granted the visa, and she nodded. 'Then there is no need to howl like a dog,' he had scolded her.

Vimala looked at him and sighed.

Neverthemore, Rajaswamy couldn't allow the American Consul in New Delhi go scot-free when a couple who had applied for visas to honeymoon in the US were refused. In their refusal form, the Entry Clearance Officer stated that their application form had been considered with the documents they had provided, and that they had performed to the best of their knowledge, but they wouldn't be offered visas, under the probability that they were a new Indian couple, who hadn't traveled out of India before and now propose to travel to the US as honeymooners. They committed suicide separately because the over two million rupees they had spent, was borrowed. They just had to die, leaving notes behind. They found no other alternative.

That same week, a young Indian boy went up the Kirti Shikhar Towers at Chanakyapuri District Centre and jumped from it, after he received a refusal form from the US Consul declaring that they had confirmed the receipts of his admission letter and tuition fee to a University in the US, but they were sorry they would not offer him a visa because he was a Kashmiri Moslem.

Anger grew within Delhi. Angry mobs protested shouting slogans with the Moslems in their midst screaming, 'Death to America and Christians.' As anger grew inside Delhi, the same took place in the Rajagopalan House. Farida, the Kashmiri cook looked at Eunice, muttered, 'fools,' and shrugged.

Rajaswamy wrote a long article in a newspaper that interested many people. They didn't believe it was the same person who had written for the closure of Pahar Ganj. Readers praised him, so the government decided to do something: they ordered the British and American Embassies to close down for two weeks. And this was in reaction to Rajaswamy's article, where he had challenged the government to 'play a superior role to let the Americans understand that without the Indians beside *them*, nothing ever works.' In the US, *New York Times* attacked the Indian government, saying that it was 'this same racist act of theirs that made the Ugandan Dictator, Idi Amin to deport over 60,000 South Asians within 90 days many years ago.' Rajaswamy had read the article and wrote a counter-article that made the Indians very happy. In it, he challenged the American government to show what was racist in closing up their Embassy for two weeks to the fact that a visa applicant had been refused a visa because he was a Kashmiri Moslem.

The controversy stopped after two weeks.

Rajaswamy entered the house and met Pankaj, the house driver, standing by the staircase, with the sleeves of his shirt folded up to his elbows. He was as straight as a pole. He was born in Assam and left for Tamil Nadu when he was nineteen. Initially, he was assisting his aged father with his tea plantation - and his sister (who later died in a train accident near Kanpur while on her bridal journey to Delhi) helped the mother on the rice fields. Then, he was 'trafficked' to Delhi, where he made his breakthrough by catching the attention of Swathi Rajagopalan.

Rajaswamy asked him to go get the things in the boot, while he entered the house to check if the salagrama stone had been cleaned by the untouchable housemaid, Basanti. Later, they had lunch of different dishes.

Helen and her son, Sunny, came over for lunch and later were driven home by Eunice who, as she drove past Khan

Market, was bewildered by chaiwallahs, bidiwallahs, hawkers and sellers shouting: '*Kala* madam, buy my vegetable.' '*Kala* madam, you buy something?' 'I make very cheap price for you, *kala* madam.' Oh, she thought these people were insane. But come to think of it, these are just the lower classes, she told herself. To calm things down, she drove on through the tarred streets of Delhi.

That evening after lunch, Rajaswamy told everyone, while he sat in the couch reading a copy of *Hindustan Times*, that he was going to India Gate, and that anyone who wanted to join him, should indicate. Without saying a word, Vimala tiptoed into her room, like a bird does when running after a moth. Rajaswamy smiled, because he knew why she had run out. Quickly, Eunice dropped the copy of *Midnight's Children* she had been reading since she gave birth to her son nine years ago ('You can't read a novel for nine years,' Rajaswamy had said to Eunice once and she replied, 'The book is so big that you can't understand it at one reading') and walked into their room.

  Funny, Rajaswamy thought. To him, he felt that it would have been David and Raghu's responsibility to hustle to join him to go to India Gate. Meanwhile, the roaches of the house - David and Raghu - had gotten the tip of the whole India Gate thing from Farida, who loved telling David (and not Raghu!) And David was happy. Then he told Raghu. They dressed up, sat on the terrace of the house like two huddled heaps of cloth.

  For the first time, Swathi surprised Rajaswamy. She walked in through the dining room and said: 'I will not go to India Gate. I need to make some jam, so that I could send them to your father's younger sister's daughter's son studying in New

Jersey.'

'Oh mama!' Rajaswamy screamed. 'Stop that! I never said that you should join me to anywhere. Moreover, there is no need of this rambling of my father's younger sister's son stuff. You are not a professional jam maker. Are you?'

'I just told you what I've made up!' she snapped.

'And who told you about going to India Gate?'

'Farida.'

'She's insane. Farida!' he called out for the cook.

And she quickly ran into the sitting room aware of why he had called her because she was eavesdropping.

'Saabji,' Farida squirmed at him.

'Did I ever ask you to go and tell our going to India Gate to mamma?' Rajaswamy muttered deeply in Hindi, pointing at Swathi, who had now slumped into one of the sofas in the room.

'*Nahin,*' she said.

'*Kya hua?*' Swathi snapped again.

'*Kuchu nahin,*' Farida bubbled and added in quirky English. 'I call her follow you India Gate.'

Swathi laughed raucously.

'Well,' Rajaswamy continued in Hindi, 'go, get me a cup of tea.'

'*Theek hai,*' and she rushed out.

Rajaswamy buried his head in the newspaper and Swathi knew that he wasn't paying any more attention to her, so she decided it was better to return to the cottage to continue making her jam. She made jam the whole day. Soon, Vimala skipped out of her room, sporting skin-tight jeans; a V-neck shaped orange shirt and black soleless slippers. Her hair, which was very long, bundled down to the curve of her buttocks, and was made into a knot that dangled at her back. Her brown skin shone under the bright scar of the yellow bulb that lit the room. She had

sandalwood paste and kumkum dot adorning her forehead. As
she came out, Rajaswamy could perceive the frangrance of her
perfume, whirring in the air. She swayed up and down, like a
model on a runway, for him to see her swirling hips, but he was
engrossed in the newspaper.

'At least, idealists like Indira couldn't have become Prime
Ministers by swirling their hips.'

'But Sonia did.'

'When?' he asked, still with his head in the paper.

'Of course, you know!'

'And I ask, when?'

'Did you watch her on TV waving to supporters in Delhi
after winning the election in Rae Bareli?'

'But never swirled her hips.'

'Who said she didn't?'

'She didn't, my dear.'

Vimala hated Rajaswamy for one thing: his political
mind. There was no day that passed without him saying
anything that was 'politically spurred' and this was why he had
been looked upon by some of the Rani Jhansi streeters as a fraud.
Even as he talked about Indian politics with much passion, he
had never been involved in it. He claimed he was not involved
because the Indian politics was bloodletting, that he could not
stand it. It was this sort of talk that gingered him to write an
article titled *The Indian Politician, the Indian Musician:*

*You cannot separate an Indian politician from an Indian
musician. Both look alike in their exterior and interior complexities,
babble inexorably about their one-sided prowesses, which they use to
attack their prey. It may not be far from the truth, when one concludes
that the same way Indian musicians tend to copy themselves, is the way
the politicians do and one can presume that it's the reason why India*

still lags behind in its economy. If the Congress politicians could abstain remotely from the Gandhi-thing and the BJP moves away from the strings its ancestors tied around their neck, and then move forward to sharpen things on their own razor! The future Congress and BJP can also learn on its path, without fear that Gandhi won't continue to rule India - look at Sonia Gandhi! The Samajwadi Party, the Third Front, the Left Democratic Front, shall be epitomes, and the immersion of intelligent politicians will enhance the smooth development of a better India.

The Shankar family has played their music, the Gandhi family has played their politics, and it is time for other families to play theirs. It is not only Nehru and Gandhi that fought for Independence. Dadabhai Naoroji, Pherozshah Mehta, Bal Gangadhar Tilak, Bipin Chandra Pal and a whole lot of people did. Why only the Gandhi family? Because they were the first to play politics?

Vimala said the article was nonsense.

Rajaswamy retorted that she *herself* was nonsense.

When he finally stumbled on an article in the newspaper that he found most wry, he rose and headed for the door of - Hers and His - room and was there lip-to-lip with his wife. He shrugged.

'Om Nath!' he screamed and called out to Vimala. 'Hey, look at your freaky sister in-law, Vimala!'

'Congrats!' Vimala came in and said to Eunice, "It fits you well, but you're not going to join us in this, please.'

'I hope you are talking to yourself?' Eunice mumbled, looking away. 'You don't tell me what to wear in my own country.'

Rajaswamy was most intrigued when he saw his wife clad in gray-blue-green sari, with a kumkum on her forehead.

'My dear,' Vimala spoke in her spurty British-accented voice: 'This is Diwali and India is changing so fast. You can hear the sounds of the metro rail, so to help change India, abandon this sari for the better.'

'*Nahin*,' Eunice disapproved in Hindi. 'The day we were wedded, I was trapped in sari, with beads, rings and gold everywhere!'

'Cut that part, dearie!'

Rajaswamy coughed and said, 'I have something too important to read from *Hindustan Times*. It is part of the India changing-so-fast thing.'

Vimala and Eunice listened attentively as Rajaswamy read from the daily.

The Delhi Police yesterday sneaked into a house at Vasant Vihar and arrested three Nigerians and four young Indians suspected of drug peddling. Fortunately for the Delhi Police officials on raid [who could have been accused of human rights violation], they discovered three bags of heroine...

'Hey, we have heard enough of it,' Eunice suddenly said. 'Each day, it's all about Nigeria and drug peddling. What is disturbing is that these reporters do not know that we do not farm cannabis and opium. India does. Pakistan and Afghanistan do. Thailand does. Asia does. You see, those Nigerians have lords in the Indian high society. Gosh!' She exclaimed. 'Next, these reporters will report the same incident, but in different ways.'

'How do you mean?' Vimala asked.

'Raj, you have *Delhi Times*?' she demanded.

'Yeah,' Rajaswamy said and turned to pick it up from the side stool, while Farida entered and placed the tea-cup-in-a-saucer on the round-shaped coffee-coloured low table just right in front of him and disappeared.

'Then read about this incident,' she insisted.

'*Kya?*'

'Do!' she said, persistently.

Then Rajaswamy shuffled through the leaves of the daily and read about that same incident audibly from *Delhi Times.*

Yesterday was the end of the road for three members of the African drug cartels that were paraded at the Tihar Central Jail here in New Delhi. The Delhi Police Chief...in a meeting with this reporter said: 'These African boys have penetrated the minds of the Indian youth and they must pay dearly for this.' In response, one of the suspects spoke contrary to the claims of the Police, noting that 'the police barged into our house at Vasant Vihar and accused us of peddling drugs.' The suspects were also found each bearing a Malawian passport and one of the Foreign Regional and Registration Officers [FRRO] spoke to our reporter: 'These are Nigerians. They are very smart people. They know that there is no Malawian Embassy here and that's why they came with Malawian passports, instead of Nigerian passports.' But their student visas are valid. Delhi Times went with the FRRO officials and the suspects to the Nigerian High Commission on Chandragupta Marg, Chanakyapuri to speak with some of the Diplomats. One of the Diplomats said: 'We've talked with these suspects and found that they are not Nigerians. And none of them could even speak any of the languages spoken in Nigeria. Not even the Pidgin English widely spoken in West Africa.' With this, the FRRO decided to deport the Malawians in a short period to Malawi, as soon as they could raise money for their air-tickets.

Like a wind blowing over the trees, Rajaswamy felt confused. He threw the papers back on the sofa where he had kept them and held up the teacup to his lip and took a sip.

'Are you ready now?' Rajaswamy asked.

'Yeah!' Eunice responded.

'No,' Vimala protested. 'You're not going to wear this and follow us, dearie!'

'Who said that?' Eunice asked and was now at the door, her purse now hanging between her elbows.

'*Tum!*'

'You missed out,' she said and was out of sight.

Vimala turned to Rajaswamy and complained bitterly in Tamil: 'Your wife is stubborn. How could you have married a stubborn black woman?'

'You are also a black woman!'

'Brown, to be precise.'

He whispered to her: 'I hope she didn't hear what you just said, rabbit.'

'No.'

'Silly lawyer'.

'I'm not going with you again,' Vimala said, as he picked up his car-key from the centre table.

And he widened his eyes in surprise. 'And who asked you to follow us?'

As soon as he said that, he was out of the room and was surprised to see David and Raghu at the front seat of the car, when he got to the garage.

'*Kya hua*?' he asked. 'Where are you going to?'

'To India Gate,' they replied and before he could say anything, they added: 'To see Bill Gates!'

Then everyone laughed - that was Eunice and Rajaswamy. They were the *everyone.*

Vimala walked quickly to the car, opened one of its doors and entered the back seat. Rajaswamy smiled and entered the car. Eunice entered.

Pankaj opened the gate and Rajaswamy drove out

You could see the beauties of India if you went to Kashmir, saw the Taj Mahal at Agra or stayed at the foothills of the Himalaya Mountains, but Rajaswamy believed that Khan Market was better than those places. Therefore, he decided to drive to Khan Market first, while the streets were crowded, with shoppers and autorickshawallahs thrusting their hands in the air for passengers, screaming their destinations: Patel Nagar, Darya Ganj, Rabindra Road, Ring Road. Through the window, David saw Delhi smiling at him, waving at him, making him feel jealous. He saw girls in saris, standing by the balconies of high-rise houses and thought they were gossiping with Kavitha's name. He cursed them, from within. As Rajaswamy steered the car, David and Raghu burst into a Hindi song, which Mr. Choudhury had taught them few days ago, when they were told Bill Gates was visiting India to donate to some charity.

We are heading for India Gate
To see the filthy wanderer, Bill Gates
He doesn't bath and has the teeth of a monkey
And as usual, he wants a lot of money

Vimala thought they were stupid for singing such lines. She didn't see any reason why David and Raghu should say that Bill Gates had the teeth of a monkey. And if he did, she couldn't tell how they knew. They had never seen Bill Gates, she thought.

We wouldn't like to see that Bill Gates
Wandering and screaming around India Gate

'Shut up!' Vimala howled at them. 'You two!'

And they stopped.

Vimala,' Rajaswamy said in Tamil, 'the way you hush these children isn't good.'

'Why not?' she said, leaning her head against the headrest. 'You are an anti-American who, I am sure, inundates these kids with filthy things about America.'

'American patriot!' he mumbled.

'Why shouldn't I be?' she asked. 'You have always nestled this hatred in your mind for the Americans. Mr Warren Frazier who lives just opposite us is not your friend.'

'That's because I don't want to be his friend,' he argued. 'He doesn't like the Indians either.'

'You just lied!'

'He doesn't.'

'And did he say that?'

'Then did I say I'm anti-American?'

'From your actions!'

'You are judgmental,' Rajaswamy said to her. 'You are just like *your* father.'

No one spoke again, not even David and Raghu until they got to Khan Market.

Rajaswamy drove into the car park, near Café Zoffiro. He halted the car and they got down from it. Vimala was much amazed and said: 'But this is not India Gate, Mr. Guide!' Rajaswamy was quiet as he locked his car and started towards the market. 'We are heading up for Anokhi.' As soon as Vimala heard this, she sashayed towards them, laughing and people turned and glared at her.

'You kid!' Eunice teased her.

'You Indian village girl!' she teased back and added

jeeringly, 'See how you are limping in that sari. Do you even have such things in your Africa?'

Astonished, Rajaswamy turned to her with his *you-are-very-stupid-and-hopeless* eyes. He stopped halfway into the building. Eunice understood. She knew that Rajaswamy could smack Vimala because Vimala had told her that even though she was a mother, Rajaswamy still smacked her in public. As he stood motionless - like he had done in that lecture hall - he thought of what to say and said in Malayalam: "You can't even hold your mouth, still you claim you are a third culture kid, right? It's not fair. Try to hold your tongue, Vimala".

Eunice felt a bit left out when Rajaswamy spoke in Malayalam. David thought Malayalam was a 'brew-tea-fool' language.

Now, they were in *Men's*, a spontaneous eatery joint just above Anokhi. They sat round a well-laid puny table and everyone ordered something to eat. Rajaswamy ordered for a cup of coffee; Eunice sandwiches; Vimala- avocado salad, while David and Raghu had Irish ice-cream buds. It later occurred to Vimala that here was where she met the man who deflowered her. Almost ten years ago, she was in the same place (but not in Men's) and was sitting with her friend, Anu, when three men - two Indians and a white kept smirking at them, as they sipped from their cup of tea. She remembered what the other Indian (who probably was the other men's guide) asked his fellow Indian, 'So you live in London country?' And they laughed. Not so relative anyway, Vimala's eyes met that of the Indian sitting just very close to the white. He made a face and she smiled. Anu smiled. Anu thought Vimala had started liking the man. She sighed.

Years later, after she married that man, even though there

was no tussle over the man being an Indian Christian born in Britain when she found out that the white man was her husband's gay partner, she divorced him.

He can't be gay, Vimala thought as she looked at her son suck on his ice-cream. And even if he is, I won't stop loving him. Swathi said that only deaf Indians heard such and didn't scorn it. She detested the times her daughter raised talks about her ex-husband. 'AIDS husband,' Swathi would say and give out a great homophobic laughter. She regretted each expense she had made to have Vimala study in England. To her, she believed that the *whole* British life had eaten deep into the fabric of her daughter's life. She no more wore saris or salwar-kameez. She never went to the ashram to pray again. That was her own headache, Vimala would say.

Finally, they drove out of Khan Market.

And headed for India Gate.

India Gate was very over-crowded. Every Delhiite who knew India Gate during Diwali believed that it surpassed the Golden Temple. But the fact remained that Rajaswamy had brought them to the right spot. The sky was lurid; the stars were bluntly appearing, making waves inexorably. The five of them walked in and the blossoming lights glistened so gloriously that it seemed like an Egyptian Pharoah's palace had been lighted during a festival of lights.

'Mum,' David said, pointing at about five black boys who had gathered in a circle, sitting comfortably on the green grass. 'Look at those people.'

Eunice turned and saw them. 'Yes, I have seen them.'

Now, they walked past happy families, screaming children, firework displaying uniformed boys, and some sensation-seeking journalists, while Japanese (maybe Chinese) tourists chortled in different languages.

'Delhi has it all,' Vimala concluded as they lowered themselves near the black boys.

'Of course, Delhi does,' Eunice added.

2

The Thinking Black Prince

DAVID WAS in his room. The air of Diwali was still around. And he felt such a seething wound in his deep skin, for being born to a chocolate-skinned mother who swore that her son wasn't going to 'absorb' all Indian names. Because he was nine years old, he believed he knew what was good and what was bad. Period.

He felt isolated in the midst of his friends, his classmates and family. He was drabbled between two worlds, so he knew that his world wasn't a simple one at all. Others had Indian fathers and Indian mothers, but he, so unfortunate, believed he was unfortunate to have a Nigerian mother.

Before his birth, his grandfather had had the same feeling: 'Those drug-peddlers! I can't believe my son is getting one into this house,' Justice Anantha Rajagopalan, his grandfather, had said, when he overheard Rajaswamy saying he was getting married to Eunice (the daughter of the then Diplomat at the Nigerian High Commission in New Delhi)

But to David, having an Indian father was also ridiculous. Brown and black

Soft hair and thick hair.

He jumped into his bed in the posh Rajagopalan House. Roof-tops and airy winds, but nothing stopped David from thinking about his identity. He coughed, so subtle and incongruous. 'How could I have brown blood running with black blood in me?' He soliloquized. Yet, no one could tell him why. But to an extent there was a reason to be told. A puny reason, maybe, one that would have broken his heart.

Nevethemore, the Rajagopalan House was a house of terror. Windowpanes could talk when they wanted, birds could sing and trees could whisper when thunder rumbled. That was a trouble-house. Not that every other person could hear them, except David, who even opened his windowsills to talk to the noisy monkeys, parading at the treetops.

Yet, the Rajagopalan House was heaven.

Built in a sordid English style, it looked sweet and fashionable with brand new French furniture. Four rooms on the top, three down. And David had his room, on top, self-contained.

'A black prince,' his mother had once called him. But his father argued that he wasn't. He was an Indian, a Maharaja. His identity continued to trouble him. He knew that he was either a ghost, or maybe, a scoundrel. He was mad at himself, at his mother, at his father, even at Swathi, his Indian grandmother, who never stopped using the phrase: 'Doing now?' In her pale bluish glasses, as fat as she was, she still cat-walked.

She dreamt of being Priyanka Chopra.

David felt alienated in that house. He couldn't even talk to his cousin, Raghu, without feeling that the young boy might think he was one of those kids from Africa who were shown dying of hunger on the television. And Vimala was to him, a not-a-good lady who thinks that she can live the life Paris Hilton is living. Not even in a single day. She had her room down the house, and all the study had been left for her.

'Mummy,' David had once demanded to know, 'why does Aunt Vimala own the study all to herself?'

'You ask too many questions, Dave,' his mother had replied. 'Don't you think she should feel comfortable for one single day? She is a lawyer and needs a large place to practice her law, alright?'

'Whatever,' he sneered,' but she should know that this is not her husband's house.'

Vimala was divorced from her husband who lived in London ('We aren't separated, we're divorced,' she would say) Her husband, a Christian, had traveled back to London after their son's birth and that was it. Years later, she was on a holiday trip and found her husband, in bed, with another man. And she asked for a divorce to get things over her head. For the sake of their son, Raghu, she scooped on vodka and Kingfisher beer and began to drink heavily.

Nothing mattered much to Vimala though. She was comfortable with all that she had. She had a Toyota car (which Raghu had said he would drive when he clocked eighteen) Yes, people clocked in years, like clocks do. And she had the kind of row of clients that gushed her. 'You are such a brilliant a lawyer,' one of her well-to-do clients had said to her, knees on the ground, in the sitting room, at a certain time. But to her, she was just like any other lawyer out there, who could get to the court. And mess up. Or mess down. True, she practiced Her Law, because that was Her Cause - her study was filled with fearfully thick Law Books. Even compiled versions of Sydney Sheldon's books. 'He's a crime fiction writer and we deal with criminals everyday,' Vimala had said when the trouble-minded inquisitive David demanded to know.

As he thought of his identity, a knock sounded on the door: *Kpoi! Kpoi!!*

'Yes, come in.'

The door hung open, Farida walked in, carrying a tray of vegetable fried rice with a tumbler of lemon juice. She placed it on a table, facing the long ruby-framed mirror, looked around the room, looking so stout, with her brown-coloured sari-knotted so strongly around her.

'Hey, Farida,' David got angry. 'What are you looking for?'

'For nothing?' That was a question, but wasn't meant to be.

Farida was a middle-aged Kashmiri Moslem woman, who was employed into the Rajagopalan House to let the spirits have a taste of some of the Kashmiri delicacies. Well, to David, there wasn't anything too special in what she cooked.

Her stature was like one of these Pygmies in the Congo, and it terrified David.

'She might come from Africa,' Raghu had once whispered to David, on a certain day, as they sat playing in the garden facing the bungalow house, just opposite the cottage where Swathi went to make jams. Jams for toast. Jams and juices, Swathi did all that because she could do them. Outrightly.

'Then go,' he told Farida, who was now standing by the door.

'Yes, going?' she repeated, and fled, banging the door after her.

'That woman is a bitch!' David protested, and gently pulled the window by his bed head open and looked out onto the serene street.

Rani Jhansi Road, by the Delhi Heart and Lung Institute was really a haven. Like a fenced and gated fortress, the street was quiet, and the houses, the six on the left and the five on the right, looked so still. Trees lined the street and it seemed that old people were only the ones that lived there, because in the evenings, you could see them rushing out of their houses and strolling down the lanes. Some with walking sticks and some, holding onto their hips. Feeling tired and gritty. But that wasn't all that David saw at that time as he watched the panorama from the window. He also saw other houses, which were brown-bricked. Then the tall Metro railway line. Even as the street was a quiet one, the sound of the Metro station abraded people's brains. Ooh! It really devastated David's brains, and the more he lived up on the high-rise house, the more it worsened the issue because he couldn't sleep till 10pm, when the station had closed for the day.

Now, David thought of his grandfather, whom he had never met, as though he was a ghost haunting him.

Justice Anantha Rajagopalan was (before his retirement) a great judge, and presided over the cases of crimes filed at the Delhi High Court. It was a wonderful experience for him because he ended up being harsh. And Saturdays were the days he reveled in, banging the hammer on the desk, over the 'filthy' lawyers (that couldn't speak English in courts) who were to defend some helpless inmates from the Tihar Central Jail. To him, those lawyers were cheap. They couldn't perform. They couldn't do what his daughter, Vimala, could do in courts. He thought of them as 'filthy.' He knew, because someone had told him that those lawyers went to the jails to beg those inmates to buy them as their lawyers. That was ridiculous because he saw and perceived such an approach as hopeless.

Rajagopalan was an alumnus of St. Stephen's College under the Delhi University and he was overly proud of that.

Like a moth, spying over a beetle, he couldn't agree with

his son getting married to an African. He saw them as hungry and helpless. Still, when David's Nigerian grandfather (his mother's father) Onwubiko Udoka was the First Secretary at the Nigerian High Commission in New Delhi, and invited him over to the Nigeria House for, maybe, Independence Day Celebration dinner, he came in a suit, because he despised Indian traditional clothing very much, and a tie. And while the celebration and all the eatables and drinkables went on, he chatted up with some of the diplomats, and moved intimately with Onwubiko.

But things changed in one day, when he introduced his only son, Rajaswamy to Onwubiko, who in turn introduced his only daughter, Eunice to them. And the two thought that it would be alright to be *one*.

First, they fell in love.

Second, they fell in bed.

But they had strong rules they were going to hold on to. And these rules were the ones that changed their lives. For Good. For Bad. For Better. For Worse.

1)   *Overlook your skin colour.*

2)   *Look deep into your heart.*

3)   *Don't listen to gossips.*

4)   *Tell your parents what you are doing.*

5)   *And trap them with a baby.*

They decided to hide the word 'pregnancy' because they thought it was insane to be written like that. Practically, the rules worked for them.

As they traveled together through the metro, from the R.K Ashram Marg to Chanakyapuri, when Rajaswamy accompanied Eunice back home to the Nigeria House, where some of the diplomats lived, passengers in the train giggled. That got Rajaswamy enraged. He summed that the Indians didn't know how to behave.

'But,' he would suggest to Eunice, 'these are the lower classes and they know nothing.'

And she would nod.

But things went out of hand the day they were sitting opposite each other inside Coffee Café at Rajouri Garden and a 'randy' short Indian man walked up to them and stared into Eunice's eyes, thereafter he muttered to her, touching her hair: 'Your hair, like foam!' And things couldn't calm down that fateful day. Rajaswamy hissed into the air and in few seconds, he rammed some heavy blows on the defenseless man, who squatted and then took to his heels. He felt really embarrassed and left the café immediately with her.

It wasn't as though Onwubiko felt inferior to Rajagopalan, but the issue was that, since Vimala was the Embassy's appointed lawyer, he wanted to be closer to the Rajagopalan Family, and he did as much as he could for that to happen.

Few nights went by and mornings came, before Eunice's mother found her throwing up into the sink in the bathroom. *Is she pregnant? Who could be responsible?* Eunice was blunt and truthful. Neither her mother nor her father screamed at her. The pregnancy was from a responsible family, so they thought, but unknown to them, the monster that had swept their daughter's legs off the ground, right into the bed, was already prepared to wed.

'Look, Eunice,' her father stood over the counter, at the bar in his parlour, with a shot of whisky in his hand. 'It's not as though I don't like your relationship with Rajaswamy. But the truth is that I don't like the Indians…'

He'd paused and taken a sip.

'Yes,' her mother had said. 'I don't like them either. And for sure, I knew that Rajaswamy was at something. Now that he has got you pregnant, I wonder where he is hiding his head.'

'He's not hiding his head,' Eunice had defended. 'We love each other and…'

'*Mechie onu gi*, Eunice,' her mother had screamed in Igbo. 'I said, shut your mouth! These Indians think of us as hungry and think they are superior to us.'

'No woman,' Onwubiko had cautioned. 'You don't say "us", say "you". They aren't superior to me. Not even Justice Anantha.'

Still, Onwubiko brought himself down.

It was the age at which he traveled to England as a Diplomat that flabbergasted the people.

There, Onwubiko recounted what he saw while in England, how he had saved an Indian girl named Indrani who lived on Brick Lane with her parents. Indrani had told her parents over the phone: 'There's this guy who saved me yesterday when the redheads attacked me.' And they asked her to bring him over for lunch to thank him. Drums drummed differently when Indrani's parents found that 'this guy' was an African with a chocolate skin. Therefore, they deserted the dinning table for the two. Onwubiko understood what had happened.

Like riddles riding rude rats, Indrani's father asked the house cleaner to clear the table after they had finished eating, 'and throw the plate that *the outsider* has used into the bin.'

When Onwubiko heard this, it ignited his hatred for the

Indians

'I understand your feelings,' Eunice had said softly.

Still, Onwubiko agreed to her getting married to Rajaswamy. He gave his blessings, and waited to see how Anantha would react when he would hear about his son getting ready to marry his daughter.

It was when Rajaswamy told his mother about his intention, of getting married to Eunice, that Anantha overheard this and said, 'Those drug-peddlers! I can't believe my son is getting one into this house.' But Swathi retaliated. 'What's wrong with them?' she asked. 'That you preside over cases of some jobless youths from Africa who come here and get themselves into crime, it does not mean you have to generalize … '

'But these are poor blacks.'

'Not all blacks are poor, you know that,' Swathi became so wild that she would have knocked the sense out of Anantha.

'Many are,' Justice Anantha argued. 'I have been to Africa, woman!'

'When, Mr. Justice?' she shooed him. 'When? Since we have been married or before?'

'I have read about them. '

'Cut that crap!'

'This,' he paused, 'all I know is that I wouldn't want my son to get cobwebbed into African untouchability. Remember, he is our only son '

'Then he needs your blessings,' Swathi swirled.

But Anantha couldn't. He carried his suitcases into his car and sped off that midnight, swearing never to come back.

David watched from the window and remembered that Farida had placed his food on the table, and he gently pushed the chair towards it and began to eat. He spooned the rice slowly and turned up to look at himself in the mirror.

'Farida is bad,' he said to the David in the mirror. 'How can she think *you* would eat this vegetarian food?'

Then there was a knock on the door. He gasped. Farida is listening. She is around. *Kpoi, kpoi, kpoi.* Stop that Farida, because you have given me bunkum.

And the door flung open.

'Ah, Raghu!' he said, somewhat surprised.

'You were taking long time to answer the door,' Raghu said, not asking a question.

'Farida was knocking, that's why.'

'Where, Farida?'

'Just downstairs. '

'Alright,' he said. 'But you know that Farida is a bitch?'

David looked around and smiled. 'If you ask my food, it will tell you that I called her the same.'

'But,' Raghu suggested, 'don't you think we should send her back to Africa?'

'She doesn't come from Africa, Raghu.'

'Where then?'

'India.'

'Not my India '

'Then whose India?'

'Your India.'

'Look Raghu,' he said. 'I think we should summon this woman up here and ask her something.'

'Should we?'

'Should we? Yes, we should.'

Raghu quickly walked out to the corridor and his voice echoed Farida's name and then he returned to the room. They stood facing each other, while she walked in, barefooted, with her sari knotted around, so smoothly.

'Welcome Farida,' David said, thrusting out his left hand with Raghu's.

And Farida smiled.

'We want to ask you something,' Raghu said in Hindi.

'Ask me,' she replied, also in Hindi.

'Are you from Africa?' Raghu continued. 'Because you look as ugly as an African.'

'Not from Africa,' she said, partly in English. 'From Jammu & Kashmir.'

'But why are you so ugly?' David asked. 'And why do you have a face not so Indian?'

'Yes, Kashmiri people, Israeli people.'

The two young ambassadors looked at themselves. Kashmiri people, Israeli people. These people look alike and Farida is one of them. Farida is not an African, still she is ugly. It was at this point that David decided to dismiss her, and as she left, she carried the tray of the food with her.

'Farida is not from Africa?' Raghu asked.

'Yes, not from Africa.' He moaned. 'So Raghu, what happened today in the garden? I didn't want to play with that girl.'

'David,' there was serenity in Raghu's voice. 'Kavitha wants to be very intimate with you. She talks about you all the time.'

Kavitha was the ten-year-old daughter of Mr and Mrs Gopalakrishnan from a Hindu Brahmin home in Tamil Nadu and they lived on the same street as the Rajagopalan Family. Although Swathi didn't like seeing Kavitha around her garden, she kept on 'pestering' around and Raghu knew that she longed for David. To the young girls on the street, David was a hero.

Everyone wanted to see him. They wanted to see his blend of deep chocolate and brown thighs show when he was on his Ferrari bicycle, riding alongside with Raghu, who had been so abusive to them all.

'So what do you think?' David had demanded to know.

'We should ride with her on our bicycles to the cinema and buy her some ice-cream.'

'You think that's okay?'

'*Theek hai.*'

'What else, apart from ice-cream?'

'Write her love-letters.'

'And?'

'Play hide and seek with her.'

'To the cinema we must go!'

David quickly opened his box and put on a red shirt that smelled of Zatak perfume. Then they ran down the staircase and on getting to the door of the corridor, they rammed into Farida, standing with another maidservant, Basanti from Haryana (that grandma asked not to touch anything in the kitchen because she was believed to be an outcaste, an untouchable) and they stopped.

'Farida has been listening to us,' Raghu said in a fluent English, whispering to David.

'No, she hasn't,' David argued and said to Farida, 'when grandma comes out of the cottage, tell her that she should keep a bottle of banana jam for us because we would buy her an ice-cream.'

'Ok,' she said. 'You buy for me?'

'No, Fairy,' Raghu teased her. 'You are too old for ice-creams, and meanwhile, if you take it, your teeth will fall off.'

But David shrugged and said, 'Farida, I will buy you an ice-cream.'

And they vanished on their bicycles, down to the lane and it was at the end of the street, overlooking the Delhi Heart and Lung Institute that the Gopalakrishnan's house was, and on the lawn, the slender girl with her hair knotted behind, sat.

'Hi Kavitha,' David said.

'Hi Dave,' she called out, in her so lovely voice.

'We are heading for the Imperial Cinema,' he said. 'Would you like to come with us?'

'Of course,' she replied shyly, and then climbed on the backseat of the small bicycle. Thereafter, David rode gently, while Raghu followed.

Through the Panchkuia Road, they rode and the air swivelled. They rode past where the rickshaws were parked and the bus stop, and then headed downwards. After the kiosks. Before the Ashram Marg Metro station, and on the left side of the road was Sri Ramakrishna Temple with the statue of a turbaned man. The air blew Kavitha's hair and she held David, with her hands around his stomach, as he rode and it was then that he rode into Main Bazaar.

Shops, local restaurants, STD/ISD booths and Cyber Cafés filled the almost rowdy street. On the right as they rode, traders sold fruits: bell shaped cashews, green and red apples, large oval-shaped mangoes, tomatoes, vegetables and papayas. Cows and cars moved sheepishly and auto rickshaws babbled with the potholes.

Then as they got to a junction, they turned onto the left and passed the Continental Hotel and then the other shops.

Actually, Main Bazaar was what it was and nothing could undermine the fact that it was a business avenue. A flow of tourists, all were gushing in, especially those Israelis. Restaurants were so cheap that one could die of eating.

But there were people who couldn't find what to eat.

Later on, David halted in front of the not-so-impressive Imperial Cinema and Kavitha got down and the ice-cream seller (who they had beckoned on) came around, pushing his ice-cream box. That evening was one that David hadn't expected, because of what Raghu came back to tell him.

'Rakesh Roshan's *Krrish* will be screened in a few minutes,' Raghu said to David.

And yes, *Krrish* was the movie every Indian and every lover of Bollywood longed to see. Girls gurgled like children at cinemas to see Hrithik Roshan and Priyanka Chopra meddle it out; he - flying in the air to save her, she - doing all her best to bring him to Singapore, to love him, to admire him, to *want* him.

'Then we should get tickets for that,' he replied.

They licked their ice-creams as they walked leisurely into the cinema hall and bought their tickets from the hard looking man over the ticket counter.

Seats in the theatre were filled

Buttocks glued to them and eyes watched.

The film began.

Krrish is a love-story and as usual, it ended with a happy note. All the three enjoyed the film very much.

3

Ambassador J.K.V Handlebroadman and the Spirits

IT WAS Saturday. Rajaswamy had been out of bed early and was reading a newspaper in the verandah. Eunice and Vimala were in the kitchen with Farida preparing breakfast. And as Rajaswamy heard his wife's giggles rise and die in the kitchen, he began to think pensively. He remembered the Aishwarya Rai-face shaped girl who sat with him under the sal tree whispering to him: 'Remember we had taken an oath. We drank each other's blood, swore that nobody leaves each other, except in death.'

He frowned as he remembered this, repositioned his glasses on the tip of his nose and continued reading - and then raised his head to watch David and Raghu.

Raghu was in pink knickers screaming, while David splashed water at him. They ran around in the garden, Basanti used the cutter for gardening, and they splashed water at her. She only smiled and continued with what she was doing. She had learnt to be too quiet since she learnt that she was a dalit, an untouchable.

Farida watched the kids through the window and she

was elated. She enjoyed everything David did. Even annoying things. Eunice and Vimala spoke completely in English. Farida couldn't understand.

'What happened at the FRRO yesterday?' Vimala asked.

'They renewed the visa, anyway,' Eunice said. 'But Vimala, I'm really pissed off with your Indian immigration. They said they aren't issuing any passport to me.'

'What is the problem?'

'They said they haven't finished their investigation.'

'What?'

'To know if I sold drugs.'

Vimala squealed. 'They are sick!'

Eunice couldn't say anything but smile as she cut the tomatoes on the chopping-board. Vimala was busy peeling the Irish potatoes in the purple bowl, while Farida rinsed the teacups in the sink.

Farida then listened to the rhythm of the Beatles song David and Raghu sang, only in knickers, having had themselves wet.

> *Dear Prudence, won't you come out to play*
> *Dear Prudence, greet the brand new day*
> *The sun is up, the sky is blue*
> *It's beautiful and so are you*
> *Dear Farida, won't you come out to play?*

David was 'back-swiping' like Usher Raymond and tilted his voice, like Craig David.

'You don't do backswipes, when you sing the Beatles,' Raghu corrected.

'Why?'

'You only do that when you sing Usher and Michael

41

Jackson.'

'But it's always good to-'

'Not good enough, Dave,' he snorted. 'There is never a time those shouty things the Beatles do could work out with the swipes Usher gives.'

'You could blend them, you know.'

'Never,' Raghu said and walked out angrily.

David loved the Beatles very much and tried to learn to dance like Usher Raymond. But what he loved more was reciting poems of Rabindranath Tagore. Last year, he won the first position at a poetry recitation competition in his school, the British School, for reciting poems of D H Lawrence and Tagore. His father said he was going to be a better writer. 'Better than Salman Rushdie?' Swathi had asked. And he had said yes.

Raghu wasn't in love with books, because he preferred watching television or playing cricket with the American boy, Picard. Raghu had in the past said to his mother: 'I'll be like Rahul Dravid, Mahendra Singh Dhoni or the great Sachin Tendulkar.' She had slapped him on hearing this, adding: 'Your grandfather is a lawyer, your mother is a lawyer and your father is a lawyer in London, so you don't dare dream of being a cricketer.' It was when he asked tearfully, 'And where is my father?' that Vimala understood she had made a mistake.

She slammed her tongue into her mouth and closed it.

Never to talk again.

So, David knew, when Raghu walked out on him in the garden that he was going to his room upstairs, just opposite his, to watch the television and he knew that he wouldn't want him to come around and watch it with him - although they hadn't had their breakfast.

As David got to the door, he knocked on it furiously. Without saying a word, he entered. Yes, it was a rule that the two

of them must keep. *Knock before entering.* Down to the chords, as
he entered, Raghu was engrossed in the television.

'Raghu,' David called. 'You have started behaving like a
bitch.'

But Raghu didn't say anything.

Something fell from the top of the wardrobe onto his bed.
It was his school bag, he found out immediately, a black and
white old picture of his father slipped out of it. Raghu caressed
his right palms over the glossy paper and smiled, turning to
David, he said, 'Hey Dave,' showed him the picture and added:
'That's my father.'

Actually, none of Raghu's father's pictures ever existed
in the parlour (there was one, with him sported in his black suit
and white wig in the study) But David hadn't bothered to see it,
though he read in the study. He said that seeing the picture
brought bad luck.

'My father is handsome,' Raghu said, smiling into the
picture. 'He looks so cute.'

'He's ugly, Raghu,' David concluded, looking away. 'Like
an African.'

'Oh, why do you say that?' Traces of bitterness ran
through Raghu's face.

'He doesn't like you or your mom.'

'He does.'

'Well,' David said, by standing up. 'I don't know him. I
haven't seen him and you don't expect me to admire him, either.'

Raghu shook. He could feel hotness protruding in the
inside of him and felt goose bumps on his skin. He watched as
David walked to the door and muttered something.

'What did you say?' he asked.

'I'm off to the cottage to see grandma,' David said.

Swathi was making strawberry jam in the cottage when David entered through the backdoor. He walked into the room where she was at work, through the door that connected with the room where the jam pots were packed.

'Namaste,' he greeted, going closer to the table, on which the jam-pots were set.

'Doing now?' Swathi began in her halting phrases.

'I woke up and mom told me you were already here?'

'*Achcha!*' she beamed, with her gloved hands patting David on the left shoulder. 'I had to do some new jam today. I would be off to Jammu's house this evening and she needs some strawberry jam.'

'Grandma,'he said.

'Yes, boy?'

'Did you learn making jam at school?'

She coughed and chuckled and said nothing.

Of course, you could say she learnt doing jam at school. Having being born in the year 1919 (that same year Britain passed the Rowlatt Act) into a rich but conservative Tamil Hindu Brahmin family, Swathi never tried hiding her passion for jams and juices. Her father's father was a politician and was one of the people who advocated reforms in India and he was said to have organised the Indian National Congress in 1885 with Alan Octavian Hume (who was then a retiree from the Indian Civil Service), Dadabhai Naoroji, Pherozeshah Mehta and W.C Bonerji and her father had joined Bal Gangadhar Tilak, Bipin Chandra Pal. She once said that it was her father who should be respected more than any of them. She recounted that she had then seen her father and Subhas Chandra Bose in a verbal war. 'Not only Nehru and Gandhi fought for Independence,' she had told her children many years ago.

'Can I ask another thing?'

'Ask.'

'Why does grandpa hate me and my mother?'

She froze - and all the smiles on her face disappeared. She didn't know what to say. Her eyes grew bewildered and looked large. If only she could quietly walk away from David. What the young man said troubled her because you don't expect her to tell him why his grandfather hated him.

'Well,' she said, 'maybe that's because your mother doesn't make jam.'

But...

On the contrary, Eunice's mother swore never to see her daughter get wedded to a Hindu because she was a Christian, so she couldn't attend their wedding. To her, the Hindus worshiped idols and the Bible forbade it. Ah, Swathi retaliated. As she sat in Eunice's mother's parlour at Nigeria House, she lectured her. She told her that all of them were idol-worshippers; that Jesus Christ died and was buried somewhere in Jerusalem, while Christians in a place like Nigeria believed He died for them and claimed He was a Living God. How? She had asked.

Eunice's mother didn't say anything, and she didn't consent to the marriage. But before Swathi left her house, she added: 'Remember the idol of Mary, the Virgin.'

The wedding took place on a Saturday in Vasant Vihar - in a beautifully decorated hall; although it should have been in the bride's house, Onwubiko had paid a wedding junkie, a middle aged woman, Shobha to appear as the bride's mother - but before this, the tilak had been done, and this was actually in readiness to welcome the groom, coming around - and the groom was Rajaswamy in his silver trimmed churidar, draped with a sherwani. The priest then fixed the day of the ceremony. When the ceremony started, it took a long time to finish.

Rajaswamy was laid in a wonderful procession that swirled open on the road, as a group of musicians led the groom, while he sat majestically on a horse - and male members of his family followed. There, Onwubiko and Shobha welcomed the groom at the entrance of the hall - where they had set up as theirs and had the dwara-puja. The bride's mother, Shobha ran out with a bowl, dipped her finger in it and put a sandalwood paste dot on Rajaswamy's forehead. There were no women in the procession. The hall in which the ceremony was to take place had been decorated with roses, hibiscuses, lotus and morning sunflowers. Then as evening neared, the couple dressed in richly made clothings, sat cross-legged side by side, in front of a sacred fire as the priest sat on one side, chanting the sacred verses, so also did Shobha and Onwubiko, the parents of the girl on the other side.

Then it was time to pray and worship Lord Ganesha ('this is something I don't like! You don't worship idols, they worship you, for Christ's sake,' Eunice's mother would have said) who was - and still is revered as - the Remover of Obstacles. The bride had her face veiled, and then the priest tied one end of her bridal sari to Rajaswamy's dress and the other end to Eunice's.

Onwubiko was meant to chant prayers as he gave Eunice's hand to Rajaswamy. *I am no Hindu. But should I chant these prayers to Kristi or Krishna?* He couldn't tell when he finished and the two clasped their hands together, crushing the mehendi tree leaves and started throwing it into the fire as the priest instructed and chanted Sanskrit verses. They did the rice throwing for seven times and the fire crackled.

Still Anantha swore never to set his milky-eyes on the

chocolate-skinned daughter-in-law because he had wanted his son to marry a typical conservative Tamil Hindu Brahmin girl.

And there he was trying to bring in a poor black, he told his friends the next morning as they sat in a teashop in Mumbai.

Then the bell rang.

David knew it was time for breakfast and before he left, Swathi asked him to help her carry a jar of jam to the dinning table. When he got there, he saw the table well-matted and decorated and the plates well-laid out. Open-mouthed, David walked to the table and gently placed the jar. After a few minutes, everyone was at the table, except Farida and Basanti.

At the end of the long table, Rajaswamy, who placed a newspaper he was reading beside him, sat dream-eyed opposite Eunice who sat at the other end, while Swathi faced Vimala - then Raghu and David sat opposite to each other.

Shiny plates filled with freshly fried egg (for Eunice and David), Irish potatoes, spinach and a jug of juice.

Then a jar of jam, with saucers filled with toasts.

Eunice served everyone what he or she wanted to eat and they began to eat. Swathi held the jam jar firmly, had a spoonful of it cemented on her toast. She grinned and David imitated her. Raghu was busy eating.

The television crackled and Rajaswamy turned to it. It was Shashi Tharoor and the Prime Minister on air, after a UN congress. Or whatever. Rajaswamy told Vimala that Mr. Tharoor was a symbol of pride to the South Indians. Vimala agreed. Good, that was how to get Vimala to agree more. He said Mr. Tharoor was a misfit for any post. Vimala called him an anti-Indian and said he should go and live in the US. But Rajaswamy said that he would rather live in Afghanistan than in the US.

'Prime Minister, Prime Minister,' Rajaswamy muttered as he ate. 'Yes, the Prime Minister is brilliant but I don't think he did a brilliant thing by connecting with the White House and that is why I think he has lost that power to push Tharoor forward because other Asian leaders are not behind him.'

'Anti-American,' Vimala stopped eating. 'The Prime Minister is not in any way doing anything unbrilliant. Tharoor as an Under-Secretary General for Communications and Public Information gives us the impression that he has performed well and must be supported to become the Secretary General. Simple.'

'No, Vimala,' Rajaswamy muttered, taking more spoonfuls of the spinach. 'The Prime Minister should abstain from getting close to White House.'

'But daddy,' David said, as Rajaswamy made his what-is-it eyes and continue:. 'Do you think the Prime Minister could do jam and juice like grandma?'

Everyone laughed. It was as though he had interrupted their argument. But true to the fact, Raghu was not one of *the* everyone who laughed because he himself had thought the Prime Minister could do jam. Just like Swathi.

'No, son,' Vimala said to David. 'The Prime Minister may not be able to do jam now because he is always busy.'

'Or does he live alone like grandpa?'

Vimala was startled. 'No, he doesn't,' she continued. 'Grandpa lives alone because he is just an individual but the Prime Minister is not. He needs guards around him for protection.'

Deep inside, Swathi was sweating. She was visualising things. David could simply bring up the issue of Anantha hating his mother because she couldn't do jam. Or maybe, say that it was Swathi who told him that. No matter what, Swathi knew, she was

not in any mood to despise Eunice because she had been married to her son for a long time. Not so good, not so good. Breakfast was over and everyone deserted the table.

Not even Farida alone could clear the table. So she asked Basanti to come and help her. When Swathi saw Basanti holding some plates in her arm, she screamed: 'Om Nath!' 'Farida ... no one asked Basanti to clear the table. Did anyone? Why did you allow her to touch those plates? Alright, take them from her and throw them in the bin.'

Eunice heard this and remembered what her father had told her; how Indrani's father had treated him. Like a stray dog. ("Oh, don't you know that Africans are stray dogs?" Mr. Frazier, the American, had asked Vimala the day they first saw the movie, *The Gods Must Be Crazy*. And he'd added: "You find them in every part of the world") Eunice got enraged and asked Frazier if he had taken a bath since the past weeks. Frazier said he didn't need to do so because he would still 'look white.' Something snapped in Eunice's head. She told Frazier that he had no trace of 'whiteness' in him. She said that he was colourless; that his colour didn't exist.

It was Jamuna who quelled the argument by saying: 'We are all racist.'

So as Eunice watched Swathi howl, she kept calm and didn't want to say anything that would breed hatred. She didn't want to say anything that would bring her into the pothole. To be hated. Or be told she was a racist.

'And you, Basanti,' Swathi screamed. 'If you don't listen to us, you'd be fired!'

Rajaswamy, with his glasses still on the tip of his nose, in a Bermuda short, walked barefoot, holding a newspaper in his hand and glared at his mother, who continued raising her witch-like fingers at Basanti.

'Ma,' Rajaswamy spoke in English. 'You don't know what it takes to be a mother, do you?'

Silence.

'Listen,' he continued, 'I know that you can't allow anyone tell your child that he is untouchable, can you?'

'Absolute nonsense.' Swathi waved at him. 'She was picked up from the slums in Haryana and imported to Delhi. She was a dalit, before I brought her here-'

'And she has been here,' Rajaswamy grinned. 'Since the time she has been here, our Basanti has been loyal.'

'She is born to be loyal,' Swathi commented, sitting into one of the back chairs by the dinning table. 'These people are born to be loyal. They are meant to be subjected to irresistible retribution. They are to be suffered.'

'*Bakhwas*!' Rajaswamy screamed. 'They are not meant to be so. We make them like that. We try as much as we can to suppress those we can. It is wrong. Where is the democracy we claim we practice when we degrade some groups of people? We are the ones who make them jobless and if I were to rule India, people who humiliate these so-called dalits, like you mamma, would have faced trials.'

Swathi glared back at him and walked away.

That evening before Pankaj drove her off to Jamuna's house at Artist's Colony, she called Farida and Basanti to the gate and said: 'I think the two of you should start helping each other.' And that meant that Basanti was free to touch the cooking utensils and was able to touch the dishes and wash the cups. For Basanti, a burden had been lifted off her shoulder. She smiled.

Before she left, when everyone had gathered in the verandah to see her off, she cat-walked. The long verandah was her runway.

'You are better than Priyanka Chopra,' Eunice teased and everyone broke into laughter.

'But ,' Vimala suggested. 'Ma can't believe that she is as sexy as Aishwarya Rai.'

Hearing that remark, Swathi walked elegantly into the car, and Pankaj started the engine and drove off.

Rajaswamy went into the study to work on his book. He had started his third book, after he was paid a two-book deal advance by one of the foreign publishers in Delhi over his second, *The Trouble with Third World Paisa*. It sold in millions. In the book, he argued that 'for any Third World country to challenge the West, it must withdraw intentionally from the world economy and have a self-centered trade union that would exclude the US and the European Union.' He said that for the naira to be valuable and most respected than the dollar bill or pound note, the Nigerian government should trade within the African continent, without wheeling any oil to the US. In one chapter of the book, he called upon the OPEC countries to abandon the US and the European Union, and that by doing so they will 'play a much superior role in the decentralisation of the world economy, so no economy raises the chart of largest economy for itself, like the US does.'

He attended lectures and seminars all over Asia and

Europe but swore he would never accept any invitation to the US, forgetting that he had studied there.

Eunice was in the room, sitting before the mirror, a towel tied around her and was clipping her long thick shampooed hair together. David entered and said he wanted to go to Frazier's house.

'Why?' she asked.

'Just to play.'

'Well,' she suggested. 'You have to be really, really careful with his slangs, ok?'

'Alright mom,' he said and was off.

Picard was really, really excellent at using the *slangs*. Actually, David and Raghu nicknamed him Ambassador J.K.V. Handlebroadman for no reason. For the last time they played, the two Rajagopalan boys went home, having learnt a new word. *Bitch.* The Ambassador had said it once, but it continued ringing in their heads. They could call anyone, anything bitch. They loved the word.

Finally, when the two boys got into Frazier's house, Mrs Frazier, a blonde-haired woman was at the doorstep with a winsome smile.

'Good evening Ma'am,' David and Raghu greeted her.

'Ram Ram!' she said, still smiling. *'Aap kaise hain?'*

They looked at themselves and said: 'We are fine.' She stood up and walked away smiling. Since she came to India (three years ago) with her husband and child, she promised herself to polish her Hindi. She said that Americans had better brains than Indians and learnt easily. Once she had run into the Rajagopalan house and screamed that Vimala tell her what 'sisterfucker' was in Hindi and she did. As she left, Vimala whispered to Eunice: 'Has that woman bathed? She smells a lot.' Another time, Rajaswamy - while very angry, after he'd had a brawl with an American at a gas station in Delhi - called Mr. Frazier to the parlour, sat him down and asked him: 'Your visa has expired, hasn't it?' And he nodded. 'You came with six months visa, but you have been here for three years?' He said yes. Rajaswamy said he would write to FRRO to come and pick him up for deportation. Hearing this, Frazier went on his knees and begged.

Picard was sitting on the rug of their sitting room, when the two boys entered. He sat cross-legged. 'I am Swami Ramdev,' he boasted.

'Americans can't be swamis,' Raghu argued. 'Like uncle Rajaswamy said yesterday, the Prime Minister should not get near the White House.'

'That's nonsense,' Picard said. 'Your uncle knows that your Prime Minister is not fit to be inside the White House.'

'Don't be insulting.'

Picard never mentioned their Prime Minister again.

He ran into his room and reappeared with a Sony digital camera. David and Raghu came and sat around him.

'This is a reality,' Picard said in a confusing American accent. 'Tonight is our fesrival.'

David and Raghu looked at each other. Confused.

'Ain't you understand me?'

'Yaar!' David nodded.

'Alrigh,' he moaned. 'I look at Indian polirics and I shudder.'

'It's so nice, right?' Raghu said.

'Das absolure nonsense,' John Kennedy Vulture

Handlebroadman groaned.

'Why?' David asked.

'En America where I come from, polirics is no' somerin a rich man struggles for, alrigh?'

'Awesome!'

'Yeah, ir shoul be,' he continued. 'No' this derry stinking smelly sherry nonsense bawdy polirics you play here.'

They laughed boisterously.

'I was joking,' he said, making them silent. 'I have a camera here and I just think you guys should come to that mosque over there with me this night.'

'Why?' they asked him.

'I just want to photograph the terrorists as they pray,' he said.

David was stunned. 'Don't call the devotees terrorists!'

'Look at you!' he whimpered. 'These guys blew up the World Trade Center, while my granny was in there, with my aunt and cousins.'

'Aw!' David shuddered. 'Sorry.'

'It's okay.'

There was more traffic, more cars on Panchkuia Road as Ambassador John Kennedy Vulture Handlebroadman led the two Rajagopalan spirits through the street, and they crossed the other part of the road, abridged by the metro flyover. It was getting uttermostly dark.

On one such night, Picard, who was then eight (and now eleven) had been walking alone on a street in New York and after a few minutes, a car screeched to the gate of a house and he heard gunshots. A woman screamed. A child cried audibly and he heard, 'Fucking mulato! We could blow you up in the same way those jihad-minded idiots did to my family back in the country.'

And he began to run. Later on, he found that he was also running now and David and Raghu joined him. They tripped and leaped over a barbed wire into the mosque on Panchkuia Road. From the tower, the bell tolled forlornly and a man in a long robe, wearing a straw cap came out to the top, with his fingers in the holes of his ears and screamed: 'Allah-ho-Akkbar! Allah-ho-Akbar! Ashadu-Allah-illah-illahu...' Unlatched, everyone thronged into the mosque and the three of them - the American and Indian Ambassadors - ran in through the back of the mosque.

The American Ambassador, who deep in his heart, wanted to be addressed as Ambassador-fucking-John-bitchy-Kennedy-dicky-Vulture-pussy-Handlebroadman, said he was an expert on South Asian politics and geography no matter his age. He thought that Jashim, the Bangladeshi was as Pakistani as any Pakistani. 'He's a Muslim, you know', he would explain to the beery-eyed Indian Ambassadors who saw themselves as one Nehru, one Gandhi. No. One Gandhi, one Nehru, because Gandhi was there first before Nehru.

But that's just politics!

So, Picard, the American-bitchy-Ambassador, because he thought he was one, said that Mr. Naif and Jashim were bitches. Oh, David liked the sound. *Bitches bitching bitches.* Raghu liked the sound. In the inside of him, he was afraid his mother could be a bitch. He was afraid. Plainly afraid. *Bitches bitching...* Shut up, David!

And he shut up! Because there was nothing to shut down

for. Seriously. Only he felt *bitches bitched bitches!*

Right there at the back of the mosque, Picard, like an American president, addressing his Indian and Pakistani counterparts, with loads of trepidation and intimidation, wanted David and Raghu to understand something about India. 'You bitches might be Indians, Pakistanis and Bangladeshis,' he began, perplexed, 'but you know nothing about India, Pakistan and Bangladesh...'

'Oh *bitches*, let's start with India,' Picard told them.

'You could be Indian, but you don't know the history of India.'

'You could be Indian, but my mother speaks better...'

'Better what?'

'Better Hindi!'

'Oh yes, you could be Indian, but Indians don't know anything about Pakistanis bitching around with them.'

'I am more Indian than you both' said Picard. 'Yes, bitches, I eat with my bare hands, I can write the history of India. I can write about Indians the way Indians can't. Yes, bitches, I can.'

For Picard, as an American Ambassador, he was observing India with diplomacy. He had his camera. He had his eye. He had his ears. One ear to get the news of India, one to get that of the US. He said he observed India with fuck-keen-interest.

And that made David think of when Swathi had begun to get pissed off by Picard parading her house with swear words.

Bitches. Fucking. Pussy. Dicky. Arsey. Lickey. Mickey. ('Was that a swear word, Swathi?' David thought to himself. 'Oh, Swathi, you don't know anything. Only jam, jam, Swathi'). But no, everyone thought *Licky-Mickey* were swear words. Only Rajaswamy didn't. Eunice half-thought, because half-thinking meant you were better than those who thought and those who didn't. So, Swathi tried all her possible best to alert Warren Frazier and his wife over the 'diminishing return' of their son. What 'diminishing return'? Frazier had asked. Swathi tried so well to explain so well but she couldn't do it so well because she didn't know so well how to tell Frazier that his son used swear words so well. So it stuck. Still Swathi could explain to herself what that ('diminishing return') meant but couldn't understand it herself. She tried to give up warning David, *Don't bring that American boy into a Hindu home with swear words, bhai.* Oh, if Mrs Frazier had heard that, she would call Swathi *bhainchute* –sisterfucker. But our God, Swathi had no sister and was really no fucker. How then, oh dearest heaven, how did these Americans come to the conclusion that they had better brains than Indians?

No brain Americans, no brain, Farida would howl back anytime she felt Picard was taking David's attention from her. For that Farida, she hoped that David would become her son. Ah, if she had known, she would have escaped to Kashmir with him that time he was still growing up. This she couldn't do, so she decided, very very well to love David. With all her might. To her, David was India and India was David. Indians were most patriotic, so Farida loved David as any good Indian would love India and hated Picard as any bad Indian would hate India to want to ask for the independence of Kashmir.

Fuck it, Picard swore.

David's thoughts zoomed back to the mosque.

Picard was observing the mosque with David and Raghu. Picard said he was writing a book, titled *A Passage to India*. Yes, he was saying this as he stood in the mosque. And when he said that, David and Raghu sneered. *A Passage to India?* No. *A Passage to India, I mean.* What? Oh, *A Passage from India.*

'You lie!' Raghu said. 'One Forster wrote *A Passage to India*'.

Picard smiled. 'You see,' he mumbled and then added, 'that he didn't write *A Passage to India*. He observed it. He observed *A Passage to India*'.

Raghu was surprised. 'Really?'

'Really, yes. Can't you see? One Forster wrote *A Passage to India*. Then two fraudsters wrote *A Passage from India.'*

But David couldn't buy that bitchy-trash about E.M. Forster. E.M. Forster, David tried explaining to the mosque-minded Picard and the 'diminishing returned' Raghu, was a British writer who loved India. And India had a fucking American Ambassador who...

'Terrorists!' Picard mouthed. 'You Indians are fucking terrorists. You Indians...'

'Did you see my face the day your granny was blown up?' David sarcastically asked.

'No, *What I saw was your dicky head, pussy-sucker.'*

'Diplomatically speaking,' Picard-the-great--American-Ambassadorial-observer-again, 'India is a beautiful country with beautiful minds. But those beautiful minds, diplomatically speaking, are beautiful terrorists... now I want to get down to my job as an observer, to understand terrorist India, to analyze, to marginalize, to criticize, to photographise...'

'Photographise?' David almost laughed.

'Yes, photographise,' Picard beamed. 'Photographise as in, when you photograph, you ice it. It makes sense, doesn't it?'

Two heads nodded. *Yes, it fucking made sense.* But it didn't really make sense to them. Raghu really didn't understand. What was that thing about photographing and icing? Icing what?'

'You know,' Picard said, 'that Jashim is Pakistani Muslim?'

'No,' Raghu said.

'He's Bangladeshi', David added.

'No, Dave,' Picard mumbled. 'You fucking don't understand why he's in India. Now let's get down to it. He is a Pakistani trying to appear as a Bangladeshi in India... when he gets to fucking know every nook and cranny of India, he goes back to Pakistan, alerts his terrorist group and they come back and bomb *Inn-mere.*'

Bomb *Inn-There?* Or India, arsehole? David thought, wanting so much to think out loud. But those kinds of thoughts were meant to be left inside.

Well, if Jashim were Pakistani and claiming he was Bangladeshi, he should *fucking* Pakistan himself out of India, Raghu kept saying to himself. And oh yes, he had never liked Jashim. Jashim was dark-skinned as Eunice, but that wasn't why Raghu didn't like Jashim. He half-liked Mr. Naif and it seemed Mr. Naif full-liked him.

Mr. Knife, Mr. Knife, always humming the Beatles. In the bathroom (while masturbating, thinking of Raghu or his grandfather, Anantha), in the kitchen (frying pakora), in his car (driving to anywhere), in his dream (thinking of the Yemeni girl his father wanted him to marry).

Very simple.

Mr Knife (Oh, Mr. Naif, Raghu!) came to India to sit out 'a coup'. The 'coup' was his father's decision that he must marry a Yemeni. Naif wanted to marry an Indian girl or a good American woman. He told his father. His father was roundly angry with him. What did he think? How dare he think he could marry an Indian? Even an American? And Naif had the money to run out of Riyadh and he did.

Now, he was in India, on Rani Jhansi Road, where there were all races, trying to hum the Beatles, masturbate when he could (he had no name for masturbation. No he did. He called it *salaaming sperm*), fry his pakora, drive and dream.

Drive and dream he took very serious.

But then masturbation he took less serious. He said it was a normal thing any man could do in 90 days. If he were to think about the implications, he would smudge at how many dollars he was losing.

A bottle of sperm = Rs 50

A pinch of sperm = $3

A gallon of sperm = N150

Raghu made the first calculation.

The second appeared to Picard,

And David had the third.

So… as they stood in the mosque, Picard, diplomatically undiplomatically abandoned politics and like Rajaswamy, always in a lecturer-in-a-seminar-mood began to teach them, lecture them really, on sperm.

'You know,' he began, 'sperm has the colour of milk and that's why most children are beautiful when they are out. Two, when you mature, you'll get to understand this, that as soon as you discharge, you'll become weak. Sex is sweet when you've not discharged... most immature minds will start fucking to hate their partners in sex... sperm is like condensed milk. It spills out gradually.'

A bearded man, who had been listening to Picard's sperm-lecture, said: 'Shoo'.

'Picard, let's go.' Raghu suggested.

'Why?' Picard wanted to know.

'Shoo!' the bearded man said. 'Prayer in the mosque going!'

Oh, Picard fucking understood. Terrorist understood. Terrorist prayer, he said to himself. You blew out my granny, eh?

'Shoo!' the bearded man said again. 'Prayer in the mosque going!'

The Ambassador ran away with his camera and the spirits flashed out with him. They passed St Thomas and stopped at a kiosk. The owner was a blind man and had no sales person. He sold everything himself. Picard said he was a fraud; that he was playing a blind kiosk owner so that he could get into the Guinness Book of Records. They bought Hide and Seek biscuits and left.

David and Raghu sneaked into the house and walked into their rooms. But before they could come down to the dinning room and have their dinner, Jamuna had arrived with her children, Pradip, who was twenty and Supriya, who was eighteen. Whatever, David hated his cousins. Reason? Because they were older than him ("I hate intimidation,' he had said) For Pradip, he knew that if he had married earlier, he would've had a child of his age. For Supriya, David wouldn't even count himself as high as someone who could woo her to some of the nightclubs in New Delhi. Like Inter-Continental.

Eunice sat in the couch, with that same copy of Salman Rushdie's *Midnight's Children*. And David walked in - she sprang up from the seat and said: 'You overstayed, David.' He said: 'Sorry, mom.' 'No, you overstayed. Why?'

Silence.

'Why?'

'Nothing, mom.'

'Alright,' she moaned. 'Have you taken a bath?'

'Yes, mom.'

'Then go to the dinning room and say hello to your aunt.'

'Ok mom.'

Jamuna and her children had already lined up in the dinning room waiting for Farida and Basanti to set the table, when David entered and walked to her side and said: 'Hello aunt Jamuna.'

'Hi Dave,' Jamuna said. 'How are you?'

'I am fine, thank you.'

'Your mom told me you were out to Picard's house?' she said. 'How was today?'

'Fine.'

Later on, Farida set the table and everyone was seated. The dishes were brought out and it was Eunice who started serving the food. Because Diwali still smelt. Actually, that night was a special one because Farida had prepared some Kashmiri dishes and that bubbled through the dusky kitchen.

Riddles ride rude rats.

Moreover, Farida knew what the Farida inside *her* could do.

She could make delicious rogan josh, tabak maaz, goshtaba and meatballs in red tomato sauce.

She could play the sitar.

She could sing Celine Dion in her dialect: Kashmiri.

But David believed that was nonsense. That no one could sing *Power of Love* in Kashmiri. For that, Farida decided to bring out the inside of her. To an extent, what still frightened Farida was that she had once misbehaved. She had once lied to Swathi, but Swathi wasn't someone who bore things in mind. She knew how to forgive, but with a hard face.

No soft face. No soft back. Swathi loved to love and hated to hate. Her mind was open, but only to those who couldn't steal her jam. No, her mind was open, empty. She bore nothing in mind for some lazy riff-raffs, but Farida wounded her that year.

That was then.

It was the season for the Mela Hemis Gompa festival and Farida left the house and took the next available train to Srinagar. This was a sort of a Buddhist feast (though it was a guise to get close to the Buddhist monks) and it celebrated the birthday of the founder of Lamaism, Padma Sambhava.

Farida sat concentrated in her train apartment in that Swaraj Express number 2472.

When she finally reached Srinagar, after a sleepless night journey in that compartment with some white tourists (who spoke in tongues she couldn't understand), she had another feel of embrace from her children, her three children who bumped around her and rattled her Delhi bags.

Later, Swathi was mad at her.

Many years ago.

It was fear that made her run away, she said. She said that

she knew Swathi would not allow her go to see her children. "That is just a flimsy excuse,' Swathi had snapped, when she knelt in the cottage (while she did jam) begging her.

Swathi decided to forgive her if she did a Kashmiri delicacy. She did a dish of roast lamb and saag. When she finished, Swathi poured some away for Eunice.

Vimala tasted it. And Jamuna was angry.

Jamuna was always angry whenever she remembered that she was born the year war broke out between India and Pakistan in 1948. She was born in a train, as her parents ran off from the Punjabi state of Kurushektra.

That was the most painful.

Being born in a train. In war.

It wasn't Swathi's fault. It was Anantha's. That year, Swathi had dreamed (virtually every night) that Pakistan was going to make trouble, so she was adamant when Anantha asked her to open up, for him to do.

For two weeks, she refused.

Anantha went out and got drunk, forgetting his wig on the bench at the bar where he'd drunk himself to imbecility. He returned home with a hard face--he grabbed Swathi by her hands and made her kneel (as she was making, not jam! but juice in the kitchen) on the floor of the kitchen in their three bedroom flat on Lukhwinder Singhji Road. Moreover, Swathi struggled, but what could she do? She couldn't escape the grip of the monster because he held her so firm. She screamed though, as if he were a rapist, not her husband. None of their neighbours came around because Anantha, the Law-Man could file an FIR against them. Swathi became pregnant.

But no one told Jamuna this part of the story.

She only knew that she was born in a train. And felt really, really angry. And now as she sat, speaking to David - who was born at Apollo Hospital - while they ate, it occurred to her that people who were born in trains, were not privileged to face those born in hospitals.

She knew all that, but it escaped her mind, she told herself.

4

When Jamuna Felt Angry

THE NEXT morning, while Diwali still unfolded, Rajaswamy woke up early because of another horrible dream. In that dream, he had seen the albino dwarf running after that Aishwarya Rai-face shaped girl who had told him about the oath they took. He couldn't exactly understand what that was. And while he had gone to the study to write, he visualised that same girl. He felt depressed. Why should that girl keep appearing to him? Of course, he knew the girl who had that face. What they had in common was gone. Now he was married to a more beautiful woman. She should leave me alone; Rajaswamy thought to himself and left the study for the parlour with some printed pages of his third book, yet to be completed.

Eunice's Liberian friend, Helen, was in the parlour when he entered.

'Another?' she asked, excitedly, as though they had greeted.

'Yes,' he replied, politely.

'And what's the title?'

'Still untitled.'

'And what's it about?'

'Many, many things, you know,' he said. 'Politics, business and diplomacy. And it's from it that I'll borrow some tips for my seminar in Nigeria.'

'You are going to Nigeria?'

'Yes.'

'So, Nigerians know about you?'

'Not all Nigerians.'

'What are you to discuss at the seminar?'

'You know,' he mumbled and slumped into a cushion. 'Nigerians as I know them. Don't tell my wife anyway...'

Helen laughed and said, 'Ok.'

'They are too much in love with foreign things,' he grinned. 'As the Asians in Nigeria mingle their way into the lives of the high class Nigerians, Africans in Asia can't do that. It's rare. So, I think it's time to go and lecture the Nigerians to be proud of their product. Here in India, which you can see, it's rare to find the Indians selling foreign products. I think I've got a lot to tell to the Nigerians.'

'And the Liberians, huh?' she chipped in.

'The Liberians are yet to get out of the trance of war,' Rajaswamy teased. 'They even respect Nigerians, talk more of Asians.'

'But what makes the Africans feel inferior?'

'Because they have always been at the back,' he pushed his glass to the tip of his nose and read from the paper. ' "The Asians and Africans, especially the black Africans believe that nothing ever works on their side, since Jesus Christ is riddled to be the Saviour, therefore He has to to answer the cry of His fellow fair skinned - the Middle Easterners, Europeans and Americans - before getting to *him*, the black man" '

'Ah!' Helen screamed. 'Your publishers must expect a bombshell!'

'Why do you say that?'

'You create a lot of controversies.'

'Really?'

'Yeah.'

'I don't think I do.'

'But, that's...'

The phone at the extreme end of the sitting room began to ring. Rajaswamy ignored it for a while. He hated the persistent ringing. Oh, why not the caller be silent for a while? When he doesn't get answered, he should just stop. Stop. Stop. Full stop. But the phone kept ringing and he went and answered it: 'Hello,' he said. 'Yes? Alright.'

He turned; Eunice was now standing by the doorway with a scrap of paper in her hand. He stretched out the desk phone to her and said, with a winsome smile: 'Your brother, Nduka, is on the line.' She froze completely. Where was he calling from? From the US? Or Nigeria? She had to find out and something like this interested her. Nduka was one her few brothers who visited her in India every year. But he hadn't come that year because they said he was taking a bar examination to qualify as a lawyer.

'Hi honey,' Eunice said happily, as she held the phone to her ear, while Helen blinked at her. 'Yes...we are alright. Yes...back from Harvard, huh? Alright. *Kedu maka mama na papa?* Ok, what's that?' There was a silence that followed before she continued, 'This December? Great. So? All right. Raj sends his greeting...yaar...he's alright. Yeah, you know he's facilitating a workshop in Lagos by December? Yeah. We'll join him. Yeah, David is really doing well. Ok love. See you then and take absolute care of yourself.'

She dropped the phone and turned to Rajaswamy and Helen with smiles.

'How did he say your parents are doing?' Rajaswamy said, sitting tight in the couch.

'They are alright,' she said. 'And you know what, honey?'

'What?'

'Nduka said that my father wants me to come home for his Thanksgiving celebration over the accident he had.'

'Oh yeah. When?'

'This December!'

'Great.'

'You'd be in Lagos for the seminar in one week,' she said. 'After that, we'd then get down to my village in Imo State.'

'*No problema,*' he teased in a flawed Spanish accent.

'You can't even speak any other language apart from Hindi and English, huh?' Helen asked.

'Oh, you missed out,' he smiled. 'I can speak Urdu, Tamil (my language), Malayalam, Sanskrit, Kannada and Bengali with equal fluency as Hindi.'

Of course, Indians were apparently known to be multilingual. But that wasn't what Eunice was after, when matters connecting her father arose. She could purchase her ticket along with David's, since Rajaswamy was being sponsored for visiting the country by an organization. What excited her the more, was that her father, who saw himself as half-atheist, half-Christian, but was actually agnostic, had finally agreed to thank God for having made him live, after a ghastly motor crash that crippled him. 'No, it's the Bishop I want to go and give ram,' he might have scolded his wife, Eunice thought.

He had the accident nine years ago, after he received a phone call from Rajaswamy that Eunice had delivered 'a chubby baby boy,' so to tell his wife of the good news, he traveled from

Lagos with his driver, but his car rammed into the bush, near the River Niger Bridge. 'Thank God he didn't jump into the river,' his wife had said. His spinal chord broke and he was completely crippled. The wheelchair became his home. He hated it, but couldn't do anything about it. In fact, he despised God, but his wife said he had no reason to despise God, for Christ's sake.

Eunice couldn't stop smiling and the scrap of paper she found in David's trouser pocket gingered her happiness.

'Honey,' she said softly. 'While I was washing David's clothes, I found this...'

She stretched up the paper to Rajaswamy, who pushed up his glasses to his nose. Eyebrows rose. He pushed the paper close to his sight and smiled. Then asked: 'Did he write this?' She replied: 'Yes, he did.'

He read it aloud for Helen and Eunice to hear.

Once upon a time. in the animal kingdom lived a monkey, that go out in the morning to pluck benana and in the same place, a rabbit live, with her family because she is a woman-rabbit: two female child-rabbit and her husband is dead. The monkey is a man and he begin to admaya the rabbit. The monkey want to do a man and a woman thing. Letaron, a lion that is a man, begin to plan his way to take the rabbit but the Monkey say no. and they begins to kworel. 'She's mine,' the monkey say. 'no, she belong to me,' the lion say again.

Nevadeless, as the monkey and Lion are friend, they tok about it evryday. the monkey become jealous and want to talk it to the woman Rabbit.

And he go to rabbit and tell her. she become afraid and begin to take her children out of the kave, where they lives. the monkey wait for her in the garden and offer her a basket of carrot. The lion go and bang on her door, but she don't come out and he start searching for her, but before he can rich, they do a man and a woman thing.'

Eunice smiled, while Rajaswamy chuckled, like a little boy being tickled in the ribs.

'He writes so well,' Rajaswamy said. 'His story is excellent and I think he has a bright future ahead of him.'

'I agree with you, honey,' Eunice said. 'But I think he doesn't know spellings.'

'Of course, Eunny,' Helen mumbled. 'Still, several great writers could just write the way he does and they would say that it is the character's language. He writes so well, believe it.'

'Yeah, he does.'

'So?' he asked. 'How do we talk to him about this? We need to make him understand that refining his language will actually bring out the true writer in him.'

'Shouldn't we send him over to Mr. Singh?' she suggested. 'I heard he is starting a class from tomorrow for teenagers who have a flare for writing.'

Rajaswamy widened his eyes. 'The writer?'

'Yes.'

'Oh!' he exclaimed. 'Where does he intend to open up the class?'

'At Connaught Place.'

'Great,' he said. 'We could simply ask Pankaj to drive him over for the class and make the necessary payment.'

'But honey,' Eunice suggested. 'Don't you think Raghu would love to go with him?'

'*Yaar!*' he sighed. 'I don't think that's a big problem. Since they are on vacation, they could just go there and spend the day, rather to stay around and make trouble.'

'Alright.'

Eunice saw Helen off.

During lunch, everyone sat peacefully, even Swathi who lazily fingered her rice with dal into her mouth, Rajaswamy told David that he had read his story and thought he should be sent to Mr. Singh's Little Writers' Club. With Raghu. Because Raghu had almost started crying when he didn't hear his name. Anyway, Vimala felt there was no way she could intrude - she wanted her son to be a lawyer. But she didn't say it out now. Then Eunice broke the news that she and David would join Rajaswamy to Nigeria. It was a shock to Raghu. He began to visualise being left alone in the Rajagopalan house. Without David. He would become sick. He shivered.

'Nigeria?' he asked. 'Oh no, not my David would go there. It's not a good place. There are so many mosquitoes there and everyone is so black and poor. Not my David.'

'Shut up, Raghu!' Vimala became furious. 'You don't be flipant with your mouth, ok?'

Eunice cleared her voice and said: 'Nigeria is not like you think sweetboy.'

Sweetboy was an Aryan, with a Dravidian blood. He became silent.

'Well,' she continued. 'As you feel the bites from mosquitoes from the garden, so you feel them there. You will simply find out that it is not what you think of it.'

'But there are so many black people there,' he insisted. 'Our teacher, Mr. Choudhury said that Africa, as a country, is as poor as Rajasthan. I don't know, but he showed us the pictures of hungry-looking African children.'

'Mr. Choudhury said Africa is a country?' Swathi snapped.

'Yes.'

'Vimala,' Swathi said, staring at her. 'Don't you think it would be better that you withdraw Raghu from that school?'

'Why, ma?' Vimala asked.

'Didn't you hear what he said?' she queried. 'That Mr. Choudhury told them Africa is a country and it is as poor as Rajasthan.'

'Well,' Vimala assumed. 'Mr. Choudhury would have said so because Africans look alike.'

'No, you fail like your son, Vimala,' Rajaswamy said, anger rising in his voice. 'Africans don't look alike. Well, I think I should lecture our brilliant lawyer.' He folded his hands and looked up in a lecturer-at-a-seminar-mood. 'Africa is a continent, with different regions. South, North, East, West and Central, just as we have in Asia.' He paused and started. 'Zimbabwe is in the South, Egypt is in the North, Kenya is in the East, then Nigeria in the West, with Malawi in the Central. It is a continent with almost fifty-three countries.'

Eunice's heart swelled. She was relieved that her man knew all these things before he married her.

'But,' Vimala suggested, 'does that make any sense?'

'Yes, it does,' he said. 'The skin nature of these people is not the same and their accents vary a lot. A Southerner would know a Westerner and a Northener is more or less a Middle Easterner.'

'Vimala, you should learn,' Swathi said. 'That people praise you for being a brilliant lawyer doesn't mean you are a brilliant person'.

'It's alright ma,' Vimala muttered.

That night, David dreamt - everything - about Nigeria. He visualized sitting in the balcony of the Onwubiko house, which he had seen in the pictures that his mother had shown him. He thought of it as Onwubiko House of Horror - because of the things Eunice had told him about it: it had all kinds of animals, even a fierce-looking Abyssinian cat.

In that horrible dream he first had of Ezeoke, the wildflower sprinkled hilly village, where the Onwubiko House was built, David was standing on the balcony of the bungalow when he saw a dwarf standing in the morning sun, with his hand clasped behind his head. To him, the dwarf wasn't one of the people of Ezeoke. He had a deep pink skin. It was then that he found himself moving to go talk to that dwarf. He quickly ran down the staircase to the garden, but before he got there, he couldn't see him. 'Where are you, little man?' David had asked. 'Please come out and let's play. I am feeling bored here. My cousins don't play with me, because they can't understand my accent.' Like magicked stars, the dwarf reappeared behind him and said: 'What do you want, David?'

'You know my name?' David startled. 'How come?'

'I know everybody's name,' the dwarf said. 'Why do you want to play with me?'

David began to fiddle his fingers. 'I know that you may not understand my accent, but -'

'I understand every accent,' the dwarf murmured. 'I know that your cousins don't like you, because you are more brilliant than they are.'

'Yes,' David said. 'And they don't want to play with me either.'

'But what kind of game do you want us to play?'

'Hide and Seek,' David said. 'I used to play that with my friends.'

'Picard and Raghu?'

'Yes.' He was surprised. 'But how did you know?'

'Well,' he said. 'I know everything God should know.

Anyway, I should go before Akajiegbe, my captor returns.'

'You want to go?'

'Yes.'

'Alright,' David said. 'What do you think I should call you next time we meet?'

'Nfanfa,' he said and disappeared.

David had never seen a dwarf in his dream for the first time, so when he woke up, he sat straight in the bed and thoughts filled his head. *Nfanfa is a dwarf. He knows everything God should know.* He folded his pillow in his arms and weighed the darkness. He felt the dwarf screaming his name from within the walls. David. Dravid.

Next morning, David and Raghu were ready to be driven to Mr. Singh's. Pankaj was cleaning away the drizzles of storm that had pelted itself all over the car, with a rag, while Eunice and Vimala stood at equal heights watching the kids.

'You two!' Vimala said. 'You have to be careful at school because Mr. Singh seems to be a harsh person.'

'Yes,' Eunice added. 'Make sure that you listen with concentration to whatever he says. He must know that his new pupils are strong headed.'

'Newton and Einstein we are!' they screamed and laughed.

Eunice laughed, but Vimala only smiled. Oh God, Eunice laughs anyhow, Vimala said to herself. They entered the backseats of the car, their little rucksacks hanging on their shoulders, while Pankaj started the engine of the car and wheeled out of the compound.

As Pankaj turned onto Panchkuia Road, he stopped and asked Raghu - because he knew that he wasn't in his father's house - to come and sit in the front seat, that he wasn't his boss. Raghu flamed up. 'No, I can't,' he said. 'You are born to be loyal, Pankaj. You are meant to be subjected to irresistible retribution. You are to be suffered.' But Pankaj couldn't understand any of the things he said because he said them in English. He drove on.

Raghu had perfected Swathi's demonstration when she talked to Rajaswamy about Basanti being made to suffer.

When they got to the traffic light - at the metro station - the light turned red. David turned to his left hand side and met a dazzling sight: a cow waiting for the light to turn green. As the light turned green, the animal found her way and vanished. This could be the Abyssinian cow, David thought, but Raghu didn't know what he was thinking.

Pankaj headed for Connaught Place through Main Bazaar and still as it was morning, the street was roughly crowded. He drove slowly into the ambience of Pahar Ganj, the sun looked at him and smiled. David felt the filth in the street crush at the bonnet - like a bomb being exploded in Kashmir. The dampness of the street muddled theatrically. He saw some Japanese tourists.

'They could be Chinese,' Raghu assumed.

'Yes,' David added.

'You never know!'

He got a glimpse of a restaurant waiter (inside a restaurant) taking a tray of food to a customer. Raghu smiled.

'Why you smile?' David asked.

Silence.

'These Pahar Ganj people,' Pankaj began in Hindi, 'know how to make aloo gobi, mushroom curry, korma, biryani and dal makhani.'

'You have eaten all that before?' Raghu asked.

'Hamara to hoga!' Pankaj squealed in Hindi.

David and Raghu looked at themselves.

'He doesn't even speak good Hindi,' David said in English.

'Yes, he speaks better Assamese.'

'He's insane!'

They all said these things in English because if Pankaj was to hear it, oh, they would have themselves to be blamed for what Rajaswamy would do to them. He would take them into the study and ask them to read J.K Rowling's *Harry Potter and the Philosopher's Stone* in a day and tell him what they had learnt from it. David would say he learnt how to fly and never stop. While Raghu would say he learnt how to enter a train without paying.

Vimala would smack them on the head.

Eunice would call them Vag-Are-Bonds. Or Muggles.

At the New Delhi Railway station, David saw something that startled him again: he saw a porter who had the size of the dwarf he had seen in his dream. Nfanfa, he said to himself and the porter turned. Raghu pinched him. He choked and asked what. Raghu told him, right into the face that he was staring uncontrollably at the porter.

'Do you like him?' Raghu asked, smiling.

'No!'

Connaught Place has traces of London, except for the spits of betelnut and gutka that have been used to paint the British-styled bricked buildings there. You try to take a picture there, come out and tell someone that it was taken in London, and that person will sure agree! But not when you took them standing near those dhabas that sell tobacco and bidi. The shops look elegant, and Piccadelhi can be said to be a London in a

Delhi. But the smells of dungs and urine really belittle the whole place and the number of dirty ragged beggars with unshaven beards and shabby hairs does a disservice to the whole of CP, Eunice used to say.

'Sahibs, I like this place,' Pankaj said, watching David from the rear view mirror. 'London it looks like.'

'You have *gone* to London?' Raghu asked in Hindi.

'You've *been* to London?' David corrected.

'Yes, you've been to London, Pankaj?'

'*Nahin*,' he said. '*London kaise hai hamari...*'

'You don't know Hindi, Pankaj,' David blushed.

Pankaj was silent. He drove through Piccadelhi and headed for the address Eunice had given him, which was where Mr. Singh held the class.

David and Raghu came into what looked like the size of their parlour. He saw many children and few he could recognize. They were his classmates at the British School in Delhi, but they couldn't say anything to each other, because Mr. Singh walked in.

Mr. Singh's full name was Sukhwinder. Sukhwinder Singh Kohli. He was a Sikh and had a stomach that looked like a balloon. ('It could deflate anytime,' Raghu whispered to David) Although he was fat, he was tall as well, but didn't look like Denzel Washington because he admired the black hunk. He had a Yokozuna-shaped body and Hulk Hogan-shaped eyes.

He introduced himself, as he was in front of his class.

David felt depressed. Instantly, he became angry. There was a time he had behaved this way, and his mother took him to the family therapist who spoke to David and after asking him questions had concluded: 'He's a manic-depressive, so you should be light on him.' Eunice wanted to know what that meant. 'He is suffering from bi-polar disorder.'

'No one has suffered that in my home before,' she had said.

'You mean Nigeria?' the therapist asked.

'Yes.'

'Oh!' he exclaimed. 'Nigerians don't have any idea about it. Do they even have doctors and psychological therapists?'

'They don't suffer what is the name?'

'Bipolar disorder?'

'Yes.'

Angrily, the therapist had added: 'Because they don't know anything.'

Raghu coughed and David turned to him with an angry face.

Mr. Singh heard him, he said to them in his easy flowing Punjabi accent. 'Goodmorin chudren!'

'Good morning, sir,' they chorused.

'Ai see,' he smiled. 'We 'ave new studence here today, and this makes me more 'appy.'

Silence.

'Wellu,' he continued. 'Ai don' 'ave mush to say, but that evri chudren here should be alert. We 'ave to do this homework, when we get home; write a love-story of no more than two hundred words and pass it on my desk tumorow.'

A love story? David thought.

When he got home that afternoon, he saw his mother still reading *Midnight's Children* and he asked of his father. 'He went for a seminar in Singapore,' Eunice said. 'He would be back tomorrow.'

'Bullshit,' he said and ran upstairs, entered his room, padlocked the door from the inside, and fell into his bed, pulling out some sheets of paper and then began to write frantically.

Raghu went to Picard's house to play cricket.

In the night as David slept in his room, he found himself sitting in the balcony of a house he had never seen, having tea with the dwarf sitting beside him. They talked, but he couldn't understand what they were saying. He only had to laugh when he saw the dwarf laughing.

The dwarf took him down from the balcony with a rope and went to the garden of the house and showed him a grave - and then laughed so loud.

David asked him whose grave that was and he said it was his and laughed. David asked him if he would take him into his grave and he said, 'I will, when the time comes!' Through the rays of his black-blue-gray-green eyes David saw himself.

'You look like me,' he told him.

The dwarf laughed and asked: 'So you don't know I am you and you are me?'

They laughed and danced along.

In her own dream that same night, while she cuddled the pillow her husband would have used if he was around, Eunice saw David entering the grave with the dwarf. She screamed. Oh,

David had mouthed, turned and asked her: 'So you don't know he is me and I am him?' Eunice knew exactly where she was in that dream. She was in her father's compound in Nigeria.

She knew the grave very well. She had been told several times that the grave was that of Nfanfa, an albino dwarf, who was buried there long ago.

Now, his ghost was coming after them, she told herself.

In a three-star hotel in Singapore, Rajaswamy battled with the pressure of being a celebrity. After a hectic evening at a seminar, he had retired to his hotel room, slumped into the bed and slept off. He began to dream.

In the dream, he was in a seminar in Lagos, when a dwarf sporting a French suit walked up to where he was delivering a paper and slapped him across the face.

They all woke at the same time. It was 1:32 am.

David was silent in his bed, with the pillow in his arms, when the door of the room he had padlocked, gently opened. He looked toward it, so surprised. There, was the dwarf, standing akimbo. The lights went off.

'Nfanfa!' David echoed his name.

He rushed out of the bed and switched the lights on again. He couldn't see the dwarf. He sighed. He opened his door and saw Pankaj racing through the hallway, down to Basanti's room. Ah, this night? He tiptoed and followed him. He eavesdropped as soon as he got to the door.

Pankaj and Basanti spoke in Hindi.

'Are you sure no one saw you when you entered?' Basanti

shivered.

'No one,' Pankaj said.

'Alright,' she nodded. 'Let's do it.'

'*Theek hai.*'

Things began to happen and they seemed *untellable*. The two felt warmth. Pankaj held her around her soft black body, kissed her on the neck and gently began to pull off her kurta. She held him too, mumbling and moaning. Quickly, as though he had been bitten by a termite, Pankaj removed his shirt and began to go deep into her, penetrating her through the silk kurta. Groaning. He jabbed her in the inside, softly, tenderly, softly and slowly. Again and again, muttering things to himself: '*Hamari nahin hain,*' even though Basanti couldn't make out what he said in Hindi that wasn't his.

Pankaj felt tired, but couldn't tell it. David watched from the keyhole as Pankaj looked up to the rooftop, breathing heavily and moaned.

He couldn't move, couldn't pull over him the knicker he wore or the shirt, and couldn't just do anything while there. He gobbled.

'*Tum* problem *kya*?' Basanti asked him. 'What's your problem?'

'*Main kha kharu*?' he replied, his eyes asking what he could do when he was tired.

But Basanti wanted more, as she wasn't satisfied. Oh, she was untouchable and now somebody was touching her. Here. There. Everywhere. And Pankaj was really, really feeling tired.

'Please,' Basanti begged in Hindi. 'Please do me.'

'Wait a minute,' muttered Pankaj. 'You don't know how tired I am. I can't even rise here. You are a tree.'

She smiled. 'Not a tree,' she protested in English and quickly added: 'But you haven't done anything yet?'

'Who said that?'

'Tum.'

'Kya?'

'Because I didn't feel anything.'

'Kya?'

'You didn't do anything,' she said. 'Do me. I want to feel
you.'

'But I'm tired.'

'Don't feel so.'

'Please.'

'Please, na!'

'Please,' he begged persistently. 'Let me rest.'

'Just do the last one,' she sniggered. 'You won't regret it.'

But he didn't. Because he wanted to regret it.

On the next day, Rajaswamy returned from Singapore and sent
for an astrologer he knew very well in Pahar Ganj. Pankaj drove
and picked him up. When the astrologer came, he was offered tea
and a saucer of Bharat biscuits with pakora. He ate quietly.
Rajaswamy told him the dream he had. He said his journey to
Nigeria was auspicious, but that he would loose his gold. He said
okay because he thought he had no gold to lose.

As he left, with an autorickshaw, Pankaj gave Rajaswamy
the letter Mr. Singh asked him to give him. He read it, smiled and
called David, who sat in the terrace watching Picard and Raghu
play cricket.

During dinner of chapatti and dal makhani, stapled with
rice and mashed tomato, Rajaswamy read the letter:

MR. SINGH'S LITTLE WRITERS' CLUB
Hamilton House, Connaught Place, New Delhi 110 001, India

Dear Mr. Rajaswamy Rajagopalan,

With strong and deep regret, I wish to send back your son, David to you. He is an ingrate, although he is a polite child. His homework is such that insults, maligns and degrades me as a person.

I apologise that I note him as a lark. I refund the payment you made and please, don't ever try sending anyone from the notorious and rich Rajagopalan House to my school because they are all completely spoilt.

Sincerely,
Mr. Sukhwinder Singh Kohli

Eunice got the story David wrote and read it.

It was a love-story, about a Sikh who entered the gurdwara with his shoes on, and his hair uncovered.

Not so good. Not so good.

'Come on,' Vimala said, her mouth filled with a lump of chapatti. 'We Indians still don't know how to ignore things like this. I have read the story and there is nothing much to be paid attention to.'

'*Chch!*' Eunice coughed. 'I'm surprised at Mr. Singh. He's a writer and should at least behave like one.'

'This is India for you,' Vimala said. 'I am Indian, but I don't agree with this Indian sensibility.'

When Jamuna heard about the letter, she was really angry. But the day Jamuna felt really angry was when Eunice told her that in Igbo, her name really had a foul meaning. She looked at Eunice and frowned.

'That's a stupid language,' she snapped.

5

The Tongue-Twister

MR. CHOUDHURY was David and Raghu's schoolteacher. The next morning, he came knocking on the door. Swathi, in a silk nightgown and socks, met him at the doorstep. She yawned into his face without saying anything and used the back of her palm to wipe her eyes.

'Goodmorning, Ma'am,' Choudhury said.

'Goodmorning, Choudhury,' replied Swathi. 'How do you do, Choudhury?'

'How do you do?' Choudhury asked in a schoolteacherly voice.

'Come in, come in, Choudhury.'

Not Choudhury, Ma'am, he said to himself. Why not say Mr. Choudhury?

Choudhury walked in, clad in a leather winter coat, which he claimed he bought in London. He believed he smelled of London, and Swathi would ask him: 'How does London smell, nitwit?'

'Would you like some tea?' Swathi asked and quickly

added. 'Pink tea? Lemon tea? Assam tea? Or Kashmiri tea?'

Choudhury, while seated majestically, said: 'Coffee I take.'

Swathi widened her eyes. 'Oh no, Choudhury,' she paused. 'You take black tea. I make you coffee in the afternoon. The swami condemns coffee, Choudhury.'

'The swami?'

'Yes, the swami.'

'What do you think he knows?' Choudhury stood and began to pace the room. 'You turn around onto the inner lives of these swamis and find out that they are not celibates as they claim.'

'Oh Choudhury,' Swathi mumbled. 'You don't slander the swami, Choudhury. The swami is the only one who is holy in the ashram, Choudhury.'

Choudhury frowned and resumed quickly, 'Go get a cup of black tea.'

'Now you want it?'

'Yes.'

Swathi limped in the gown to the dining table. She uncorked the blue Falcon flask and poured some hot water into a tea cup, then put it on a saucer. She opened a tea carton, took a bag and dipped it into the cup, and the water made it toddle. She sprinkled some ground sugar into the black tea and carried it to Choudhury. He held it firmly and said: 'Enough sugar?' She looked at him and said yes. 'How do I know?' He asked.

'Taste it.'

'It's very hot,' he grumbled. 'You have cakes?'

'This is morning, Choudhury.' Swathi was saddened.

'Morning? How do you mean?'

'You manage the tea only, Choudhury.'

Swathi was angry with Choudhury. Her face changed

and she gently slumped into a couch. Choudhury sipped from the cup. He inhaled. It hurt his tongue. It retched and he squealed.

'It's too hot,' Choudhury said.

'Don't complain, Choudhury.'

'Why?'

'You woke me up so early,' she said. 'You don't expect me to give you anything.'

'Oh!' screamed Choudhury. 'When I was in London, I brewed coffee in the mornings.'

'But not eaten with cakes?'

'I was a student then, with no money'..'

A Punjabi, Mr. Choudhury was the kind of teacher who was loved by every pupil in David's school. Funny, jovial and above all, accommodating. But parents hated him. He was always drunk and taught his pupils nonsense, so they said. People believed that he was a viper, but he saw himself as none. Swathi bore a heavy grudge against him, and didn't want to show it for one day.

'Well, how do you feel about this paltry sultry weather?'

'Paltry sultry?' Swathi looked at him, agitated.

'Yes, paltry sultry,' he said, went to a window and pulled the curtain curves open. The sun blistered into the room and Swathi yawned. Choudhury said: 'The paltry sultry of the weather. Look at it, ma'am. Like wobbling sunburn, the smouldering sun cracks the glass. Very tipsy. Unadorned. Anyway, where are my pupils, ma'am?'

Swathi made a face, pointed to their rooms upstairs and started walking through the dinning room over to the staircase. She put on the light, looked around, pressed a red button on the wall and a bell rang upstairs. David's door opened. Raghu's opened. The two began to walk down the staircase. Swathi sighed and returned to the sitting room, where she met Choudhury sitting in a chair at the dinning room eating cheesecakes and biscuits with milk tea.

'Oh Choudhury!' Swathi shouted.

'I'm not an ingrate, ma'am!'

'You are only a fool, Choudhury.'

'I won't finish it, ok?'

She tiredly slumped into the couch. Choudhury walked to the window and said: 'Look at the paltry sultry pearl of the fuming weather, disrupting the ambience of the escalating moon, the stars squeal, the monsoon mottles, the winter wiggles and all the monsters - '

Swathi cut in. 'Your pupils are here.'

He turned to them. 'Oh!' he said, when he found out that Rajaswamy, Vimala and Eunice had assembled along with David and Raghu. 'How do you do?'

'How do you do?' David said.

'How do you do?' Raghu said animatedly.

Choudhury smiled and nodded. 'Yes, my sweet paltry sultry pupils.'

'What you want, Choudhury?' Swathi said in English.

'*Hamesha!*' he said in Hindi. 'I know it is a wonderfully kept surprise that you have me visible in your house this paltry sultry morning. Well, I learnt from a close source that one of my pupils is going to the Land of *Kala*.'

Swathi sat up. 'Land of *Kala*?'

'Yes,' Choudhury said and sipped from the teacup. 'Nigeria.'

'You must be sick in the arse, Choudhury,' shouted Swathi uncontrollably. 'I know you have a boil in the arse, Choudhury?'

'No boil, Madam Rajagopalan,' he said. 'My arse, so

chilled and cold.'

'Lazy teacher,' Swathi released her grudge. 'You don't know anything. You claim to have read in London.'

'Stop that, mama,' Rajaswamy was furious. 'You have to respect teachers as judges.'

'You are also sick in the arse,' Swathi said to Rajaswamy. 'For your information Ramesh, no, Rakesh, no, Rajaswamy, lawyers are the pillars that hold the world.'

David and Raghu smiled. He knew what was happening behind the loaded truck. So, Rajaswamy had those names and didn't even tell him, David said to himself.

'Choudhury, get out!' Swathi swore. 'Get out! Get out!'

Choudhury laid the teacup on a side stool. He made for the door and shrieked. Then stepped out. Of course, he knew that Swathi was power herself. She was born a Brahmin, married a Brahmin and had Brahmin children, all living in a Brahmin house, filled with Brahmin things and even dreamed and redreamed Brahmin dreams. And Swathi was ready to tear him into shards with her Brahmin fingers.

When the morning sun finally came up and the smell of the watered garden rose, Swathi walked in a blue gown through the carpet grass to the cottage, passing the dwarf flower trees as they bade her good morning. She shuttled between the smell of the pakoras their Bangladeshi neighbour made on the thrashing pan. Swathi now remembered softly how Jashim had left East Pakistan and ran to India. He brought with him a picture of his beautiful wife, cuddling her daughter. He told Swathi that one day he would make enough taka and go back to his home in Dhaka. Suddenly, Swathi hit the top of her biggest left toe at the taproot of a mango tree and squealed. 'That monster!' She wept. 'That monster. He shouldn't have come here this early morning.' She was referring to Choudhury. To her, Swathi, she believed that Choudhury was bad luck. She retched as her eyes turn red-brown, as though she had been drowned in Kingfisher beer. She screamed and began to limp back to the house, holding her left leg, as if she was holding another person's leg for the person.

She reached the verandah and slumped into a cane chair there. Jam, jam, she said inside, her curly long hair draping the edges of her spectacle. The memories of the day she and Anantha made love in the kitchen came back to her, like haunting ghosts. Although she felt like a rape victim that day, she also enjoyed it - and then she remembered how she had felt the day she met Anantha.

It was in the summer of 1946 - when the British Labour Government of Prime Minister Atlee offered self-government to India - that she met her prince charming: young Anantha in a café in Bombay, while she worked in a suburb jam factory and they winked at each other. Anantha was working with a well-known law firm in Bandra.

They had lunch at Shiva Ram Restaurant, where he held her left hand and kissed the back. She fell in love. He proposed. She agreed and then she paid the dowry.

They wedded in a posh room lit with incense and sweet smelling candles.

Mr. Frazier and his wife were sitting at the dining table, having roast lamb and rice for breakfast, when David and Raghu came into the parlour, while Picard sat cross-legged on the rug, eating the chicken chips burger they had ordered from a local restaurant in Pahar Ganj. David greeted the American couple and they nodded in approval with their mouths filled.

Picard looked up at the two of the spirits. 'You are too happy, David?'

'Yeah!' He jumped up excitedly. 'I'll go to Nigeria this December.'

'This month?'

'Yeah.'

Picard frowned. 'You know Nigeria is not good, Dave?'

'How?' David asked, so surprised.

'People are kidnaped almost everyday there,' Picard had begun. 'You don't have to go, Dave. There is too much malaria there. I felt depressed the last time I saw black kids on BBC. They looked very thin.'

Raghu cut in: 'I've told him that as well.'

'You are a bitch, Raghu,' David swore.

Mrs Frazier turned frantically and asked in Hindi. '*Kya?*' She paused and then added more quizzically, 'You should have said it in Hindi.'

'Sorry,' David apologized. '*Teri...teri...*' and he shut up.

'No problem,' she said, because she did not understand.

David turned to Raghu and Picard. 'You know,' he said. 'When my uncle Kezie came to India last time, he told us that Nigerians believe that we Indians live on trees, cook with the dung of cows, sleep with cows and eat like cows!'

'Are these things true?' Raghu asked, tears filling his eyes.

'No,' David responded. 'That means that you don't say bad things about a place where you haven't been to.'

Mr. Frazier looked at his wife and they smiled. Their going out was followed by a long silence that had Picard, Raghu and David all staring at each other. Tears filled their eyes and then flowed down onto their cheeks.

Pinkcolouredcheeks.

Browncolouredcheeks.

Chocolatecolouredcheeks.

They embraced warmly, and David visualized himself as Krishna dancing with the gopis. It was actually after he watched a play by Radhakrishan based on the life of Krishna staged at the Indira Gandhi National Centre for Arts on Rajendra Prasad Road that David began to see himself as Krishna, Vasudeva became Rajaswamy, Devaki was Eunice but there was no Balarama. If there was one, that should be Raghu, but Raghu was the son of another man who had abandoned him and his mother for a man there in West End.

When Anantha tried dashing David at a stone, he became a gigantic figure and grew eight good arms and each wielded a weapon. He then attacked Anantha.

In Mumbai, Anantha gathered his friends in a bar and asked them to drink their heads off. They would drink and drink and drink into intoxication. His friends - who were not drunk - would get him into a cheap hotel and pay a prostitute to spend the night with him. But no matter how drunk he was now, Anantha would never make love to any of those prostitutes. 'I'm married,' he'd tell them and show them his wedding band. One day, he'd called Swathi over the mobile phone and she screamed back at him. 'You left me to go and make love to those *homoners*!'

'Who *homoners*?'

'Those boys that fuck boys!'

'*Nahin,*' Anantha screamed.

Swathi had always suspected Anantha of that. But there was no evidence. She knew that their marriage wasn't a forced or arranged one. That was why she couldn't even talk to her friends about it. She nearly hit the Saudi Arabian, Naif who lived on the same street as them for checking on her husband the other time. When Anantha asked her why she had behaved that way, she replied: 'These Arabians who don't have the opportunity to fuck women prefer men!'

'You are close-minded!' Anantha snapped.

It was Naif who said that tomorrow was pronounced as Two-Moron.

And it was he who taught David the Beatles. So, David, Raghu and Picard sang the Beatles for Raghu.

> You say it's your birthday
> It's my birthday too - yeah
> They say it's your birthday
> We're gonna have a good time
> I'm glad it's your birthday
> Happy birthday to you.

'Will you invite bin Laden's brother?' Picard asked.

'Yes,' Raghu nodded.

'Why?'

'So, he wouldn't terrorise us!'

They laughed.

> Yes we're going to a party party
> Yes we're going to a party party...

'And Kavitha is coming, Dave?'

'Yes,' David said.

'You think this is the last supper?' Picard boldly asked.

No.'

David sang.

You say it's your birthday
It's my birthday too - yeah
They say it's your birthday
We're gonna have a good time
I'm glad it's your birthday
Happy birthday to you.

Picard sang the last lines with much dexterity. He swung into the air and smiled. He raised his leg, high into the air and danced like a happy nun leaving the church after a mass to roam the streets of Kingston, Jamaica. His head twisted as the song flowed ceaselessly.

'Can you backswipe?' David asked Picard.

'Backswipe?' he asked. 'Or swirl?'

'Whatever,' he muttered. 'Dancing like Usher Raymond.'

'Yes, I could.'

'Do.'

Picard tilted his legs, tried to move backwards in a quick movement (like Michael Jackson did in one of his music-videos) and fell on the marbled floor. David grabbed him quickly, while Raghu burst into a hysterical laughter.

David was out immediately. Alone. He ran into the cottage and found Swathi sitting in a padmasana style on a mat, just below the table where she placed her jam-pots and jars. She was doing yoga. She said she wanted to be the female Swami Ramdev.

Swathi was so close to David that she taught him how to do yoga. She wrote out the direction on how to do yoga for him on a scrap of paper.

1) *Sit straight in siddhasana and inhale the oxygen gently. Then keep your palms on your knees.*

He began to do it.

2) *Lower your neck a tad infront and your chin would touch the deep in your neck.*

He had begun to shiver.

3) *Focus on your brows. You will find your chest coming forward on its own.*

Swathi told David that the Pranayama was called jalandhara bandh. That she had got the instructions from the swami himself. She told him it was necessary for him to do that pranayama, so that his voice could be sonorous like Craig David's.

One certain Wednesday morning, while Swathi had gone to the ashram, David sneaked into her room and found a copy of *Pranayama: Its Philisophy and Practice* by Swami Ramdev. He read it and saw many of the things Swathi had told him in the past. They were all written there. He labeled Swathi a thief.

Now Swathi was sitting in a comfortable yogic asana, inhaling through her two nostrils persuasively, then she exhaled. That was part of the yoga, she would explain to anyone who dared to know.

'No ma!' David screamed. 'You don't do that!'

She turned, opened her legs (still cross-legged) and said: 'Why?'

'You have blood pressure, ma.'

'But I have asthma.'

'But you have blood pressure?'

'Yes.'

'Please ma,' he pleaded. 'You love me and I love you too. If Pa is the one doing this, I'd allow him do it.'

Swathi stood up. 'Doing now?'

'Alright,' he said.

6

A Witty Raghu's Party

THE RAJAGOPALAN house smelled of curry and spices. Vimala was overly busy and was throwing an extravagant party to mark Raghu's ninth birthday. There were white long laid tables decorated with pots of flowers. White rose flowers larded the tables and exotic bottles of French wines, which Raghu's father had bought in Paris, specifically for the party and sent it from London through one of his Indian friends. He sent Vimala an e-mail noting that he wouldn't come; since he hadn't been able to overcome the shame he put himself in. Vimala replied and said it was alright, but promised that the party would go fine.

Eunice made light French dishes (to match the wines, you know), of grilled fish, cheese and fruit.

Rajaswamy read the names of the wines: Puligny Montrachet, Champagne, Fixin, Cotés de Beaune, Chatéaneuf du Pape, La Mouline and La Landonne, with assorted types of grape wines.

Swathi said it was too much: 'So, that AIDS husband of yours knows what is good, eh?' she asked Vimala, who snapped happily.

Farida and Basanti were busy arranging things, while Pankaj was in the garage stuffing crumbs of rice and beef into his mouth. Everyone knew he was a vegetarian, but why was he taking the beef? He ate and ate, then gulped a bottle of water at once. He breathed in. If Rajaswamy had seen him eating that way, he'd surely call him a Sri Lankan refugee, who needed a tent in Tamil Nadu. Or he would lecture him on how the Cambodian refugees in 1979 had spent their years in Thailand. 'This was genocide,' he would say. 'You can imagine children dying without food and nowhere to be buried.' Then Rajaswamy was reading for another BA in the US. He wrote an article in a US newspaper, praising President Carter and calling upon the world to condemn the genocide in Cambodia. It was a Baltimore-based newspaper and the editors were too impressed with his article. They sent him a mail, asking him to take a foreign correspondent job with them. He agreed ("I was a journalist in the US',' he would tell Jamuna when he felt he should)

The newspaper sent him on his first assignment to report on the situation in Cambodia - to be assisted by Miss Kelly White, a black young woman who looked really smart. He, Rajaswamy, wondered why a black should answer white. But that didn't matter then. Because what mattered was what was underneath the skirt.

Kelly White was the first black woman to have Rajaswamy groaning under her thighs. During the time the Cambodians were buried in common open graves, Kelly made love to Rajaswamy. But they wrote their articles and when they were published, the UN awarded them for Human Rights Report.

Rajaswamy returned to India with a first class in International Politics and Diplomacy.

Vimala said that was his business.

Raghu, who was the celebrant, was sported in an Italian suit that fitted him so much. David said he looked like James Bond. Picard said he looked like Adolph Hitler. And he made a face. Then walked upstairs alone. He was looking for Pankaj, Farida and Swathi. He wanted to show them his suit. But he saw Basanti. No, he couldn't go without showing anyone.

'You see my shirt?'

'Yes,' Basanti smiled.

'I look like James Bond?'

Basanti was surprised.

'You don't know James Bond?'

'Yes, not know him,' she said. 'Who's he?'

'A movie actor!'

The way Raghu said a movie actor in English startled Basanti. Moo-vee-ractor. But he did not know he had pronounced it too quickly. Move-you-tractor!

When he returned to the parlour, the whole place was filled with people. Their neighbours. The women in saris, kurtas and salwars. Raghu looked around, got sight of the Saudi Arabian.

'Mr. Knife,' he called out to him.

'Yearsboy!' Naif blabbered in his Saudi accent.

'Did you see my brother, Mr. Knife?'

'No, see no brother, youngboy.' He paused and pointed to an end of the room. 'See one litul boy over dear one satin time. He lukes lark a black boy.'

'Yes, Mr. Knife.'

'I shore he is some wear around hear,' he said. 'He most be haiding in the dark. You can only faind him two-moron.'

'No, Mr. Knife.'

'Why you faind him?'

Raghu looked around frantically to see if he could get a glimpse of David, but withdrew from giraffeing when he couldn't. 'I have to cut the cake with him,' he added.

'The keik?' Naif asked excitedly.

'Yes.'

'Bought we can cot the keik togeda,' he demanded.

Raghu said no.

'Why you say no?'

Raghu didn't say anything. He could hear David's voice floating in the darkness, like a balloon. He listened attentively. He turned and the party guests disappeared; the decorated tables vanished and there was no party. He shook in fear. Now, all that he saw was darkness and in the midst of that deep darkness, he could see a black hut with a dwarf clad in white dancing around it. He was singing.

'Lizin,' Naif said to Raghu in a soft whisper. 'I hear his voisi. He is a speak inside that dark. He is there. I shore he is a dear wit his friend. Years. I see him wit a litul man the size of a cat.'

Raghu eyed him angrily and walked away. He passed through the shrinking dry leaves and walked to the cottage. As he got to the wooden door of the cottage he could now hear David's voice. He gently pushed the door open and saw David and Kavitha sitting on the long jam table. David smiled. He frowned. Kavitha smiled. He frowned, hissed and then walked away. David looked at Kavitha, jumped down from the table and ran after him. 'Raghu!' He echoed his name. 'Wait.' But Raghu did not wait. He continued walking, as fast as he could. 'Happy birthday!'

Raghu stopped, without turning.

David stopped. 'I'm sorry, Raghu,' he said. 'Happy birthday!'

He turned and smiled. 'Happy birthday, too!'

David didn't know that. His mother had planned it that way; they hadn't celebrated his previous birthdays on the same day as Raghu's. So, it came today as a surprise. Strange things were happening to him at nine. He couldn't understand. Vimala had told Raghu that the two of them were born the same day, month and year. While he in London, David was born in Delhi.

'Just a minute,' David said almost to himself. 'Oh God!'

They sang.

> *Happy birthday to you*
> *Happy birthday to me*
> *Happy birthday to you*
> *Happy birthday to me*

They danced round the trees and left Kavitha in the cottage. They danced into the parlour and to his amazement, Raghu found that the guests were back and they had been served wine. Toasts began when they came in.

The guests sang *'Happy Birthday to You.'*

7

The Last Bidi, the Last Sitar

THAT NIGHT after the party, Rajaswamy had signed into his email box and got a mail from the Consular Section of the Nigeria High Commission asking him to come over for a visa interview. He wide-eyedly asked Eunice if Nigerian visa had finally become as difficult as the American visa. She said it was difficult only for the Indians. 'You know Indians are too many in Nigeria,' she'd quickly added.

On the next morning, they drove to Chandragupta Marg, Chanakyapuri and got their passports stamped with tourist visas.

While they drove home, Rajaswamy said that the Entry Clearance officer insulted him by saying that it was the Indian government that ballooned the schism in India; that it was the Indian government that gave Indians the power to discriminate blacks. He said that it was an insult to someone of his status and reminded Eunice that it was one of the reasons why he hated Indian politics. In his mind, he piled up his reasons. He had once told a group of Indian students at Victoria University, Manchester that they should not allow their fellow British or white students to intimidate them. 'Without you,' he had told them, 'they won't have anyone to envy. You are the Indian Ambassadors. You represent the never-to-be-shaken Indian culture and these white kids are jealous of you because they have finally fallen from the ancient European culture.'

A student of Bengali parents asked him what he thought of Robert Clive's defeat of the Nawab of Bengal at Plassey in 1757.

Rajaswamy said that Robert Clive was 'a downtrodden racist pig.' Brawling on with his lecture, he said that Warren Hastings was on the same terrain with Clive, because 'he consolidated his conquests.' Although there were few white students there - who were studying Sanskrit and the history of India - Rajaswamy said that the British should be scorned because if they hadn't controlled virtually all the lines of India south of the Sutlej River and completely erased the powers of Mysore and the Marathas in 1818, they would have remained completely independent like Sind and Punjab. He disappointed the students, so they believed, when he ended the lecture by saying that 'Mahatma Gandhi wasn't a hero, because it was his weakness that made the exportation of cotton goods to Britain possible.'

David ran into the cottage to see Swathi as soon as they got home. He was depressed to have found Swathi smoking bidi, a leafy cigarette-shaped puddle. He frowned as Swathi looked at him drooling and their eyes met. He stamped his feet on the ground and made a *kpaah kpaah* sound. 'This was why John Lennon and Yoko Ono were arrested in 1969, grandma,' he said.

'Why?'

'Cannabis.'

'No child,' she felt relaxed, blowing rings of smoke. 'I'm depressed.'

'You can't be depressed, grandma. Why?'

Getting near David, Swathi threw the bidi down and stepped on it, so the light would wane. She held him by the shoulder. 'You see! This world is like Varanasi. You come and go.' With a deeply-grumbly eye, David said yes. 'Alright,' Swathi moaned. 'When I was young, my grandmother told me a story of a girl named Parvathi.'

David was astonished. 'You have a grandmother?'

'I had, child,' she corrected. 'She's dead.'

'Did she love you the way a grandmother loves a grandson?'

Swathi paused and said yes. Then, she told David that the girl Parvathi loved a dwarf and they were strongly in love. That the girl lived in Shillong with her grandmother. The dwarf married Parvathi and wanted to take her back to his home in Manali, so the grandmother asked her to kiss her before she left.

Farida got her sitar ready that evening. She rehearsed the songs she was going to sing. On last year's Lakshmi Puja, she had sung a song in Kashmiri to an accompainment of the sitar, but Swathi warned her, that she shouldn't 'play those terrorist-songs again.' So that evening, Farida sang in Kashmiri.

Snakes bite thatch-huts dwellers
Cloudy nights bewilder them
And waters flow thro' their skulls

She bubbled the strings of the sitar labouriously.

A naked python dances in the silver sea

She thimbled through the clenches of the strings. It occurred that David was enjoying the song, because Farida didn't claim she was Celine Dion.

The whispers from the lizards mottle
Ghosts move untapped in cradles
Gurgle of blood flows in the man's head
The poor man smashes in fear

They all loved the song. And they applauded her. Rajaswamy said she performed better than Ravi Shankar, but that she should make sure that she didn't go on again copying people's words, from English and putting them in Kashmiri. Then Farida rose and walked into her room. She was surprised when David and Raghu walked into her room, without knocking. 'Kya?' She had asked, wide-eyed. With eyes filled with tears, David told her that he had seen that she loved him the way a grandmother loved a grandson. They embraced, Farida cried, and to David, the memories of last year's Diwali haunted him. He remembered what had happened that evening, while he was sitting on a dwarf-wall at the Gopalakrishna's house. He had come with his bicycle and then was teaching Kavitha how to ride it. He hit his leg at a mislaid stone in the process and screamed at the spree of a bitter pain. Earlier that day, Mr. Choudhury had visited the Rajagopalans and after a lunch of white boiled rice and butter saag, he asked David and Raghu to write an essay on How I Spent My Diwali Holiday. The wound retched and then he saw blood reeling out of it.

Fortunately, Farida passed and heard him. She rushed for him with her breadloaf-shaped heart and carried him home with the smell of roast lamb on her skin.

Like a potted palm tree, he was heaped into his bed.

Farida began to tend to his wound. She had a bowl of cold water and a tiny pink towel that she dipped into the flushing water and slowly kneaded his legs. He was grim-faced. Oh, this had happened to him, while he taught a lover bicycle riding. Everytime you love a girl, his mind was telling him. Blue-shaded now, he looked up at Farida. 'You tell Ma?'

'No!' she said in English. 'Ma I not tell.'

'Who you tell?'

'Nobody I tell, baby,' she kissed his forehead.

There was a knock on the door. Raghu walked in gently and went to David's side.

'Get out, you!' Farida shouted. 'You get out, you!'

'Why I get out?' Raghu asked her in English.

'You disturb David,' she babbled. 'You go!'

Raghu rushed to the door. 'Idiot,' he cursed her. 'I'll tell my mom and you will leave this house and go back to Kashmir, vulture!'

Farida ignored him.

Swathi's voice was so loud, when she spoke, strapped loosely in the large cushion. Rajaswamy, Vimala and Eunice were there. She wasn't telling them about the bidi she had smoked, but was screaming wholeheartedly at Vimala who had raised issues of going back to her ex-husband in London. Swathi said she was insane. Vimala said she loved her husband, Rajaram and that since he had apologized and accepted his guilt, she wanted him back.

'You can't, Vimala,' she looked at her critically.

'Mama,' Vimala reproached her. 'You are trying to ruin my life, mama.'

'Om Nath!' she exclaimed. 'How? Oh, you children make things seem wry. I can't abet evil. I haven't even lived through the shame you brought to me by marrying a *homoner* or what do you call it?'

The question was for no one, but Eunice answered, 'Homosexual.'

'Then let me remarry, mama,' Vimala pleaded tiredly.

Swathi rose angrily. 'Not now, Vee!' She paced the room. 'But for you to say you want to go back to that *homoner*, huh, I can't pull the shame to my face!'

'He's not a homosexual,' Vimala muttered.

Surprised, Swathi smoothened, 'Not *homoner*? What's he?'

'Bisexual,' she said.

'What's the difference, nitwit!'

'Look mama,' Vimala adopted Rajaswamy's mood-in-a-lecture. 'He's the father of my son. I love him, can't you understand?'

'But he doesn't love you,' she argued.

'He does mama.'

'*Theek hai,*' she nodded. 'But he has many flaws. The swami said he should be stalked to death because of his act.' Swathi snapped and walked away.

Vimala slumped into the couch and broke into tears. She had wanted to settle this out with Swathi before Rajaswamy could travel. That afternoon, she had called Jamuna on the phone and informed her that she wanted to talk to Swathi about going back to her ex-husband. 'Yes, you have to, Vimala,' Jamuna said. 'She needs to understand how you feel about Rajaram, ok?' Vimala thanked her and she concluded, saying: 'You know, Vee, any man could be gay.'

The next day, Eunice drove herself to *Twenty Four Seven* on Lajpat Nagar II. She was quick for the shopping. She shopped for beverages, noodles, toiletries, canned jams, sauces, juices, milk and butter. Others were soaps, pomades, toothbrushes and pastes.

She returned home immediately.

And Jamuna was there with her children. She told them that her husband had traveled to Beijing for an official assignment. As she stepped in, Supriya greeted her. 'How are you?' she asked her and she said she was alright.

David and Raghu were sitting in the couch.

'You will have another girlfriend?' Raghu asked.

'No.'

Farida called David from within and said that the 'Amerikan boi' wanted to see him. Then, Picard entered and eyed Supriya. Raghu pinched her skin. She screamed, began to walk away, flat-soled and crying.

Eunice was reading *Midnight's Children* in the verandah, sitting in a cane chair, when Warren Frazier and his wife arrived. They sat opposite her and Farida served them Darjeeling tea. They sipped and while they did so, Eunice buried her head in the book.

'I heard you are going to Nigeria?' Mr. Frazier asked.

'Yes,' she said, without looking up.

'You gotta be careful there,' Mrs Frazier added.

'That's my country, my friends,' she kept reading.

'*Theek hai,*' Mrs Frazier polished her Hindi. '*Aap khana khaey hain?*'

Eunice looked up at her angrily. '*Nahin,*' she replied. 'We have no food here.'

They stood and as they got to the gate, Jashim, the Bangladeshi was struggling to enter. Mrs Frazier said: '*Namaste.*' He said: '*Namasteji.*' And they passed. Eunice cheered up briskly when she saw Jashim, holding a polythene bag in his right hand. She offered him a seat and asked him if he wanted Nilgiri tea or chocolate. 'Thank you, Madam Eunice,' he said. 'This -' He stretched the polythene bag towards her. 'I buy from Chandni Chowk and this from Chowri Bazaar. Gold necklace worth ten-carat purity of coins. You take. Inside, I buy wrist watch for sir Rajaswamy.'

Eunice didn't stretch her hand to take it. 'No!'

'Why you not take, Madam Eunice?' He asked, ashamed.

'I just can't, Jashim,' an astonished Eunice said. 'No, thanks.

'You not take, why?' He made a face. 'You not know what you do me? Sir Rajaswamy help me get job. I make enough taka now I wan go back to Dhaka.'

Eunice lightened up. 'Oh, but thanks.'

'No Madam Eunice,' he insisted, dropping the polythene bag beside Eunice. 'I write my address inside there. I not go back to Dhaka, without thanking you. If you wan come Bangladesh, call me and I make hotel arrangement. You do me good.'

'When are you going?' Eunice finally asked.

'Now,' he said. 'I call taxi, carry me to airport. I fly to Dhaka.'

'Safe journey!'
He thanked her and left.

Swathi walked slugghishly to Rajaswamy's car. It was 8:31 pm.
Everyone gathered near the cars in which they would head
towards the airport. Rajaswamy, David and Eunice were leaving
for Nigeria. Jamuna was going to drive back Rajaswamy's if he
drove it to the airport. Pankaj would drive the other car. Vimala
would go in her own car.

David embraced Farida warmly and left her.

At the gate, they saw a ragged, dirty and smelly old man,
with shabby curly hair.

'What does he want?' David asked Eunice thrusting his
right hand, in deep fear, in hers.

'He said he had a dream,' Eunice began, 'and in his dream
his dead father appeared and told him that he should come and
meet us to take him to Mauritius.'

'Why?'

'He said his father is from Mauritius.'

'And where is he from?'

'Gujarat.'

'Let's take him, mom.'

'*Mba, chineke ekwela ihe ojo!*' she screamed in Igbo. 'No,
God forbid bad thing.'

8

Farewell, Oh Breast-Sucker!

THE WELL-TARRED road, larded with beautiful and colourful flowers that draped to the Indira Gandhi International Airport was lit with sparkly street lights that beautified the whole grandeur of Delhihood. And David felt the soaring wind, as if it would tear apart the sky, as he sat in the backseat of the car with Raghu, while Pradip sat in the front seat, speaking to Pankaj, while he drove.

David looked at Raghu in the dark car and his face turned to that of the albino dwarf he had seen in his dreams. He slushed. Because it was all he could do. He made to wind down the window, and hummed. Because it was all he could. He sweated and prayed that the car got to the airport quickly. Then Raghu, with the face of the dwarf said: 'You are me, I'm you!'

Pradip turned and stared longingly at them.

David bent his head in shame.

Pankaj steered towards the International Lounge of the airport. They got to the Parking Lounge and he reversed and stopped. David, ran to Swathi, asked her to bend, so he could whisper something to her. When she did, he kissed her on the cheek and said: 'Parvathi and the dwarf didn't go like that. You lied, grandma.' Swathi froze, looked at him and her hands shook. Yes, she loved him. And he loved her back. That was equal love. *Love-me-I-love-you.* He held her hand and said wittingly: 'Whenever grandpa comes back, tell him that I have taken my mother to Nigeria. I will teach her to make jam.' She nodded and kissed him on his forehead, without saying a word, while airport people watched them sheepishly.

Supriya was most annoyed. She was going to miss David. So much. She walked to the railing where airport people, who waited to wave goodbyes (and even badbyes) to their loved (and hated) ones, leaned. Tears flowed down her smooth cheeks. Although Rajaswamy traveled frequently from the Indira Gandhi Airport, he hadn't had the time to read one sign that angered Eunice. It was the *British Airways Passengers Should Enter Through Gate 2* sign. He said when Queen Victoria was crowned the Empress of India in 1877 was when India became 'a part of the British prisons.' 'Look at it,' he said. 'They are still surfacing in India so much.'

Jamuna embraced Eunice. Vimala kissed her by the sides. Swathi asked her to look after Rajaswamy and David very well. And after herself.

Raghu held David firmly. 'You can't leave me alone in India, David,' he screamed and broke into tears.

The airport people turned to them.

Vimala walked to him, held his face in her left palm and slapped it. 'Shut up!' she scolded. 'You're being too stupid, idiot!'

He fell quiet. He knew he couldn't do anything else. David stopped half-way as he ran into the Waiting Lounge and shuddered. He knew he couldn't do anything else. Tears flowed ceaselessly down from his cheeks. He knew he couldn't do anything else. Rajaswamy who was behind him, pushed him to go further. He knew he couldn't do anything else. Pradip smiled and entered the car. He knew he couldn't do anything else. Pankaj started the engine and gently drove out. He knew he couldn't do anything else.

Jamuna drove the other car back home.

'Passengers boarding Ethiopian Airlines 0901 to Addis Ababa are advised to head for the flight through Gate Four,' a slender black woman of East African origin said in a British accent.

They were checked in by the Indian Customs and as David walked behind his parents to the Ethiopian airlines lounge, he saw the albino dwarf sitting in the midst of some Japanese on the steel benches in the Waiting Lounge. He stopped and looked at him closely. David smiled. The dwarf smiled. Rajaswamy turned and met his son standing in that crowd staring at someone he couldn't see. He smacked him on the head. *'Chalo!'* He shouted. And David followed him immediately.

Now, they were inside the plane. David thought that a plane was a bird that only grew large when it touched the ground. He said that his father traveled to those countries he went to, in caravans. When he entered, he saw many people. Japanese, blacks and whites. He held on to his mother, who was sporting a dupatta. She held her ticket and David's. 24B for her and 25B for David. Rajaswamy's was 24A. David was lowered into his 25B seat. 25A was empty.

After some minutes, a tall Sikh gentleman (who looked exactly like Mr. Singh) walked in and gently lowered himself into

24A. David choked. His heart began to pound. He shivered his legs, just as a child possessed by an evil spirit would do, and let out a great yell. The Sikh felt astonished. Eunice turned and when she saw the Sikh gentleman, she understood David and what he was going through. There was a black boy who Eunice begged and he exchanged his seat for David's. Near David now, was that same dwarf. He smiled. David smiled. 'You are me and I am you.'

'You are Abyssinian!' David mumbled.

One day, Eunice had found a diary kept by David. In it, he wrote in his slanting handwriting: *Today I sow a cow at road and it stop when trafic light go red. I call it the Abyssinian cow, because it look like a cow from hell and behaved strangely. I rememba mumi tell me there a Abyssinian cat in Nigeria. I go and find out.* Eunice had laughed and laughed. There's no need to correct him, she assumed.

The dwarf muttered something to himself.

'Hey,' David said. 'Where are you going to?'

'Nigeria.'

'Why?'

That's my home.'

David frowned. The dwarf frowned. David looked away and when he turned, he saw no dwarf again, but a Japanese sleeping softly in the seat, with his head bent backward. He shrugged and shivered, then held his legs up and sat.

The air hostesses served food. David had mashed tomatoes, sliced fruits, butter, toast, grape jam, and an empty paper cup for tea and a plastic spoon. Another hostess poured boiled water from a flask for him. For tea, she said. Pink tea? Lemon tea? Darjeeling tea? Black tea? Milk tea? Or coffee?

Hours passed.

The plane landed at Addis Ababa and the passengers moved to the Transit Lounge. David's eyes roamed the large apartment. He couldn't find the dwarf. Maybe he had gone to Nigeria, he concluded. He sat on the steel bench in the Lounge near his mother who sat like a Nigerian woman: sit straight with your legs slammed together, so that no man would see your thing. David widened his eyes to search for the dwarf. He saw a man in a leather coat shop and he had the face of the dwarf. The dwarf smiled at him. He looked away and burst into laughter. Eunice looked at him. He frowned. Abyssinian boy in an Abyssinian land, she intoned inaudibly.

A Customs Officer called for the passengers heading for Lagos. Passengers checked in, with their Duty Free bags and handbags. Even legbags. That was what the dwarf, in David's mind, carried.

David said the sound of the plane was voo-voo as it left for the sky.

'We are in heaven, papa,' a young Indian boy said to his father.

'Yes,' his father replied.

When the plane landed at the Murtala Muhammed International Airport in Lagos and the passengers headed for the Checking Counters to be purloined by the Nigerian Customs, David went near the young Indian boy who had told his father that they were in heaven and said: 'You disgraced India in the plane, sahib.' The boy looked at him in shame and began to sob uncontrollably.

PART TWO

18th December, Twenty Hundred and Six

Nigeria

9

A Dusty Welcome to the "Giant of Africa"

THE DUSTY December wind flapped itself through the squashing rumbles of the airport, like a lightening, sending objects into chaos. Rajaswamy held David by the hand and headed for the counter where foreign nationals were checked. A woman at the counter tossed Rajaswamy's passport, read his name. 'Raj-as-swarmee Raj-a-go-palan?' she asked, looking up at him. Rajaswamy smiled and said yes. But in the inside of him, he was saying, 'That's Raj-ash-wamy.' Then the woman while stamping the back of the page where the visa was placed, muttered something in Igbo to herself. 'Yeah?' Rajaswamy asked and she said boldly, 'You Indians are becoming too much in this country with these your horrible names. What do you want?' Before he could say anything, she placed his and David's passports for collection and added abruptly: 'You Indians shouldn't kill us in this country.'

Eunice still had a Nigerian passport, so she was cleared with no hassles.

When they got to the carousel, Rajaswamy told Eunice

that he had gotten a nasty welcome from an Immigration Officer. 'What about the average Nigerian?' He asked absent-mindedly. Eunice didn't say anything. While she looked out for when their luggage would roll out, Rajaswamy went to get a trolley. He held one and as he made to go, a uniformed boy asked him if he had paid to collect it. But it's not like that in Delhi, he said. But the boy said he must pay to have the trolley. He asked how much it was and he told him that it was fifty naira. He said he didn't have naira. 'What currency do you have?' the boy asked. 'Rupee,' he replied. 'No,' the airport boy said. 'Do you have dollar?' Rajaswamy said yes. He opened his wallet and gave him one-dollar bill, then carried the trolley. He went back to the carousel.

David was now standing by his side. Right in front of him stood a black dwarf in a denim blue jean trouser and a Reuben V-neck shaped shirt. He smiled at the dwarf and the dwarf smiled. David frowned. The dwarf smiled. David smiled and said, 'You are funny.' Rajaswamy looked down at him, stared at him, and then watched his gaze. 'Do you know him?' He asked David and he said no. 'So why laugh?' He became silent. In a while, Eunice appeared with three travel-bags, with airport stickers, placed them in the trolley and they began to wheel it towards the Arrivals Lounge. An airport official detached something from their boarding passes and smiled at David. He had envisaged Eunice as a Nigerian and fondly he asked in Pidgin: 'Him be your hussy?' She said yes and he said it was good.

At the Arrivals Lounge, people held placards that read Yoruba, Igbo and Hausa names. Oba Oladotun Oyinlola, Igwe Akuoma Agunaechemba and Alhaji Baba Ahmed.

Rajaswamy found his name. A young man in a white long-sleeved shirt and black trouser had it printed neatly on the paper.

When he saw Rajaswamy, he rushed to him, because he had his picture in the car he had come with. 'Sir, are you Dr. Rajaswamy Rajagopalan?'

'Yes?' Rajaswamy asked, as if he didn't know why.

'I'm from the University of Lagos,' he stressed. 'You are delivering a lecture there.'

'Yes,' he said, then turned to Eunice whose gaze was fixed on something else. He turned towards her gaze and saw Nduka, a lean handsome effeminate young man, well-shaven and slightly tall.

'Hey!' Nduka said as he neared them. 'Welcome home.'

'Oh!' Rajaswamy sneered. 'Here is someone picking me up from the University of Lagos.'

'Come on,' Nduka sniggered. 'Let him go. You gotta stay in my house and from there you attend the seminar or whatever!'

Rajaswamy told the young man the same and he left, with anger swarmed all over his face. David slushed. Eunice admired Nduka as if he was a model on a runway.

'You look really great, smallie!'

'Do I?' He drooled, as though he didn't know he looked *really* great. Come on, jolly good, jolly good, boy, you know you look great, his mind kept telling him.

'Yes, you are,' she teased him.

Nduka eyed David and then clicked his cheeks with his fingers. 'He now looks like his grandfather,' Nduka said to Eunice.

David paused and in protest, he said: 'No. I can't look like my grandfather. He hates my mom and me.'

Rajaswamy was astonished, but didn't say anything.

Eunice held David's ear. 'Don't be silly, Craig David.'

And he smiled. 'Alright ma,' he said. 'Craig David is not silly.' Then Nduka ran his left hand through his oiled hair and led them through the airport people who kept staring at them. Maybe because Eunice was dressed strangely. In a dupatta. Or partly because of her 'white husband.' Eunice hated such things. She thought that Nigerians were very stupid and didn't know *how* to stare at foreigners. Rajaswamy muttered something in Hindi and Eunice said, adding in English: 'Yes, Nigerians worship foreigners!' As they got to the car park, a smartly dressed boy ran to them and asked: 'You wan change?' Nduka said no. Nduka hated such mannerism. He said that in a civilized country, it was the buyers who went to the sellers, not the sellers going to the buyers.

'You know,' Eunice said, helping David into the frontseat of Nduka's Bora car. *'Ukwu jie agu, mgbada abia ya ugwo!'*

'You can imagine!' Nduka said shyly getting into the driver's seat. 'You still speak Igbo very well.'

'Of course,' she said and got into the car. 'That's why I love the Yorubas. No matter where they are born into, they tend to speak their language wonderfully and fluently. Even the Hausas. But the Igbos are so stupid that they forget so easily.'

'That's true,' Nduka said. 'Even Igbos born in Igbo land don't know how to speak and write Igbo.'

Rajaswamy called a newspaper vendor and bought a copy of the *Guardian*. He entered the car and Nduka drove away towards Bank-Anthony Way. Rajaswamy saw one of the captions in the newspaper and trundled. It was *An Indian Hacked to Death at Ikorodu by Agberos*. He asked Eunice what agbero meant. She said it was a Yoruba word for 'miscreant.' He read the article. His widened eyes grappled with the reality. He had come for his slaughterhouse. There was no way out.

'Yeah,' Nduka said as he drove onto Opebi Link Road. 'The Senate House is debating over the status of the Indians in Nigeria since it was reported last week that a Nigerian was killed at Old Delhi Railway station by the Indian police.'

'Old Delhi Railway station?' Rajaswamy was surprised.

'Yes.'

'But it wasn't reported in India?' He asked, feeling ashamed.

'It couldn't have been,' Nduka added.

'So what is the Senate debating?' Eunice asked with interest.

'Over the deportation of all Indians,' he said in a dimpled smile. 'Both the ones born in Nigeria and those who came from India.'

'Oh, that's depressing!' she slushed. 'At least Nigeria should demand for the diplomatic ties with India to be severed, than deporting all.'

'Come on, sister!' Nduka sneered. 'The Presidency called upon the Indian Prime Minister or President to have some words with him. But they sent a party leader...'

'Really?' Rajaswamy asked.

'Yes,' he mumbled. 'But you know it's an insult to send a party leader when the President of a large country like Nigeria wants to speak to his colleague. So the President asked the Senate to debate over it. Anyway, some Senators who have business relationship with Indians are standing in for them. But you know, in the Senate, the majority carries the vote. One of the Senators lamented how he was harassed by the Indian Immigration Officers at the Indira Gandhi Airport, even while he had a diplomatic passport. He supports the deportation wholeheartedly.'

'That's why I hate politics,' Rajaswamy said, almost to himself.

Rajaswamy buried his head in the bulky newspaper, which he bought for one dollar, as soon as Nduka turned onto

Ikorodu Road. So this is where that Indian was hacked to death, he said to himself as he watched the high-rise houses pass the sills of the car. Eunice looked away to the other side of the road. She was highly depressed and hoped that the ground would open and swallow them. She made a face and sighed as she saw Indian-shaped faces of beggars. Nduka told her that those beggars were from Niger. She inhaled in relief. She thought Indians shouldn't be begging in a country like Nigeria. It would seem degrading. But she was startled when they got to the traffic jam and in the car next to theirs, she saw an Indian man with his family.

'You know this is Ikorodu,' Nduka explained to her. 'Indians are too many here, even where I live.'

'Oh!' she was disappointed. 'And what are they doing here?'

Nduka let out a laugh and David looked at him.

'Some of them have spent years here working,' he said.

'Working?' Rajaswamy asked.

'Yes. Why?'

'Ah!' He exclaimed. 'Why won't the Nigerian Government deport these Indians? You know, the only thing I hate is inequality. Frankly speaking, Indians don't employ black people and why then should they be allowed to work here?'

Eunice turned to him fiercely.

'Yes,' he nodded. 'Stop staring at me. You never told me all this before!'

'I should have?'

'Of course.'

'Sorry that I didn't.'

Rajaswamy frowned. Oh, maybe that was what his hosts were going to ask him during the seminars and interviews. He looked away and allowed the breeze at Onipanu slash his face, as the car drove into Oyewole Street, then to Tinubu Road. David played with the buttons on his shirt and when they stopped because of the traffic jam, passers-by watched them. Stared at them. A black woman with a white husband. Nigeria was full of black people, David trudged. At least, he was a sahib in the midst of untouchable black people.

Nduka turned onto the driveway, near a gas station. David looked up at a cone-shaped sign and read: PALMGROVE ESTATE. A uniformed man at the gate, on recognizing Nduka gently pulled the large gate open and he drove in. Rajaswamy saw the sign, NO OKADA ALLOWED IN, but he didn't understand what okada meant. He asked Eunice and she told him that it was a Nigerian way of saying motorcycle. To his amazement, Rajaswamy discovered there were autorickshaws in Nigeria, but the ones in Nigeria were larger than the ones in India. Then, Nduka slowed towards the farther right passing an orphanage home, a Cherubim and Seraphim church and then turned on the left, to India Street through D'Alberto Street. When Rajaswamy saw the India Street sign, he grumbled. 'How come?' He had asked. Nduka smiled, saying: 'Yeah, this is where I live.'

He stopped in front of a duplex, blared the horn of his car and a tattered-looking man opened the gate. He drove in. Ah, Eunice was flabbergasted. How could her kid brother be living in such mansion? Such beautifully decorated house? She helped David out. The gate man opened the boot of the car, after greeting Rajaswamy and Eunice, and hauled the three travel-bags into the house.

'Look at you!' Eunice jounced and embraced Nduka. 'You own this whole house?'

'Yeah, sister,' he said and beckoned on them. 'Come on inside!'

They followed him as he led them into the sitting room

Nduka was Onwubiko's last child. He was born some few years after the Biafran war. Then Onwubiko was on diplomatic mission as Nigeria's Ambassador to South Africa. And his wife agreed to go with him. She also didn't feel comfortable with the apartheid, for Christ's sake. She cursed the white oppressive government for treating the blacks like pigs. Years later, it was reported in the newspaper that a notable Nigerian writer and activist was held in South Africa over immigration rules. 'Those bastards!' she had screamed. 'We helped those bastards out of the claws of the whites, for Christ's sake!'

As soon as Khotso Seatlholo called upon all the blacks of Azania to stay at home on strike on November 1, 1976, Onwubiko's wife was in labour at a hospital in uptown Johannesburg. To tease Nduka, his siblings (except Eunice) nicknamed him Hector Peterson, who Kezie said 'roasted himself in the front chapters of history.' But Dada Felicia, Onwubiko's younger sister who was still a spinster at the age of sixty-two said that Nduka should instead be called Tsietsi Mashinini. Or even Seatlholo. Kezie said no, explaining that the two she'd mentioned were destined to live briefly. That they were like chickens being squirmed at by a mob of angry hawks. He said that Mashinini's death was mysterious and that he died in exile while the Soweto Uprising was high. He quoted Seatlholo as saying in farewell note to Mashinini: 'I will die in an accident, fall ill or simply get mugged.'

Kezie studied in South Africa and returned when the Nigerian Head of State, General Olusegun Obasanjo arrived in South Africa, heading a Commonwealth delegation to visit Robben Island to see Nelson Mandela and the others.

Kezie became a father at the age of twenty-one. In the middle of war. That was during the war that broke out between

Nigeria and the new state of Biafra. It was a war that changed the lives of people. Not for good. Not for bad. Not for better. Not for the worse. But for a tortuous life ahead.

When the war broke, while Ojukwu screamed for secession, Onwubiko was already off to Iraq as a Deputy Ambassador. His wife said that she wouldn't go to that part of the world, for Christ's sake. She said she would stay back with her three children - Kezie, Udunna and Eunice - who met with their demons during the war. Moreover, Onwubiko's wife believed that war was a natural thing that every nation must pass through. But she was enraged when Igbo people were massacred in the north. She said that the Hausas were 'ethnicist beasts.' She hated them so much and said that if the war ended, she'd be happy to have some Hausa people employed in her house as maids and cobblers.

'These Nigerians are bestials,' she had muttered to her children. 'The Hausas are stupid.'

It didn't take long when the enemy helicopters started nearing Ezeoke, their village. And Onwubiko's wife asked the children to get anything they could lay their hands on and take to their heels, for Christ's sake. Things began to change. Overnight. Wonders started to end. Like scars on a dog's nose, it began to appear for all men to see. The village became a troubled one. Families began to scatter, but Onwubiko's wife, whose name was Ashiagbalam (though she didn't like that), held her children so close. She made sure that they ran to where she ran to.

Conscription began and Kezie was conscripted into the Biafran army. She hid Udunna, for Christ's sake. Eunice wept when Kezie was taken to the Biafran army camp in Umuahia. What disturbed Eunice the more was how the Igbos were slaughtered in the north. One day, she was sitting on the terrace of their house when the headless body of their neighbour's son was brought back to the village.

Kezie met a girl in Umuahia and as a soldier, used intimidation and had sex with her. She became roundbellied. He decided to marry her. But how was she going to cope with a soldier-husband? They had a child and called him Uche and then a daughter, Pamela.

Nduka's mobile phone rang, he answered the caller. 'Yeah?' He said. 'Oh brother. Big sister has already arrived with the husband. Yeah. Ok.' He stretched the phone to Eunice, who was now seated in a couch, near Rajaswamy. 'That's brother Udunna!' She took the phone from him and they conversed.

Udunna was the most quiet and humble amongst the Onwubiko children. He was married to a Japanese woman, Hatsu. They had two children - Yvonne and Jerry. Smart looking. Dog eyed. Small-mouthed. And wore glasses.

Eunice was the most pampered. She never lacked anything. In Igbo tradition, girls are treasures and fortune harbingers to their families. As a girl's dowry brings good things, they are taken care of very well. But Ashiagbalam - whose name means 'Let Me Not Have Badluck' - was disappointed when Eunice married Rajaswamy. 'Oh!' she had screamed. 'How can my daughter marry into a tradition where a woman pays the dowry, for Christ's sake?'

She was spoilt, really well. In their house, they had so many maids, from Nda Lydia - who made melon cakes for the Ibo-Uzo feast; prepared nsala soup, pounded yam and cassava; Mgborie who made rice and stew, beans, spaghetti, egusi, agbonu and achi soups. And the kitchen couldn't be more warmed up without Babiana in it. She fried eggs with carrot and cucumber, indomie noodle and washed the kitchen utensils. Above all, there were Labata, the driver; Mama Benji, the cleaner, the gardener, the washerman (who opened the laundry on

Saturdays) and the animal keeper, so they called him.
     But Kezie despised all this. He said that Papa-Nkeukwu,
which was what Onwubiko, began to answer, because he was a
grandfather - and Mama-Nkeukwu (Ashiagbalam) were
'polishing themselves up to laziness by employing all those
people in the house, while Dada Felicia stayed in the house.' He
believed that if Papa-Nkeukwu had fought during the war, he'd
have been more agile.

Nduka's Lebanese cook, Malik made a delicious meal of fruit
salad (with its cream), cakes of white rice drooled onto their
plates and stew, a red sauce garnished with sweat meats. Then a
bowl of richly made spinach, for Rajaswamy and they ate
lavishly.
     'You can't tell me this guy is your maid?' Eunice asked
Nduka.
     'Lee nu gi,' Nduka spoke for the first time in Igbo. 'That
guy is a Lebanese and his name is Malik. You know, sister?'
     Rajaswamy was listening.
     'No?' Nduka continued. 'I wanted to have Lebanese and
Asians for maids.'
     'Really?' Rajaswamy asked.
     'Yeah,' he said. 'My former cook was a Chinese. My
friends would tell me that one day, if I am not careful, this guy
would make frogs for me.'
     David laughed. 'You won't eat?'
     'No, honey,' Eunice poked him on the shoulder. 'We don't
eat frogs in Nigeria.'
     'Come on, sister!' Nduka shrugged. 'The kids in the

village eat frogs.'

'Really?'

'Yeah.'

'So smallie?'

'Yeah.'

'Ain't you...' Eunice paused and added in Igbo, so Rajaswamy couldn't understand what she was saying: '*O bu na i choghi ilu nwanyi?*'

'*Mba, adanne!*' He grobbled. 'I will when the time comes, you know?'

'*Kedu mgbe o bu?*' she asked in Igbo, between mouthfuls.

'Soon, sister.'

Well, suspicions had, in the past risen about Nduka. He had been effeminate from childhood, but no one could gather up the courage to tell him to his face what they thought about him. Papa-Nkeukwu's friend, Chief Mobutu had told him one night, as they sat on the terrace of the house smoking their pipes: 'Onwubiko, I was stunned today during my rally at Ndiama when someone said your son could be Elton John.' To the politician's surprise, Onwubiko laughed a tiny, but loud laughter. He told Chief Mobutu that if his son was what they said he was, that he would 'ungay' him by forcing him on Nda Lydia.

Chief Mobutu said he should better do it. 'For political purposes, you know,' he'd added. But would Nda Lydia stoop so low? She couldn't, because for her, she was both ugly and beautiful. Ugly in the sense that she was old. And beautiful that she was a beauty while she grew up. But for one to say that he could force Nduka on her was a bit of a mischief. She would open her thighs, but the man wouldn't go, without having his penis screwed. No one.

And Nduka couldn't do that.

'*Nwa ahu abughi homosezal,*' Babiana had said to Mgborie

(in Igbo) when they'd overheard Mama-Nkeukwu and Chief Mobutu's wife discussing it in the verandah. 'That boy is not a homosezal,' she'd repeated in English. 'He is polite and handsome.'

'Don't you know?' Mgborie had enquired.

'What?'

'That polite and handsome people do that thing.'

'No!' Babiana waved. 'Only ugly boys who can't talk to women do that!'

'You mean it?'

'Yes.'

'That means Labata is one?'

'Somehow,' she said and busied around.

Babiana and Mgborie were the gossips of the house. Anyway, they were surprised to note what people said about Nduka, because Nduka was always seen surrounded by women. Babiana and Mgborie were midget-sized and were always found in the kitchen the same time. They despised Labata, because he ate too much. True, Labata had so many flaws. He spoke Hindi, French, Italian and Greek and had no money. Babiana said that people who spoke many languages were always poor. 'Yes,' Mgborie supported. 'They are always poor.' Babiana nodded and said: 'They don't have shi-shi. No farthing. They are hopeless. Labata doesn't even have money, still he has twelve children.'

'His wife is pregnant now,' Mgborie broke into a derisive laughter.

'Again?'

'Yes.'

'That man is so stupid,' she clotted.

Labata didn't care a fig. He was alright with the twelve children he had, clad in their one-bedroomed flat. His wife, Uchaoma sneaked into the Onwubiko house in the evenings and escaped with the leftovers her husband might have packed for her. Till she was caught one evening (as she made her way through the backyard) by Mama-Nkeukwu.

'*Onye oshi!*' Mama-Nkeukwu screamed at her. 'Thief!' She held her by her hair. 'I pay your husband every month for driving my car, for Christ's sake; still you want me to feed you and your twelve disciples, for Christ's sake!'

'No, mama,' Uchaoma begged.

What no, Uchaoma didn't explain. And Mama-Nkeukwu slapped her left cheek. She fell down. Nothing mattered much to Uchaoma (not even the slap), she continued sneaking in for the leftovers.

On the next morning, Nduka drove Rajaswamy to TerraKulture on Victoria Island, where he was to attend a seminar on 'Boosting World Economies.' When they got there, the whole place was filled with people - students and journalists. A Master of Ceremony introduced him and he started the seminar. He was happy to see some Indians in the midst of the crowd. When he was finally settled to field questions, a student rose and said: 'Sir, in your country, we are meant to know through the media that you treat black people as untouchables?'

'Not so bad,' he said, clearing his throat. 'First, I'm married to a Nigerian. Second, we live and eat in the same house.'

But that wasn't the question, Nduka sitting at the back of the crowd muttered to himself. Could this be tension?

A journalist, standing asked: 'Sir, if the Senate finally arrives at deporting all Indians in Nigeria, do you think it will affect Nigeria's economy?'

'Not at all,' he brilliantly said. 'But the issue is that it won't bode well with the image of Nigeria. I think any problem with Nigeria today has got to do with the immigration. If the immigration is corrupt, then foreigners will come here and mess up.'

The crowd was silent.

'The immigration must not renew visas of Asians and should ask them to go back to their countries in an organized manner,' he continued. 'You know, every good country is determined by the immigration. Jobs reserved for the citizens should not be offered to foreign nationals at any cost.'

After the seminar, there was a cocktail party and students conversed. They complained to each other that they couldn't understand what Rajaswamy said. 'He speaks buru buru buru,' an Igbo said and they laughed.

Rajaswamy appeared on TV shows and asked the Nigerian government to tackle Asians and deport those who held expired visas. Newpapers carried exotic headlines:

THE SUN: *Outrageous, Indian screams*

GUARDIAN: *Illegal Immigrants Will Bring You Down, Indian Warns Nigeria*

THIS DAY: *Indian Polemicist Laments Over Nigeria's Immigration Rules*

THE PUNCH: *Indian Writer Lambasts Fellow Asians*

NEW AGE: *The Trouble With Nigeria is Immigration, says Indian*

He and Eunice were in Lagos for one week.

AT SAM MBAKWE Airport, Owerri, Labata's mind began to pound. He stood at the Arrivals Lounge with no placard, probably to pass on the message that he was waiting for somebody. He visualized Eunice. Was she still that slim girl that paraded herself, so elegantly? Or had she grown fat? He was overly scared of the future. How he may dwindle himself by forgetting how that brainy girl looked like. He was in a dilemma.

But things were not as he thought.

As soon as Eunice and her husband appeared at the lounge with their son, Labata recognised them. He walked up to them and Eunice smiled up at him. Good, because her mother had told them in the past that anyone who was poor and underprivileged (that couldn't live the way they were living) was osu. And Eunice bore that in mind, although her father tried to dispel these thoughts out of her.

'How are you?' Eunice asked, stretching out the trolley to him, so he could haul it away.

'I dey fine ma,' he replied, held the luggage and headed for the Exit Lounge.

'And your wife?'

'She dey kampe o, ma.'

Eunice sighed and as soon as they got to the Volvo car parked in the car park, Eunice lifted David, settled him into the front seat, and then glued her posterior in the back where Rajaswamy sat. Labata started the engine of the car. *Kpigbim.* And drove off. David was saying things to himself in Hindi. He began to sing a song he had heard Picard's mother sing a day before they left for Nigeria.

Aaj toh kamal ho gaya
Dhoti ko phar ke roomal ho gaya
Toh kya kar rahe ho bhai

Even though he couldn't make out the real meaning of what he sang, he went on singing.

'*Namasté*,' Labata said and turned towards Okigwe Road, then Wetheral Road.

'*Namasté*?' Rajaswamy asked, open-mouthed.

No. Eunice had to explain to him what Labata was, because Indians were fond of belittling people. Labata passed Wetheral Junction, turned towards Old ITC Park and then headed towards MCC Junction, past Dan Anyiam National Stadium and was now at Fire Service, drove round the Roundabout Traffic Control and sped through Mbaise Road to Egbu, down to Emekuku. Labata's story was a long, long one. But Eunice made it very, very short. Again, the shortness of the story heightened its intensity. The angst. The tremor. And this was why he couldn't tell more about his life in Paris, which was where he'd started from. That was many years ago, when Papa-Nkeukwu was a real Omereoha - 'A Doer For All.' The elders of Ezeoke asked him to help send one of their sons abroad (because he was then the only one to have traveled outside the country from that remote village) and he agreed. Labata was picked out. Papa-Nkeukwu - who knew the way to do things - arranged everything for him, and he was sent to France with the assistance of the elders who contributed some money for the flight ticket.

Labata was in Paris, knew no one, had nowhere to go and so had to loiter around a restaurant near George V Hotel and then swarm into Restaurant le Cinq, where an old woman, sitting opposite him winked her eyes at him.

Like a bird peeking at a worm in mud.

He sighed and looked away. Why was she staring at him? No one knew. Now, he knew that the old woman wanted him. More than an expert carver would want a crooked wood, to prove his perfectionist mind. She kept her gaze on him like a wrack above the fire. She showed a toothless smile and feeling embarrassed, Labata stood up from his seat. She got up and held him by the hand and whispered to him, 'You are handsome!'

'*Merci*,' Labata had replied unbelievably.

'Could you sit with me, *mon garcon*?' she said. 'Sit, please.'

'*Que*?' he asked.

'Sit, please.'

And he did.

'*Tu parle Francais*?' she asked, feeling roused within.

'*Oui*,' he said, '*je parle Francais*. But I speak English better...

'You are new to Paris?'

'Yes.'

'Of course,' she smiled. 'I guessed as much, because I know almost all the black boys around here.'

Then Labata was twenty. 'Really?' He had asked.

'*Oui*,' she nodded. 'I admire black people a lot, especially the boys. They look sweet and splendid. *Nous sommes est beau*.'

'*Merci, madame*.'

'*Non!*' she muted. 'I just love them. And you know the sweetest thing about them?'

'*Non*.'

'They have large dicks.'

He felt embarrassed. She must be so stupid, he cursed her. How could she say that?

'Well, I don't know,' he finally said.

'*Oui*,' she said. 'My friend Willie had two black boys in her house the other time. And you know what?'

'*Non*.'

'They made her scream under their thighs.'

'*Que?*'

'Yes,' she intoned.

Embarrassment, harassment, embarrassment. There was excitement on her face.

'You know what?' she continued, 'She felt happy after that.'

Labata smiled.

'Every night,' she said, 'she'd go into their room and .....' She bent towards Labata and whispered: 'Her body began to nourish. She began to shine like a lily in the morning. She was seventy eight then and her body swelled beautifully.'

'*Oui?*'

'That means that you can help me.'

'How?'

'You should know,' she said, low-toned.

Still, Labata did as if he didn't know. Neverthemore, it was as though the old woman who introduced herself as Mrs Siegried, had charmed him, he followed her. To his greatest surprise, the old vamp carried him in her Toyota Camry to Louis Vuitton and bought him the kind of things he wanted. As the winter breeze snudged in, they walked through Champs-Elysees. And had dinner at a restaurant near Au Petit Chez Soi.

She took him to her bungalow apartment, sprawled with a lush garden and she told him that she would be paying him monthly (and even feed him) to have sex with her. He agreed, since there was no job for him in that expensive city.

Few months after, Mrs Siegried died in a car accident near Louvre Museum. At eighty. And Labata took to the street. Like an outcast. He found himself smelling the slums of Paris, but it didn't work out. One Saturday evening, while walking through La Place Vendome, he met a Ghanaian woman and narrated his story to her. She agreed to accommodate him on one condition: that he was going to work for her. What kind of work? Labata had asked himself. When the Ghanaian had introduced him to the other boarders in her house, Labata understood the kind of job he'd come to France to do. 'You are going to deliver some brownie to our customers in London, through the underground,' she'd told him.

Unfortunately, Labata was arrested by the police on his way to the station, spent years in the jail, and then was deported to Nigeria. Labata told them this as he drove past the GOODBYE FROM OWERRI signpost.

10

Half- past, Half-present, Half-future

DECEMBER in Ezeoke has always been like it is now. Things go mad and mad goes things. It is always the time when all fresh fruits are withered and the leaves of trees start speaking. *They* weep because no rain falls on them. *They* make noise. *They* also weep of the harmattan that squashes all through them. Dust rebels against sand. *They* dance like fools in the air, like imbeciles. *They* make the colour of houses turn muddy. The high-rise houses shrink to the tone of exigency and all the time, birds chirp below their window panes. The birds sing. Sing like angels, (if angels sing). The croaking of frogs breaks through the winds.

Then that December, political rallies smelled at every edge of the village, like the smells of excrement from a broken waste pipe and families who had families that were returning from abroad painted their houses with new Saclux paints; removed cobwebs and cut elephant grasses. Some bought new cushions and cemented broken parts of their houses.

And Onwubiko's house was one. The gardener gardened; the washerman washed and the cleaner cleaned.

Mama-Nkeukwu walked through the hallway, carrying

a tray of melon cakes, because that day was Ibo-Uzo feast day, and the puny Abyssinian cat marched slowly behind her. She turned and stared at it. 'You!' she shouted at the cat. 'I'm not a witch, for Christ's sake! Only witches use you!' The cat kept following her. It belonged to Papa-Nkeukwu, who was a member of AMORC, The Ancient and Mystical Order Rosae Crucis. And as everyone was busy, he sat crippled in his wheelchair reading Harvey Spencer Lewis' *The Mystical Life of Jesus.* Mama-Nkeukwu stepped into the spacious kitchen, and just beside Dada Felicia, she placed the tray on a white larded long table and sighed. Dada Felicia looked at her and smiled. She couldn't say anything. Maybe, she, Mama-Nkeukwu wanted to say something about the Ibo-Uzo feast, Dada Felicia thought. On last year's Ibo-Uzo festival, Mama-Nkeukwu had screamed that nobody was going to cook anything in the house that day, because it might look as if they were part of the pagan feast. Papa-Nkeukwu said she should pack her things and go back to her parents. Unlatched, tears trickled down her cheeks, she said that wasn't possible. She no more had parents. And her brothers were too old. No.

'I can't believe this!' she said after all.

Dada Felicia made some *whatisit* eyes.

'That I'm exhausting myself because of that hopeless Rajaswamy.'

'Lajaswamy?' Dada Felicia said.

'Yes,' Mama-Nkeukwu nodded, ignoring her tongue. 'I don't even know the reason why Eunice should allow that idol-worshipper come with her!!!'

'Tlue,' she said. 'They are leally clazy. They need Jesus Chlist!'

'You are making a point there, for Christ's sake!'

'Good point,' she said. 'And that's why they are vely

poor.'

'*The i kwuru bu eziokwu,*' Mama-Nkeukwu said in Igbo. 'What you said is true.'

'Clazy people,' Dada Felicia said.

She knew one thing: that she didn't create herself, everyone knew. But some assumed that her tongue was pranked upon by God, because she was *talk-active*. She could say anything at any given time. Even at that age, she couldn't pronounce 'r' because she pronounced it as 'l.'

She had lived with a man at first. But as a *partly* wife. And a *wholly* unmarried woman. And when her *partly* husband threw his *partly* wife away, Papa-Nkeukwu gabled like a nun, and trundled the hills of the land. He was ready to get to the root of the matter. Then he'd just returned from abroad. He drove angrily through the potholes from Ezeoke to the police station at Orieagu and lodged his complaints against Dada Felicia's husband.

Four Complaints. He wrote them down on the long notebook before the District Police Officer on his desk.

1)   *The so-called husband beat the shit out of her.*

2)   *He screwed her arse.*

3)   *He kicked her on the belly like a thief and threw her out.*

4)   *He did not come to apologize.*

But the DPO didn't know the whole thing. He didn't write them anyway.

1)   *I don't think there are husbands named so-called, who could beat the shit out of their wives.*

2)   *What equipment did he use to screw her? Screw-driver?*

3)   *Did he kick her like a football? If not, that's not a case.*

4)   *How could he come to apologize?*

Papa-Nkeukwu opened his suitcase and placed wads of naira notes on the desk. The DPO smiled like a child at an extravagant birthday party. He promised Papa-Nkeukwu that they would 'fetch the so-called husband and have him castrated.' He said that was alright. He told the DPO that if they got the bastard, that they should keep him in the cell for two weeks.

Junior officers were sent out to fetch the rogue and when they got him, the DPO sent for Papa-Nkeukwu. When he arrived, he asked for a space to talk to Felicia's *partly* husband and when he asked him why he had to treat his sister like that, the partly husband howled: 'Your sister was involved with other women!'

Papa-Nkeukwu, ashamed of himself, went home. And promised himself not to reveal to anyone what his sister was.

Dada Felicia, wearing a sleeveless white shirt, tied a green wrapper and in her soled rubber slippers, walked through the corridor that connected the study and paused when she saw Mama Benji, in the study, cleaning and wiping away the dust that had enveloped the whole place. She coughed and Mama Benji stopped and turned towards the door. She smiled as soon as she saw Dada Felicia. Dada Felicia stepped in and stood by the doorway.

'*I boola*!' Mama Benji greeted Dada Felicia.

'*Imeela*!' she replied. '*Kedu*?'

'I'm fine.'

'Did you...'

Mama Benji cut in. 'Thank you for the mbom-uzo gifts.'

'*Enweghi ihe mele nu*,' Dada Felicia said. 'No ploblem. I just think you deserve that.'

'Thank you.'

'You are welcome,' she said. 'I believe I also deserve more than this when the time comes.'

'Eh,' she nodded. 'And what time would you want me to come today?.'

'Ugbu a,' she whispered. 'Now. My bedloom is wide open fol you. I leally would love to see that thing again. It makes me clazy.'

Mama Benji began to laugh. She dashed her feet against the floor. She was feeling shy. Nothing mattered much to her. The issue was that deep inside her, she thought that she and Dada Felicia were the paired saints Perpetua and Felicitas.

'Ngwanu,' Mama Benji said. 'Let me just finish cleaning this and I will be with you in the next few minutes.'

'Allight,' she said. 'I'd be waiting. And I'm sule that this time alound, you ale going to bellyful me with this youl potatoish body.'

'Ha-ha!' Mama Benji laughed. *'O bughi nani* potatoish. It's not only potatoish. Tomatoish *kwanu?* I will do the one I could do, ok?'

'Ok, *nwunye m,'* Dada Felicia smiled, although Mama Benji wasn't her wife.

Mama Benji was married to a woman. But the old woman she was married to was dead. It was usual in Ezeoke anyway. Women marrying women. Mostly, these women were married to women (daughters of Ezeoke) who couldn't marry out because they were the only children of their parents and needed children who could answer the family's name, so that it wouldn't be a dropped one. And Mama Benji had to go and scout for a handsome man that would give her a handsome child. Chief Mobutu gave her Benjamin. Everyone knew, but no one tried telling Benjamin.

There was a whirlwind after Labata drove past Ahiara Junction and was now at Aba Branch near Ehime Mbano Local Government Headquarters. Just at the roundabout, there was a political rally. Young boys and girls in white shirts, printed with pictures of Chief Mobutu on the chest held green-white-red coloured flags. And raised placards that read: WE WANT CHIEF MOBUTU; CHIEF M IS THE ONE WE NEED; NO CHIEF M, NO ELECTION. Rajaswamy felt repulsed, when he saw a swarthy looking man in an isi-agu black dress, sporting a red suede cap, spraying naira notes, while the crowd cheered.

'That's Chief Mobutu,' Labata explained. 'He's contesting for a seat in the State House of Assembly. He comes to the house everyday. He is very rich and none of his opponents challenge him.'

'But this is campaign theft!' Rajaswamy said. 'You don't spray money during rallies.'

'That's India, Raj,' Eunice said. 'This is Nigeria.'

'So?'

'You have to device every means to get supporters.'

'Through bribing?'

'Yeah.'

'That's terrible.'

The crowd surged ahead and Labata braked the car. There was no way out for them. The car came to a standstill and then there was the cheers and applause for Chief Mobutu.

Chief Mobutu's real name wasn't known to party supporters. On his poster, it was written Chief Mobutu only. He was born on October 14, 1940 and on learning that the Field Marshal of Congo, Mobutu Sese Seko was born on the same day, but in 1930, he took up the sobriquet Mobutu, swore an affidavit in court to be addressed as that. It worked. Finally, when the war broke out on July 6, 1967, he was off to see Sese Seko. He was determined to see him and he did. When the war ended in 1970, he came 'politically-strong' to stand his opponents.

He said that Ojukwu was a coward and a greedy pig, for wanting to rule a country. He, Chief Mobutu, founded and funded a newspaper, *The Frontliner*. He employed some Igbo graduates ('I won't spare those Hausa and Yoruba pigs,' he had told his journalists. 'I want a situation where you will flame up tribal hatred and have these fools crushed!') to write for his newspaper. In his own sulky interest, he dictated to his journalists things that he wanted published. During the 27 August coup of 1985, where Babangida removed Buhari - his fellow Hausa - Chief Mobutu dictated to his journalists that Amadioha, the Igbo God of Thunder, was on the verge of fighting for the Igbo who were massacred in the north by the Hausas. He said that the time was coming when he would take up the major political seats in the country. At the back, which wasn't in the paper anyway, he told his journalists that if he ever became the President of Nigeria, he would make sure that the Hausas would be gathered together and slaughtered. He said he would destroy them and wait for the next move. 'The one Hitler did to the Jews is small,' he said. 'I will wipe these Hausas out and feed the Yorubas to the vultures. The Fulanis I will make to wipe the shoes of the poorest Igbo man. I will kill them silently and no UN will know about it. And by the grace of God, I will rule Nigeria.'

Even as an illiterate, Chief Mobutu courageously walked into the political terrain. He said that the so-called educated people couldn't play politics. 'Don't you see Soyinka!' He would say in Igbo and let out a flat, but heavy laughter. 'That guy can't play politics. He is only criticising us!' First, he contested for a seat in the Local Government Council as a Councillor. Then a chairperson. And now, he was rallying support to win a seat in the House of Assembly. He was determined to win and his opponents were easily intimidated because of his personality. Oh yes, he knew someone who knew someone who, in turn, knew someone else that knew the party national chairman and was always in close contact with the national chairman of the National Electoral Commission. In politics, all that mattered was connection, Chief Mobutu had told a group of his friends during a midnight meeting in his duplex house in Ezeoke. And Papa-Nkeukwu was a part of them. 'You have all this kind of connection and you still spray money during rallies,' Papa-Nkeukwu in a wise manner had said. No, Chief Mobutu said, if you don't give these peasants money, they will despise you. Let them just have their share now and don't expect me to do anything for them. But in his manifesto, Chief Mobutu had promised good roads, steady power, water, free education-for-all and employment if elected as a member of the House. The editor of *The Frontliner* prepared the manifesto. Because the Chief couldn't write. But he could speak English. 'English should be a language for bastards,' he had once said. 'The language is so stupid. You get entrapped into it and can come out easily. But look at Igbo, the most terrible language. You can't write it.' If he were to give a speech, it had to be prepared weeks before the selected date, so he could read, reread and cram it for a flawless presentation.

One day during a party meeting at Owerri, chaos was almost unveiled when the party members who were present at the meeting, were asked to write their name on a scrap of paper that was passed round to them. Sharply, because he was smart, Chief Mobutu, sitting majestically asked the man who was sitting beside him to *please* write his name for him. The man did. But he had no idea that his fellow politician was afraid to take up the pen because he couldn't write his name. Or any other thing, except numbers.

When people heard his name on radio stations, they thought he had a Harvard degree.

But they didn't know he was just an illiterate. An illiterate, but a fierce member of the Peoples Democratic Party (PDP). There was a faction and the party split into two. The Federal and Grassroot. PDP (Abuja) and PDP (Grassroot). Grassroot was for the states. So, Chief Mobutu was a strong member of the Peoples Democratic Party (Grassroot). You couldn't vie for any political seat and win, without seeing that chief. He was the real frontliner when it came to politics.

Last month, *The Frontliner* had used Chief Mobutu's picture on the front page of the paper, with the caption: *POLITICAL MESSIAH*. He had asked them to write it. In a long profile of him, they had written that he was educated at Dakar and Sorbonne Universities. A picture of him and Mobutu Sese Seko was attached. In the picture, he was sitting on the floor, while the Field Marshal sat largely in a couch. His critics attacked him, saying that he was a product of tyranny. No one said anything about his educational background because he could speak English. Even better than English graduates. 'I told you that English is a stupid language,' he told people. And could speak French. It all worked.

They incidentally passed Aba Branch and headed towards Orieagu.

Benjamin in a boxer short and black singlet, as lean and handsome as ever, stepped into the Onwubiko house through the small gate to assist his mother with her evening chores, while Mama-Nkeukwu was sitting on a low steel back-chair in the wooden-floored verandah. He had to pass the verandah before he could get to the cottage where his mother worked. But this evening, he didn't want to pass the verandah; he wanted to go through the garage on the southern cape of the house and Mama-Nkeukwu had warned him in the past not to. He passed the dwarf guava tree and headed for the garage. Mama-Nkeukwu rose quickly and screamed: 'Bastard, you must pass through this verandah.' He kept on walking. 'Did you hear me?' she growled.

'I didn't,' Benjamin said, halfway into the garage. Then turned to her. 'And I'm not a bastard.'

'What are you?'

'I'm not a bastard, that's all,' he replied.

'You have no father,' she said. *'Enweghi onye i ga-akpo nna gi.'*

'There is someone I can call my father.'

'Onye?' she asked, leaning on the wooden railing. 'Who?'

Nearing her, Benjamin said: *'A ma m* my father. I know my father.'

She broke into hysterical laughter. 'You don't know,' she said. 'If you have a father, oh, I should be the one to tell you that, *nwa m.* Many kids around here have fathers, but they don't know them. In your own case, *you* have no father.' That was a fearful way to reveal to him that Chief Mobutu was his father.

'Bullshit!' Benjamin finally babbled in a fake American accent. 'Shut up, you ...!'

Mama-Nkeukwu widened her eyes in surprise. She looked around the compound quickly to see if anyone was watching them. She whispered to Benjamin coolly: 'You are using foul language? I think you are mentally deranged!'

'Chineke ekwela ihe ojo.'

Labata drove past Rosita Memorial Hospital.

He explained to Rajaswamy and Eunice that the hospital was being managed by an Indian man, Dr. Ranganatha Venugopalan. But Dr. Venugopalan was a Nepali. Well, you could say he was a fraud anyway. He was born in Tamil Nadu, but was raised in Kathmandu, Nepal, so he told people. He moved to Kenya with his parents, then to Uganda. When his parents were deported from Uganda by the great Idi Amin's administration, while his parents moved back to Nepal, he decided to move to Nigeria. When he arrived, he moved to Owerri, where he believed he would get a better job. He worked at the Federal Medical Centre, and because he was Indian (*oh, Nepali!*), he got a job as a surgeon. Nigerians apparently believed that Indians were better doctors.

One day, Dr. Venugopalan was asked to attend to a patient who was to be operated on for appendicitis and he found the patient to be pretty and beautiful. After seeing her whole body bloom in the theatre, he invited her over to his apartment when the operation had healed and seduced her.

Not to pull the shame to his face, the father of the victim (*was she?*) who incidentally was Chief Mobutu, asked Venugopalan to marry his daughter. He sponsored their court wedding. Chief Mobutu held his international passport, so he couldn't leave Nigeria without him knowing. Then, he asked the randy Indian man to take over Rosita Hospital. He renamed it Viswanathan Memorial Hospital. Chief Mobutu said he was an idiot, that Nigerians didn't need that Viswanathan thing. But he didn't know that Viswanathan was Ranganatha's father's name. And Rosita was Chief Mobutu's mother's name. Venugopalan had to reverse to Rosita.

They now lived at Umuakagu, Venugopalan and his wife Priscilia, with their twin children: Bharti and Lalwani.

As the car approached the okada park at Orieagu, Labata and his passengers met a group of ragged people. There were elderly people in the crowd. They were all trapped in a festive mood. Beside a traditional ruler, there were old men. Drunken boys and girls. That was part of the Ibo-Uzo festival. And the festival was a celebration of the home-coming of Urashi after his battle with Amadioha to save his wife, Ogbuide. As it was told, Urashi, on his return, visited many marketplaces in Nsu, with his wife before he reached to settle in Nzerem. He killed Amadioha in the month of December, Labata narrated to Rajaswamy.

'It's like Diwali, you know,' Eunice told him.

'Yeah, the Ravana thing,' he added.

'Yeah.'

One of the boys in the crowd with a matchet stood hands akimbo in front of the car and Labata stopped. The boy came over to Labata's side and demanded for money. *'Puo ebe a!'* Labata screamed at him and accelerated the car in a high speed. Past the Catholic Church, Fatima School, Agbaghara Junction and was before the WELCOME TO EZEOKE sign before St. Paul's Cathedral. On the left, coming from Ukwungwu, Eunice saw the mad man who was called 'white vagina' in Igbo, because he was fond of light-skinned women. But his sobriquet was Rommy B.

'That's Rommy B, *akwa ya?*' she asked Labata. And he said yes.

Eunice explained to Rajaswamy that Rommy B. became mad in the eighties when he was living far away in Italy.

'Really?' he asked.

'Yes,' she said. 'He was a doctor in Italy -'

'He must be brilliant?' David asked.

'Yes.'

Rommy B. in his silky long black beards, sported in a

149

dirty loincloth, with a bunch of newspaper dailies in his hands and a bamboo stick stepped through the old church. His moustache was large and Rajaswamy compared it to those in Bollywood movies, calling it a Bharati moustache. In them, one could trace morsels of what he had eaten that sunny December afternoon. Now he was on the lane that ran through the church and obiama. He began to wave his hand, to flag down an imaginary taxi, but it was like the imaginary driver who looked at him grabbed the reality immediately that there was something wrong in his head. But he never agreed, because he didn't know. He sighed, when none of the imaginary vehicles he had waved at chose to stop. He began to stroll down the alleyway.

Rommy B. was just a sobriquet. He had to accept that name, because there was no need calling him his real name, when he knew that he didn't deserve it anymore. He accepted it with good fate. Everyone knew him for one thing: he liked white women or even fair-skinned women. Anything white, he loved it. He loved those things as a way to continue picturing his Italian wife, Rebeca and twins, Benito and Carlito. He lost them completely when he had to be hounded out of Italy by the Nigerian diplomats, who'd gotten reports of his *new* development then. They'd been told (by Rebeca) that their countryman was lunatic. They screamed. Within two days, they had him sent back to Nigeria through Alitalia. And as a doctor, then in Italy, Rommy B. saw many things. They haunted him even in this depressing situation.

There was a house in Ezeoke. And only two souls lived in it. Since Rommy B. lived in it, with his other brother, Mr. Cold (who wasn't far from mad), it had to be called White House. Even though Rommy B. was insane, he knew that White House was where the US President popped up his plans for inferior countries to be invaded: 'Ah, if Benito Mussolini is still alive,'

Rommy B. would say and then reverse, 'God would weep at his feet.' Nevertheless, people believed that there was always a meaning in anything he said. But no, there was none, which was certainly what Mr. Cold would say. And it happened that nothing mattered much to him. Inside White House (although there was nothing white about it), Rommy B. read newspapers. From morning till night, except if there were places he needed to go. Maybe where a light-skinned woman had arrived.

Well, White House was an old-fashioned bungalow, trapped near Chief Mobutu's house and built with bricks. It had a balcony, where Rommy B. sat reading his newspapers. Of course, because he was educated and was non-violent, people visited him for long discussions, especially gamblers. They thought and believed that he knew the numbers that would help them win their game. They would buy him that day's newspaper, he would give his clients numbers and if they played with them, surely they'd win. That mesmerized many young people and they would throng up to the balcony to extract numbers from him. At times, it wasn't possible, unless you bought a newspaper. Still, you may not likely get the numbers if you hit the nail on the head. Once, a young man (who had heard of his miracles) traveled all the way from Umuahia to meet him with a newspaper, and when he'd given it to him, the young man demanded: 'Where are the numbers?'

'Yes,' Rommy B. said, still engrossed in the paper. 'Idi Amin thought that Michael Jackson was his son.' And he smiled.

'Let me have the numbers!' He persisted.

'But Philip Roth wanted Toni Morrison in his bed.'

The young man flamed up. 'Give me, now!'

'What numbers?' he glared in rueful smiles, still not looking at the young man who'd now stormed out of the balcony screaming slurs at him. As the young man left, Rommy B. walked to the railing and watched him. He smiled and said to himself: 'They think I'm mad like *them*.'

Now as he walked down the alleyway, he stopped, removed his slippers and hung them around his elbows.

Labata drove past the obiama and headed downwards on the right. The harmattan wind blew, as though done by an immortal flute and the trees bent and waved, smiled, waved and David thought the trees were saying to him, 'Welcome, man. Welcome, naughty boy, naughty boy.' He looked up to the sky and birds glided through. He became jealous of the birds; he wanted to be like them, grow wings and learn to fly, to fly around the world and find where the albino dwarf was. He wanted to be like the birds, but all these were not possible, so he relented and kept staring at the trees, as they waved at him. Bend. Wave. Bend. Wave. Smile. Wave. Oh, he smiled back at the trees and waved back. His father stared at him and shook his head. Whatever's wrong with him, he thought and looked out through the window of the car. There were young people sitting here and there. And Eunice really loved that.

'I kind of like this village,' Rajaswamy said.

'Really?' Eunice asked.

'Yes,' he said.

'Look at that!' David said, pointed at a child singing on a heap of sand.

'Yes,' Eunice said.

'He is singing in Igbo!' Eunice explained as the child wagged his leg in the air.

Gi mee m ka m bu nkikara akwa

(If you treat me like a rag)
A ga m eme gi ka i bu onye azu
(I will treat you like a fag)

But Eunice couldn't tell them what the child sang. As they passed a palmwine shop, they saw a man with an amputated hand, chewing on a *dogonyaro* stick and wearing a torn white singlet and wrapper. Rajaswamy smiled at him and he waved at him. The man with one hand was singing, whistling and smiling.

A turu m nwunye di m akwa
(I asked my husband's wife to buy me a cloth)
Ya azutara m akwa eh!
(She bought me an egg-eh!)
Akwa apu m n'anya;
(Tears rolled down my eyes)
Nwunye di m, kedu ihe m mere gi?
(My husband's wife, what did I do to you?)

Eunice let out a loud laugh. She translated all he sang to Rajaswamy. Labata said the man lost his hand during the war. David saw children coming after their car through the side view mirror. He smiled. His heart quickened. He watched the excited children approach. They were screaming, *'Lee kwa ndi ocha!'*

'What are they saying?' David asked Labata who had noticed them.

'The kids?' He asked.

'Yes.'

'Oh!' He said. 'They are saying, 'See these whites.''

Eunice felt repulsed and cut in, when she saw Rajaswamy's lips tearing apart to talk: 'They believe Indians are white, Raj.'

'That's bad of them,' Rajaswamy said. 'Let me just believe that it's just because of the environment, eh?'

'Should be!' Eunice said and looked up ahead. 'Oh! That's mama and who's that woman, Labata?' She meant Mama-Nkeukwu and Chief Mobutu's wife.

'That's Chief Mobutu's wife,' he explained.

The two women were coming towards their car, talking, discussing. They were in long dresses, of dabbled fabrics, walking tall.

Labata slowed and stopped when he got to them. Eunice rolled down the window glass and called out to her mother. She smiled. Chief Mobutu's wife smiled. Mama-Nkeukwu peeked at them through the window. *'Kedu, nwa m?'* But Rajaswamy didn't understand. Eunice stared at her mother and asked Labata to move on. He did.

The two women turned and followed them *nwayoly*. And the children surged into the Onwubiko compound as the car entered. The gate man beat them back. *'Anyi choro ihu ndi ocha,'* they demanded furiously and one of them repeated in English: 'We want to see those white people.'

In the evening, rich men in posh clothes gathered in the sitting room of the Onwubiko house. There were bottles of Gulder and Star beer. Some empty. Half-drank. Some full. Papa-Nkeukwu was entertaining them, to mark the Ibo-Uzo feast. Labata entered, carrying a jar of palm wine. Immediately there was power outage. The men murmured. Some mumbled slurs at the government. 'These NEPA people are crazy,' one of them said. Papa-Nkeukwu asked Labata to go and put on the Lister. He went with torchlight, passing the garage towards the Boys' Quarters, where he slept at times. He started it, and there was light. That was a soundless Lister because no one could hear the sound.

The drinking and talking went on. There was Nze Akubuiro, dressed in a richly starched agbada. Chief Kenkwo, in an up-and-down leather jean, Barrister Clement Ude in his suit and Professor Machiavelli, who was always seen carrying in his Pajero jeep, a copy of Niccolò Machiavelli's *The Prince*. Machiavelli wasn't a nickname. It was his real name. His mother (who was now dead) was Italian and his father from Ezeoke. By and large, he was the only opponent of Chief Mobutu who was never shaken by Chief Mobutu's personality because he himself knew people who knew people who knew more important people. This was anyway his first time of coming to Papa-Nkeukwu's house. To canvas for his support.

'You know,' he said, taking a sip from the glass of palmwine he had, 'Nigerian politics is such that irritates. Everybody expects you to give him money, if not, he won't support you.'

'Oh, Prof,' Barrister Clement cut in. 'D'you really read that book you carry around?'

'Yes,' he said, wide-eyed, because he knew he didn't. 'Why?'

'*Ngwanu*,' the barrister said and added in Igbo. 'Don't you see your namesake arguing that it is often good for leaders to use immoral ways in order to achieve power?'

Professor Machiavelli hadn't read the book. He was open-mouthed.

'And I learnt from a close source that you don't use *juju*?' Nze Akubuiro asked. 'You better come, let me take you to a strong witch doctor that would give you protection, or to the Hindu temples in Lagos.'

'*Onye kwuru?*' Papa-Nkeukwu said, addressing Nze

Akubuiro. 'Who said? Did anyone tell you that these Hindu temples in Lagos are real?

'They are Onwubiko,' Chief Kenkwo said, sipping gently.

'Hapu nu ihe ahu,' Papa-Nkeukwu said. 'You all know that I have lived in India?'

They nodded.

'Good,' he said. 'These Indians have no idea what voodoo is.'

That's not true, Onwubiko,' Nze Akubuiro said sitting up. 'I heard that Chief Mobutu's son-in-law, Venu, what?'

'Venugopalan,' Papa-Nkeukwu ended.

'Ehe,' he continued. 'They said that he makes charms for Chief Mobutu.'

Papa-Nkeukwu laughed. 'Anyway,' he said. 'My son in-law, Rajaswamy came in today. He is an Indian.'

They stopped and looked at each other contemptuously.

I kwuru eziokwu?' Professor Machiavelli asked. 'Did you say the truth?'

'Yes.'

'Ask him to come and greet your umunna, Onwubiko,' Chief Kenkwo said.

'Alright. Labata,' Papa-Nkeukwu called out, while Labata was already at the doorway. 'Go, tell Eunice that she should come down with the husband and greet umunna anyi.'

'Ok sir,' he said and vamoosed.

In a while, there was a knock on the door. Papa-Nkeukwu said come in. Chief Mobutu stepped in with Dr. Venugopalan and Priscilia. Chief Mobutu shook hands with everyone, even with Professor Machiavelli who was his opponent. Professor Machiavelli was a member of the Peoples Democratic Party (Abuja). During his own rallies for the primaries, he had recited his manifesto saying that he would provide good roads, quality education and employment. Critics said he had no new propaganda. But he said that since he was an emeritus professor, that he could pass motions in the House. The masses said no. That he didn't spray money.

'Mobutu Sese Seku Kuku Ngbengu Wasa Banga,' Chief Kenkwo praised Chief Mobutu as they greeted in a chief-style. 'You will live long.'

'And you will enjoy my stay on earth,' he added and sat in the leather brown cushion near him. Dr. Venugopalan and Priscilia settled into the long cushion near Professor Machiavelli.

'Happy Ibo-Uzo!' Chief Mobutu said to Papa-Nkeukwu and they laughed. 'I heard our beautiful Eunice is back with the husband?'

'Yes,' he said, while pointing at the drinks for Venugopalan. 'They came back this afternoon, *mgbe anyi gara* for the festival?'

Everyone laughed for the way Papa-Nkeukwu had spoken his English, mixed with the Igbo.

'Where are they?' Chief Mobutu asked. 'He should meet his fellow countryman.'

'That's true,' he said. 'I have sent for them.'

The arcade widened. Eunice stepped in, wearing a long skirt and V-neck shirt, followed by Rajaswamy who was now in a pink shirt and blue jeans trousers. Venugopalan rose in utter amazement. His heart bumped.

'*Namaste,*' he said, placing his palms together to his forehead.

'*Namaste,*' Rajaswamy said in the same way.

Venugopalan made to touch his feet while everyone watched them in silence.

'*Nahin,*' Rajaswamy said, holding him up. '*Aap ka naam?*'

'*Mere naam hai* Ranganatha Venugopalan,' he said.

'Oh!' He'd remembered. *'Mere naam hai* Rajaswamy Rajagopalan.'

They all heard the names and were astonished. How come? Ranganatha Venugopalan? Rajaswamy Rajagopalan? And the names? Very tall, did you see? They smiled at each other and settled in the cushion. From mere meeting Rajaswamy, Dr. Venugopalan quickly understood that he was a Brahmin. It was certain.

'Nno nu o!' Eunice greeted them in Igbo. 'Welcome!' They replied.

Rajaswamy looked at Eunice. 'This is the doctor the driver was talking about,' he said in Hindi. 'That's his wife.'

Eunice smiled up at Priscilia. 'Has he taught you Hindi?' She asked her in Igbo.

The men laughed because they were listening. The Indian men were puzzled.

'Mba,' she said. 'I couldn't learn, but he could speak little Igbo.'

'Really?'

'Yes.'

Professor Machiavelli's heart quickened.

He told Rajaswamy that he wanted to have a word with him outside. And they went outside. He introduced himself as Professor Machiavelli. Rajaswamy said the name sounded strange. He recited his credentials. He was born to a Nigerian father and an Italian mother. Had his B.A. from UNN and M.A. from Yale. PhD from Stanford. A Diploma at Leeds. Had traveled to fifteen countries as a visiting Professor. Had written ten books on Nigerian politics. Had been an observer for Nigeria to South Africa during the election that led Nelson Mandela to the seat as

President. And now was contesting (*against that swine inside*) for a seat in the state House of Assembly and was in the ruling party.

He didn't go straight to the point. But not connected to his brain, he had no idea that the person he'd just recited his credentials to was a best-selling author and a man India was proud of. This was why Dada Felicia said that Igbo people were too obsessed with themselves and were shameless self-publicists. She was one of them, if she had no idea.

Then he gathered the courage and told Rajaswamy, 'I want you to help me prepare charms, so I can win this election.'

Rajaswamy said he had no idea what he was talking about.

A car drove into the compound.

It was Udunna, his Japanese wife, Hatsu and children, Yvonne and Jerry. Smart-looking. Dog-eyed. Small-mouthed. Both wearing blue-grey glasses. Mama-Nkeukwu was heard screaming from outside. David walked up to the balcony to watch them, and as he stood there, he saw a white-coloured grave far away in the garden. He shook. Memories began to sprout in his head, like okra seeds do. This was that grave the dwarf told him he would take him into one day. It was this, he thought. He held the railing and as the darkness deepened, he slushed. He could still hear Mama-Nkeukwu screaming Yvonne and Jerry's names. He could still remember that he had seen that grave.

From the grave, to his amazement, the albino dwarf came out, carrying a large bell and walked behind the plantain tree and then the orange tree. He paced up and down. David looked away, and his gaze was now at the people gathering to welcome

Udunna and his wife. They all became dwarves. He looked away. And when he looked towards the orange tree, he saw the albino dwarf coming towards his direction.

He ran away from the balcony.

Dada Felicia was in a green long gown now and stepped out to the verandah as soon as Hatsu stepped into it. Mama-Nkeukwu had carried Jerry in her arm, while she held Yvonne by the hand leading them into the house. Rajaswamy shook hands with Udunna and he said 'Welcome to the Giant of Africa.' Eunice and Hatsu embraced, although they hadn't met before. Dada Felicia came out and embraced Hatsu. *'Ni hao,'* Dada Felicia spoke in Mandarin Chinese. 'Oh!' Hatsu laughed. 'I'm Japanese, not Chinese.' Dada Felicia said that the Japanese and Chinese were the same. Hatsu said that wasn't true.

'You are all *isolationists,* anyway,' Dada Felicia muttered to herself and racially biased, she said, whispering to Labata, as though he wanted to know. 'These Japanese people look like frogs.'

'Leave me alone,' Labata hushed her.

And she choked.

11

Little Dream in a Little Dream

DAVID WAS given a large room with a Vita foam bed to sleep in. His pyjamas seemed like jodhpurs; draped like a mongol, he strolled through an alleyway, primping himself. He hung his travel-bag behind him and stepped into an old village, where he found himself walking past an old church, and then spotted the albino dwarf sitting under a plum tree, or what looked like a chestnut tree, his wee size shaded by the tree. There were villagers who had gathered to watch him. Weary, he was neither looking up at the villagers nor feeling woozy. He was tired and sat wordless on a wooden box. Everyone stood staring at him. From the children with large bellies who looked like they were suffering from kwashiorkor, to tiny and shrunken people, who stood with teeth sticking out of their mouths, the albino dwarf, Nfanfa sat on the box staring at them. He leaned on the tree.

He gently bent down and lowered himself on the trolley, buried his head in the ground, and was engulfed with thoughts. The villagers fed their eyes on him. Some girls giggled, chortled and chuckled. Passers-by watched him. They were all like watching the performance of a naked mad woman in a marketplace. How she would glare around and show her nakedness. If he was mad, they'd know. Now, his head was raised and he saw the eyes of the villagers were focused on him. He smiled at them and they jerked into uproarious laughter, like hee-hee-hee, as if there was a circus going on. They watched him.

David looked around and found that he was different. His clothes and shoes. But these villagers were in wrappers and loincloth. He understood. It was the year nineteen hundred and thirty six. He marveled. But why was he there? Nonetheless, the villagers didn't stare at him, because they couldn't see him.

Then the leaves from the trees fell on Nfanfa, and he picked one of them. Just to distract himself from looking at the hundreds of people who'd climbed up the trees, and the tower of the old church to watch him. He held out an acoustic guitar. Well, he wasn't so much of a musician, but he liked playing with the strings that would sound so much like tini-ni-tana-na. He unbuttoned the case, or rather unzipped, and strummed the strings.

There was silence.

A Deep Silence.

Eunice was in her own bed, sleeping just beside her husband dreaming. In her own dream, she saw the albino dwarf sitting under a chestnut tree. There was silence. The girls who were chattering paused; the dogs that were barking aloud stopped; and the temple bells that tolled forlornly came to an abrupt stop. Everyone, everything, was ready to hearken to the sonorous sound of the guitar he had. But he wasn't playing any music. Still, there was silence.

Right at the garden, from the white tiled grave, Nfanfa stepped out barebodied and began to pace up and down. His legs felt damp and sticky, as he clambered towards the building where everyone slept. He felt cocky as he entered the padlocked door that led into the hallway. In derision, he stepped farther right and knocked, on David's door room.

David woke up, leaving his dream behind. He stretched back and sat up in the bed, staring fearfully at the door. Then the door opened slowly on its own. David shrieked.

Nfanfa stepped in, bare bodied. The door closed of its own accord. David mumbled something to himself as the dwarf came towards the bed. He shivered.

'Who are you?' David asked, very afraid, shaking.

'We have met, David,' the dwarf said. 'Stop shivering.'

'What do you want?'

Nfanfa stepped to the cupboard in the room and leaned on it. 'Stop behaving like a woman.'

David kept quiet.

'You know,' Nfanfa said. 'I don't know why you should keep on shivering. Do you know how long it has taken me to meet you finally?'

'What do you want?'

'Alright,' the dwarf sneezed. 'Don't feel panicky. Relax. Do you have any idea that you are me and that I'm you?'

'No,' David smiled.

'You should know.'

'But how come?'

Nfanfa lowered himself on the pouffe in the room. 'I promised you something,' he said.

'What?'

'That one day I'd take you into my grave.' He held out a pouch from his knickers. 'I told you that we would go there and drink mead.'

David rushed out from the bed, excited. 'You mean you live in that grave?'

'Yes.'

'How?'

Nfanfa laughed boisterously. 'You know you are me!'

'I don't know.'

'But do you think you are me?'

'Whatever,' David sniggered. He slushed and continued. 'Were you in the plane?'

'Yes,' he said pitifully. 'I'm anywhere you are!'

David brightened up. 'I can't just believe you,' he said.

'You can't?'

'Yes.'

He laughed. 'Then you can't believe yourself.'

The Abyssinian cat mewed loudly from within the corridor. Nfanfa rose quickly, frightened. He moved to the wall and disappeared. David stared at the wall longingly. When he finally turned, he saw Papa-Nkeukwu standing on his legs by the doorway, the cat by his leg. David gabbled, like a duck. Oh God, he screamed in the inside. Was this man not said to be crippled? Yes, he was and when David came back he had seen him in a wheelchair. He looked at the wall-clock and it was 12:00 am sharp. He shook in fear.

'Are you ok?' Papa-Nkeukwu asked him.

'Yes,' he said, staring at the walls in fear.

'Come on,' he beckoned on him. 'Let me take you to my room, ok? You'd be alright.'

'Ok,' David said and followed him. He looked at the cat and the cat smiled at him. 'Huh?' David said really surprised. He looked away and followed Papa-Nkeukwu side by side as they walked through the hallway, while the cat followed them.

Assuming it is midnight, you are trying to enjoy your sleep and someone knocks on your door. A dwarf enters. Then leaves. Someone else enters. In addition, that happens to be your grandfather, who has never walked on his legs since you were born and he stands there with a gruesome smile. Then, being surprised by what happened, you tried to scream but your voice failed and you couldn't even say anything. So he takes another step, asks you to come and join him. Obviously, you know he has never walked since you were born and he decides to take you by surprise that very night. It would be a shock. That is for certain.

It could be a surprise that Papa-Nkeukwu wanted to show David. He was the only one he did that to. Everyone in the family believed he would never walk. Moreover, that was the first secret that he kept with David. Though there was one that lurked in his inside. One that would tear apart the world. He honestly did tell David why he chose to do that. Still, David felt somewhat curious about him.

David thought that the man who was leading him through the hallway was a ghost. But no, it was him, with that wrinkled face and brown teeth that always looked agape. His aged face and everything glowed in the green light. David wondered why he decided to do it when everyone had gone to sleep, until he spoke to David and told him many things that he never knew that he was going to hear in his entire life. Some deep secrets that he strummed into his life. David never knew that such secrets ever existed.

He was a member of the Ancient and Mystical Order Rosae Crucis. From what he told David, he was in charge of the fraternity's Lodge in Owerri and was a big admirer of Harvey Spencer Lewis, the founder of the world's largest fraternity, AMORC.

In a lecturer-at-a-seminar mood, he made David

understand that the Rosicrucian group remained secretive for a hundred years, as declared by Christian Rosenkrutz. Papa-Nkeukwu showed David many things. He also told him many things. But as they talked, David felt something reeling inside him, as the cat smiled at him. He began to perceive the endless smell of the albino dwarf's cologne. He shivered.

On the wall of Papa-Nkeukwu's room, David noticed, was the Confession of Maat, which read, 'Homage to Thee, Great God, Thou Master of all Truth, I am pure...'

Papa-Nkeukwu genuflected before the altar bathed in light from red candles and said the Rosie Crucian Prayer to God:

'O Thou everywhere and good of all,' he began as David squatted at an edge of the room, staring at the cat. 'Whatever I do, remember, I beseech Thee, that I am but Dust, but as a Vapour sprung from Earth, which even the smallest Breath can scatter; Thou hast given me a Soul, and Laws to govern it; let that Eternal Rule, which thou didst first appoint to sway Man, order me; make me careful to point at thy Glory in all my ways and where I cannot rightly know Thee, that not only my understanding, but my ignorance may honour Thee.'

He paused as there was thunder and lightening outside. The thunder clapped; he made a sign of the Cross and continued, 'Thou are all that can be perfect; Thy Revelation hath made me happy; be not angry, O Divine One, O God, the most high Creator, if it pleases Thee suffer these revealed secret, Thy Gifts alone, not for my praises, but to thy Glory, to manifest themselves...'

David rose quickly. Oh, he had been having a dream in a dream. And he had woken because of the noise he had heard. A woman's voice. He opened the bed head window and looked out, saw a woman, who clapped her hands in a round-about dance, shouting, then more women ran in and joined her, as they sang.

> *Ha, ah, eh!*
>
> *Ohua! Oho! Oho!*
>
> *Chineke imeela*
>
> (God, you have done well)
>
> *Unu muru nwa gini?*
>
> (What's the sex of your child?)
>
> *Anyi muru nwa nwoke*
>
> (Our child is a male)
>
> *Eji gini azu ya?*
>
> (What are you going to grow him with?)
>
> *Ihe eriwele, enye nwa, nwa riwe, ya enye nne*
>
> (Anything you eat, give the child, if the child eats, let him give mother)
>
> *Chineke nwe nwa, maa taa maa echi niile*
>
> (God owns the child, today and forever)
>
> *Uwa ebebe - tee-hoo, tee-hoo*
>
> (Everlasting world - tee-hoo, tee-hoo)
>
> *Anyi nwe ebe a, nwe ebe a*
>
> (We have this place and this place)

Somewhere around the river, near the crab-apple tree, Rommy B. strolled through the path, soliloquizing. There had been no rain, but the grass looked sticky and damp, filled with the morning mist that had gathered around his legs. He was still hanging his slippers beyond his elbow. His hands were feeling strong as ever and in his mind, he kept the memories of his twin sons, Benito and Carlito. He began to lick one of the crab apples he had picked. He chortled as he visualized Rebecca in a bed with another man. He stopped, chortled again and walked through the bushy path. As his heart rose in a thump, he began to wave at imaginary white women. White breasts. White lips. He stopped half-way into the main-road and smelled something. Oh yes, some white breasts had arrived somewhere. 'Oh,' he exclaimed. 'No monkey told me. Yes, I eat garri with water.' He frowned and then smiled. The sky looked lurid to him. And the thick grass tried to hold his legs, he felt. He felt thin looking at it, and almost immediately, he walked the main-road and headed up towards Onwubiko's house. But the path was long and he knew.

Labata's wife, Uchaoma had just returned from the stream, when she heard the women singing. And by then, all her children were out to the stream to fetch water and her husband hadn't returned last night. She entered their bedroom, put on a calico, tied a scarf around her head, and headed towards the Onwubiko house. Her heart beat rhythmically. Let this old woman not slap me again, she told herself.

Benjamin stepped out of their mud-zinced house and looked up to the sky. Oh, the Ibo-Uzo festival had passed and it remained only Christmas to look forward to, he murmured as he stepped into their kitchen. His mother was out and before she left, she had steamed the egusi soup she had made last night, gone to Benjamin's room and told him that he should take the remaining akpu in the bucket. Now he was in the kitchen and behind the rack on fire, he saw the soup pot and the bucket where the pounded cassava was always packed. He opened the pot and set it down. He looked at his Bermuda shorts to see if anything had stained it, brought the bucket down, got a low stool, washed his hands in a small basin at the far right end of the door and began to make balls of the akpu, dipped them into the soup and after a stir, he threw them into his mouth and swallowed, making his Adam's apple rise rapidly.

He shrieked, when he heard someone calling his name from the front yard. He quickly recognized the voice and said: 'I'm in the kitchen, Emeka!' Emeka was his close friend. So, after a while, Emeka emerged through the short wooden gate and walked to the kitchen. He looked lean like Benjamin. He was now standing in front of the kitchen, watching his friend swallow ball after ball of akpu.

'Come and eat,' Benjamin offered.

'*Mba*,' Emeka said no. 'I can't eat this heavy thing in the morning.'

'Oh!' he leaned back. 'At least you have a father that looks after you.'

Emeka became furious. 'Stop that!' He snapped, entered the kitchen and sat on one of the low stools. 'Eh,' he began. 'I heard Onwubiko's daughter came back from India with the husband?'

'Yes,' Benjamin said between mouthfuls. 'Even with the child.'

'You mean it?'

'Yes.'

'Ha,' Emeka mumbled. 'I respect that family a lot. *Ha jii ezigbo ego*. They have enough money.'

'That's true,' Benjamin said reaching out for a cup of water. 'If I finish eating, I will go there, take Eunice's son and go around this village. I will pose with the boy, so that these girls will know that I have foreign connections.'

'Guy!' Emeka squealed. 'You know something.'

'What are you talking about?' Benjamin laughed. 'When they see me with that boy, any day I toast them, they will agree.'

'That's true,' Emeka chortled. 'But there is something you will do for me.'

'What?'

'I want to travel abroad and make money.'

Benjamin stopped eating. 'You make me sick,' he said. 'We are just eighteen. Money should not be our priority now.'

'You won't understand, Benji,' he mumbled. 'Your mother earns a lot of money from working in that house. You are ok!'

'That's not the issue, man!'

'So, *gini?*'

Back to the Onwubiko house, Uchaoma had just arrived, when the women were in the midst of singing and eating. This was wholly Mama-Nkeukwu's arrangement. Papa-Nkeukwu had no atom of an idea about it. It was Mama-Nkeukwu's. She had sent a clandestine message to all the women in the neighbourhood, to come and sing, for her daughter had delivered a boy. But David was born nine years ago! She said she couldn't celebrate the birth of a Hindu child. You could have slapped such a woman, but that couldn't stop her from inviting the church priest she had asked to come and cleanse the house for Rajaswamy had come to defy her house.

Eunice stepped out of the house to the verandah, and the women (who were now seated) rose quickly as though a hex had been put on them and began to sing, when Rajaswamy came out.

Onye biara Ezeoke, orikwala
(He who comes to Ezeoke, has gained)
Inyah, aha, onye biara Ezeoke, orikwala

(Yes, aha, he who comes to Ezeoke has gained)

In a flash of excitement, Eunice stepped into the circus and began to dance with them. Rajaswamy felt embarrassed. He looked like a cretin and as though he was blotto, he joined in the dance. But oh, no, he couldn't dance well. The women applauded him. They cheered. And he became shy, thereby burying his head in the ground. Uchaoma amidst the women shouted at the top of her voice: 'Ha, ah, eh!' But nobody responded to her, at least, 'Ohua, oho, oho!' Nobody. She felt ashamed, stepped slowly out of the compound; with some of the biscuits she had been given.

Rommy B. stopped at the one-handed man's palmwine shop. He walked into the shop and met a group of boys, drinking and chatting. Bleary-eyed, he sat on one of the wood benches and muttered things to himself. Some of the boys gathered around him. One ordered a bottle of palmwine for him. He was served and then shook the bottle and poured some into the drinking gourd. The boys stared at him. He looked out of the shop and saw women carrying their wares to the market. 'Oh, today is Orieagu,' he said, taking a sip from his gourd, while some wine dropped on his beard.

'Yes, Rommy B.,' one of the boys said. 'Today is Orieagu.'

'How many market days do we have?' a second asked.

'Ten men beat Adolph Hitler,' Rommy B. said and smiled.

The boy who had ordered for the wine had a pen and a scrap of paper and he wrote the number Rommy B. had called down.

'Tell us about this primary election,' a third demanded wisely.

'Oh!' he said. 'That's why I ate thirty four bokchoy in

twenty minutes.'

The boy wrote down the numbers and ran out of the shop. Some of them raced after him. 'If you win, na me and you oh!' one of them shouted.

The women had gone finally, at least to take their wares to the market because it was orie. Labata, who was beery, wheeled out Papa-Nkeukwu to the verandah. Papa-Nkeukwu didn't care anyway because Labata was a married man (*with twelve disciples, for Christ's sake!*) and so could smell of beer if he wanted. It wasn't his business; that was all.

Papa-Nkeukwu lit his pipe and inhaled. Labata told him that he wanted to go and give his wife some money for market. He said ok. In Labata's mind, he thought that he would give him the money. But he didn't. So, he had to go like that. Through the macadam near the garden, the cat stole underneath the wheelchair. It mewed.

Rajaswamy was holding a newspaper when he stepped out to the verandah with Kezie and Udunna. They sat on the chaise longue near Papa-Nkeukwu.

'You should have known better,' Udunna said. They were talking about the Senate proceedings they had just watched on TV. 'There are many of those Senators who are doing real business with Indians and that's why the deportation may not come through.'

'I kind of think that Idi Amin did his autocratically without consulting the Senate,' Kezie said.

'Oh no,' Papa-Nkeukwu cut in, smoking his pipe. 'I'm not in any way biased about this, umu m. I have served as a seasoned diplomat in many countries. Among them, I will tell you the truth, India is the only one that doesn't respect black people.'

Rajaswamy turned to him in despair

'I think that's true,' Kezie added. 'I have worked with the Indians, and I can tell you, they feel we don't know anything.'

'Awesome!' Rajaswamy said. 'But that doesn't mean anything.'

'Really?' Udunna widened his eyes.

'Yes,' Rajaswamy continued. 'Black people make themselves feel inferior. For God's sake, why should blacks behave always as though they are slaves! Oh, of course, Indians are segregated and discriminated against, you know.'

'Not like blacks, you know that,' Udunna said. 'I'm married to a Japanese. I'm saying this because I have a reason for that. Asians are isolationists, let me generalize on this. I'd say that my wife is an exception, because she was born in the US. But -'

'I couldn't believe more on that,' Rajaswamy sniggered. 'The Indians get flushed off so much in the UK. English people treat Indians as dogs or at least, try to. Worse than dogs. They make the Indians feel that they are not wanted in their land. Once, my sister's employer in London asked her not to come to work wearing bangles again.'

'And what did she do?' Papa-Nkeukwu asked.

'She resigned and sued the employer to court,' Rajaswamy drabbled. 'She got no justice and returned to India angrily.'

'Britons are known to be open-minded and unbiased,' Kezie said.

'Not when it comes to an Indian,' Udunna laughed.

'You can say that again,' Rajaswamy said. 'I do think that we are all on the wrong side. When I travel to Britain, I get embarrassed. When I speak, young Britons would glare at me and laugh. That's racist, you know!'

Rajaswamy wasn't lying. As he said this, he remembered how while passing Bramley Road, he had stopped to ask some young lads standing by the roadside how to trace Trent Park Campus of Middlesex University and they immediately broke into laughter. 'We can't understand this whole blah-blah-blah,' one of them said.

Hatsu stepped into the verandah with a silver tray filled with three plates of crisp fried pancake folded together with meat and beans in it. She served them to Rajaswamy, Kezie and Udunna. Rajaswamy declined.

'I hope this is not our breakfast?' Udunna said.

'No, honey,' Hatsu replied and disappeared through the door.

Kezie lifted his to his mouth and took a crunch. 'I kinda like the tandoori chicken Eunice made for me when I came to India.'

'Yeah,' Rajaswamy said. 'Continental dish I call these things. The time I went to Athens, my Greek hosts served me something called tarasmalata the first day I arrived.'

'Tarama salata?' Udunna asked.

'Eh,' Papa-Nkeukwu said blowing rings of smoke into the air. 'The Greeks eat it a lot. It's made from fish eggs; it looks pinky and eaten with bread.'

'Fish egg?' Kezie was quick at asking.

'Yes,' Rajaswamy said. 'I think Americans are the only people who don't eat good food - '

'Yeah,' Udunna said between mouthfuls. 'Hamburger, fried chicken, vanilla ice cream, milk - that's all and that's why they are always weak. They haven't won the World Cup!'

Rajaswamy laughed. 'You know,' he said. 'A bus boy in London once asked me if we Indians know anything about football. I said no.'

They laughed.

'That's true, Raj,' Kezie cut in. 'I learnt that there was a time India came for World Cup and played barefoot.'

'Oh!' Rajaswamy leaned back. 'That couldn't be worse!'

In the kitchen, Eunice and Hatsu were preparing breakfast with Tabasco sauce. Babiana and Mgborie busied around, preparing what were written on their routine list. Dada Felicia stepped into the kitchen, and opened the fridge and brought out a plastic plate of creme caramel. She dipped one of her fingers into it and let it drop on her lip. She moved to the sink where Hatsu was now washing some saucers and china. Hatsu looked at Dada Felicia's buckram and smiled a thin smile. Her eyes widened.

'Chink,' Dada Felicia said. 'How are you?'

Hatsu stared at her and said: 'I'm Japanese.'

'*Xiexie,*' she said in Mandarin Chinese. 'I know that you are Japanese. You must have gone to Beijing.'

'I was born in the US,' Hatsu said. 'I have only being to Tokyo to see my ancestral home.'

'Chop, chop, Hatsu,' Dada Felicia laughed out loud.

There was an embarrassed look on Hatsu's face. She looked at Eunice who winked a never-mind-that-buffoon eye.

'Do you do this t'ai chi ch'uan?' Dada Felicia asked, taking spoonfuls of the creme caramel into her mouth.

'I'm Japanese, please,' Hatsu begged.

Dada Felicia chomped. Eunice turned and stared at her. She didn't say anything. In Eunice's mind, she was saying, Get out you little spic. She hated Dada Felicia sincerely. She had never heard what Dada Felicia's *partly* husband said she did, because Papa-Nkeukwu sealed it up, if not she'd just tell her to the face that Hatsu wasn't one of them. When Dada Felicia chomped horribly, Eunice began to sing a famous song she'd learnt while a young girl. And Babiana tickled Mgborie and they laughed.

> *Felicia nne m, i chotara onye?*
> (Felicia my mother, who do you want?)
> *I chotara onye apali nne gi, o masiri gi*
> (Do you want your spoilt mother, that concerns you)
> *I chotara onye nyere gi ncha nke iji saa ahu tee mmanu*
> (Do you want the person who gave you soap and oil)
> *Ihe m kwuru gi ugwo, i nye tu la m?*
> (Have you given me what I paid you for?)
> *O ji abali agaa, onye ewo mee ewo!*
> (Night-walker, real fucker!)

Dada Felicia angrily stepped out of the kitchen shouting slurs. Eunice looked at Hatsu and they laughed. Babiana and Mgborie chuckled. Their hearts gabbled and beyond imagination, they revelled over the fact that Dada Felicia was somewhat mentally deranged. She was mad, Nda Lydia assumed. Because if she wasn't, she wouldn't call a Japanese a Chinese. She knew, because she knew that Dada Felicia could smack her on the head, if she got to know that she was assuming something about her. But nothing more could scare Nda Lydia.

Dada Felicia is a real *nightwalker*, Mgborie told herself.

Around mid-day, Labata drove Rajaswamy and Eunice through the obiama, past the old and new Cathedral, past Agbaghara Junction, past German Hill, past Fatima School, past the Catholic

Church and Orieagu okada junction, where they had met a group of marchers that thronged in for the festival. There was a traffic jam. He stopped. Oh, today is Orieagu, Labata blurted, as if he didn't know. As if he wasn't the one who told Papa-Nkeukwu that he was going home to go and give his wife some money for market.

Orieagu market day is always busy. School children carried the wares of their parents to the market before heading for school and on market days like this, no one seemed to go to farm or go to the bush to fetch firewood. Always the roadside buyers of palm kernel blocked the roads. They bought in buckets from sellers and after that, trucks would come and haul them away to the north. Then the palm kernel got made into olive oil and some hair oil. House boys, carrying piles of plantain on their heads. Roast meat thrust on trenchers, and the stiffness of the legs muddled.

Labata looked on his right and saw women shouting at customers. 'Nnem, come and by my vegetable.' 'Oga, you wan buy paw-paw?' 'Ah, my udara is sweet.' 'Customer, come I'll give you cheap price.' He inhaled and then met a group of school-children babbling at their busy-bodied mothers: 'Do fast, *biko.*' Some school boys pedaled their bicycles past the junction, down to Fatima school.

'Some school boys, Labata?' Rajaswamy said, in a guise to know if there was no vacation for them.

'They do extra-mural lessons for their certificate exam,' Labata said.

A woman at a far end of the road was frying red-coloured beancake. A gmelina tree at the junction shook for there was a surging breeze. Then through the tiny shop where the woman was frying her stuff, a young man raced, holding something firmly. A crowd was going after him, screaming: '*Onye ekwela uzo*

177

gaa!'

Eunice puzzled and stretched her head upwards to see more of the spectacle. She saw something, something that was absurd. Rajaswamy, hustling to get his ambience right, sat tiredly in the backseat. With the stares from the passing people, market-eyes watching white ears, nothing mattered much to Rajaswamy by the way. He couldn't do anything to them. The way these ignoramuses stared at him, was the way those peasants in Delhi stared at Eunice. *One is one,* Eunice said and smiled like those in the movies. He grabbed her by the hand and kissed her. Okada men who saw them mumbled. Oh yes, they hadn't seen such. In public. So what? They looked away to the boy being pursued. *'Onye ekwela uzo gaa!'* a middle-aged woman screamed at the top of her voice. Someone shouted: 'Thief!' Huge hearted boys with huge breasts stood on their huge legs and went after the huge thief in a huge way. Quickly, like James Bond in movies, they grabbed the huge thief and someone, among the huge hearted boys with huge breasts gave him a huge slide-down. He fell to the tarred road and everyone gathered to interrogate him. In Nigeria, everyone was a police officer if you were caught by an angry mob in something serious.

A man appeared with a gallon of petrol. A kiosk owner volunteered with her box of matches. The crowd cheered and some screamed, 'Burn him! Criminal.' Suddenly, a policeman came and the chants of the crowd subsided.

'What did he do?' the policeman asked the man with the gallon of petrol.

'He stole a packet of cigarette from that woman's shop,' the man with the gallon of petrol said, pointing at the middle-aged woman who had screamed at the top of her voice.

'That?' the policeman said, referring to the packet of cigarette. 'And what do you want to do to him?'

'Burn him!'

The police man came out to the centre of the crowd and asked them not to take the laws into their hands. The mob shouted slurs at him. They accused him of conniving with thieves. They grabbed him by the hands and shook him around violently. Then rolled him away and then there were screams all over. A vulcanizer rolled out a car tyre to the road and it was sneaked around the assailant's neck. Petrol was poured on him and a match-stick went up with light and he screamed as fire burned him.

Rajaswamy shrieked when he saw the burning man thrashing about.

Benjamin had gathered David, Yvonne and Jerry under the cashew tree, after he had taken permission from Dada Felicia and Hatsu, who were looking after the kids. He sat like Christ giving sermons in parables on the mountain. The three bleary-eyed monsters were his disciples. He knew he could tell them anything. He bubbled with stories to tell. One apron a thyme, he said. The three monsters didn't reply. 'When I say once upon a time,' you say, 'Time, time.' And they said, 'Time, time.' Benjamin's smiles dimpled. Oh, he was talking to white disciples. A black preacher with white disciples under a cashew tree. He knew that St. John wouldn't dare to record that in his Gospels. Therefore, he decided to tell them a different story.

'There was a woman named Akudo,' Benjamin began. 'She had a child and her husband was dead. Everyday she took her son to the marketplace to beg for tobacco because she used it. And she was a very lazy woman. One day, she asked her neighbour who sold tobacco: "Can you help me with some shillings to buy tobacco?" Her neighbour said, "No'.'

'Why did she take tobacco?' David asked.

Benjamin paused. 'I can't tell,' he said. 'She was just taking it.'

'So,' Benjamin continued. 'That night she took her child to the riverside and said to the river goddess: "Please take my child and give me tobacco'.' The river goddess came out and gave her a pouch of tobacco, and took her child away.'

'My mom can't do that too,' Yvonne said.

'Mom can't do that,' Jerry added.

'So,' Benjamin mumbled, smiling at his disciples. 'She took the tobacco and became mad. The villagers threw her out. Each night while she roamed the forests, she kept searching for her child. But she couldn't find him because she sacrificed him in for a better stuff.'

David sighed. He didn't like the story, that was all. But, he had to listen, because Yvonne and Jerry were doing so.

Dada Felicia lay on her back in her bed. She had come for a nap, but she couldn't sleep because thoughts were racing through her head. Her heart was longing for Hatsu. Oh, she had to find a way to get her into her bed. She rose from the bed, jumped into the leather slippers by the bedside and walked to the curtain-larded window. She saw Hatsu sitting on the steel bench with Udunna. They were kissing. She sighed. And looked away.

Labata turned the car on the left and drove past ITC bus park, Nsu Community Bank and wheeled the car, past Ebere Links. 'Nigerians drive badly,' she said.

'Aagh!' Labata inhaled as he drove past Bossman Hotels. 'This is where Chief Mobutu will be hosting his guests.'

Rajaswamy looked at it. 'Really?'

'Yes,' Labata said.

He went past a church, Madonna Science School, and another school and pulled the car beside Terryvene Hotels. Rajaswamy came out. Eunice did the same. When Labata finally came out, he pointed to a cyber café over the road. They crossed as people watched them like people watching movie actors on set. He didn't bother because he was playing out his role. They climbed the staircase into the café.

The dust settled under David's legs as he marched side by side with Benjamin. The gravel crunched at their feet as they walked past the crab grass that sprawled through the alleyway. In David's mind, he felt he was passing Egmore Station in Chennai. There was something familiar about these places, he told himself.

They got to the palmwine shop and the one-handed man said to some of the palm wine drinkers, 'It's yucky,' and he laughed. 'This kid is an Indian. They live on trees.'

They laughed.

'They smell of raw jackfruit churry,' he continued, then came closer to David who backed away.

'No,' David shrieked. 'We live in houses.'

'Shut up, brown pig!' the one-handed man shouted. 'Do you take bath at all?'

This was the one-handed man's way of showing anger to the Indian. He had lost his first son who had traveled to India, after closing up his electronics shop at Aba. It had been over ten years the young man left. No one heard of him again. There was never a time he wrote. No phone calls or whatsoever. And each time he saw brown-coloured people, he got angry.

'Look at them!' He shouted. 'They Indians smell a lot. These people make people mad.'

In Ezeoke, it was believed that anyone who traveled to India, always came back mad. There were many who had passed through such: Erastus, Benneth, Chilaka, Stephen. They had traveled to India to study, and on their return, they were found to be mad. Those who weren't quite mad were found behaving like mongols.

'Oh!' the one-handed man exclaimed. 'I wish the government can only allow us to have our pound of flesh from these spice-smelling Indians.'

SWATHI LOUNGED ON the chaise longue in the verandah with a bidi thrust into her mouth. She blew fine rotating rings into the air and dishevelled her hair. She rose gently and began to walk through the corridor. 'Farida!' she called. No one answered. 'Farida! Farida!' No one answered and she walked into her room, muttering things to herself. 'Wherever that wuss has gone to! She hasn't made the mor kuzhambu I asked her to make. Farida!' She screamed at the top of her voice and a withering mild voice said from within: 'I come, mama.' She stepped through the cottage into the house and while she stood by the doorway, Swathi had slumped into the bed.

'You crazy!' Swathi scolded. 'Why don't you tell me where you go?'

'I tell you,' she said.

'What you tell me?'

'I speak you I go pray!'

Swathi sighed and told her to go. She rose from the bed, threw the bidi away and through the brightly coloured door-curtain, she walked into a tiny room, where there were pictures of Krishna and Radha, standing hands clasped together before a well-furnished room, with gold laces for the curtain and Shiva standing stoutly with his left hand placed on his hip and with the right, he held a W-shaped stall that had three knotted linings at the end. Around his shoulder, there was a cowskin and a life-like cobra sprawled around his neck. His hair was matted and tied into a foaming at the upper end, his lips brightly coloured like that of a woman and just below his earlobe there were large round-drilled ear-rings that dangled. He wore long thick beads around the neck, the ankles and wrists. A red silk cloth was tied to a heavy knot at the far left side of his waist, with a cow's horn draping around. On the forehead, there were three long lines stretched across it and in the middle, a cone-shaped dot, supported with a red sandalwood paste.

The shrine had the images of Ganesha and Kartikeya as well. Jamuna and Vimala together said that if Swathi was so intent on being a follower of Shiva, that there should be no need of Krishna's pictures in that shrine. But Swathi asked them to shut up, making them understand that it was because of the pictures of Krishna in her house that brought to her handsome and beautiful children. Rajaswamy said it was her belief. Vimala said that was absolute nonsense. But she thought they were all stupid for disagreeing with her. Swathi held out a bowl of water and bathed the Shiva-lingam placed beautifully at a corner of the room. Then took up a yellow red-blue garland and bedecked it, then brought a stainless steel plate of rice and uttered some mantras. Feeling weak, she muttered prayers for the safety of Rajaswamy, Eunice and David. When she had finally finished praying, she bowed and slowly stepped out. 'Farida!' she shouted. 'Farida! Farida!' And no one answered. She had heard a knock on the door and was trying to alert Farida. 'Basanti!' she screamed and the corridor echoed. She walked to the door, turning the knob open. She met Mr. Choudhury.

'Oh Choudhury!' she said, making way for him to enter. *Kab andar aye?'*

'Aap theek na?' Mr. Choudhury asked in Hindi.

'Mein theek hoon,' she muttered as Choudhury stepped in

and headed for the parlour. As she closed the door, she made a face and followed him.

Choudhury paced the parlour. 'You know,' he said. *'Humko diwana.'*

'Kya?'

'Oh, kuchu nahin, pyar hain,' he murmured to himself. *'Kasam, teri kasam. Tum mere apne-Mere jaan.'*

Swathi glared at him. 'What?' she asked surprised at all the things Choudhury was saying. They didn't make sense to her.

'Prem dhoon laagi,' Choudhury said. 'My heart beat. You come lunch with me?'

'Nahin,' she said and patted him on the shoulder. 'You like my grandson, Choudhury. *Theek hai na?'*

'Nahin,' Choudhury frowned. 'I want to have lunch with you. You lunch with me?'

Swathi laughed. 'You see!' she said. 'I believe there are many young people out there who would love to have lunch with you.'

'Oh!' he howled. 'I lunch with big people.'

'I'm old Choudhury,' she pleaded.

'Nahin!' He said and muttered things to himself. 'Not old, not old.'

'What you talk, Choudhury?'

Swathi slumped into a sofa and inhaled. Choudhury was a snare and she wasn't going to fall in. How could she be able to fall in love with such person like Choudhury? Choudhury is too young, she told herself.

If we lunch,' he said, 'I will take you to London. We elope.'

'You are silly, Choudhury.'

'I'm not silly, Swathi.'

But there was nothing Choudhury realized. He didn't

realize that Swathi was as old as his mother. He should have known that Swathi wasn't that stupid because she couldn't stoop so low as to *lunching* with such a goon as Choudhury. The doorbell rang. Swathi shouted: 'Farida! Basanti!' In few seconds, the two appeared in the room. 'Where have you two been?' she asked. 'I in the kitchen prepare dhoka kebab, phalon ki thandi kheer aur gosht biryani,' Farida said in quirky English. 'And you?' Swathi asked Basanti. 'I prepare sweet cheeni paratha,' she mumbled, burying her head in the ground.

'You two!' Swathi howled. 'Go check who is at that door!'
And they went out.

'Madam,' Choudhury said. 'That Haryana girl beautiful.'
'You are stupid, Choudhury,' she replied. 'She is dalit.'

'Dalit not matter,' he grumbled. 'I tell you something. Caste system we make. It is not the ... ' Choudhury stopped as soon as he saw a beautiful slender young lady in a kurta walk into the room, smiling. He rose. Swathi turned. '*Namaste*,' Choudhury said. '*Sabash*, Choudhury,' Swathi said in a whisper to him.

'Good day, Madam,' the young lady greeted Swathi.

'Good day, young lady,' Swathi murmured pointing to a sofa. 'Please take a seat.'

'*Shukriyah ji*,' she said and sat loosely in the sofa.

Swathi looked at her. Oh, she knew her. But her name? Her name? She couldn't remember again and this was really becoming too much. She looked into her eyes and then turned to the coffee table at the extreme of the room. She turned to her again. 'You are?' Swathi asked in a guise to get the information she had been longing for.

'I'm Sambhavi Jayachandran,' she said. 'I'm sure you remember?'

Swathi shook. Of course, she remembered that

Aishwarya Rai-face shaped girl. Swathi sighed. She had remembered that girl.

It was the summer of 1990 when Rajaswamy and his family were on vacation to Chennai. He had not married Eunice then and had not even thought of such. He was sitting in a café near St. Andrew's when a beautiful woman walked in, draped in a salwar-kameez that made her look as sexy as any sexy woman. The young woman was alone. Rajaswamy thought it was the only way to get to her, he smiled at her.

'You don't mind me joining you?' Rajaswamy asked softly.

She smiled and said, 'I don't mind.'

When he got over to the seat, they began to talk over cups of tea. About the weather. About the best Tamil film produced that year. About the elections. About anything. Having run out of what to say, Rajaswamy blurted out: 'Do you enjoy Mexican dishes?'

'No,' she said, frowning. 'I don't like Mexicans, let alone talk of their food.'

'Pescado a la veracruz?' Just to let her know he knew the names.

'Oh come on,' she frowned. 'No!'

'What African food do you enjoy?' He added.

'Not a bit,' she felt repulsed. 'Those people stink. They are lazy. Ugly!'

'But it has nothing to do with their food.'

'It does,' she said, sipping from her cup. 'You can't eat something from someone who stinks and is ugly.'

Rajaswamy looked at her and choked. 'You know,' he

said, 'you sound racist.'

'Not that!' she sniggered. 'I just don't like them.'

'Why?'

'Because I don't like them.'

'Tell me. Why?'

'I. Hate. Them,' she slowly said. 'They stink.'

Before now, Rajaswamy was just talking and talking without even realizing that he didn't even know the name of the girl he was laughing with, when she mimicked Italian accent.

'Ours is not even better,' Rajaswamy added.

'I sound like a chauvinist, huh?'

'No, racist,' he corrected.

She paused and then asked, 'What's your name?'

'Oh!' He inhaled. 'I'm so stupid. I forgot we are mere strangers!'

'Are we?'

'Of course,' he said. 'I'm Raj. Rajaswamy Rajagopalan.'

'Nice name,' she smiled. ' And I'm Sambhavi Jayachandran.'

'Single or married?'

'Married,' she said, laughing.

'To?'

'To whoever.'

They laughed. And the whole thing began to move smoothly. Sambhavi had Rajaswamy introduced to her family. Her family was rich and her parents were well-educated. In turn, Rajaswamy introduced her to his family. They loved her. Like the Jayachandran's family loved Rajaswamy. They began to go out together. Hand in hand. Lip to lip. They became the real tourists in town. Japanese and European tourists stopped to watch them. They walked past shops, smiling and laughing at themselves like lovers in a Bollywood movie.

One night, as they sat huddled themselves like heaps of clothes, sitting on a steel bench, outside the road that led to the train station, ideas rose from their heads. Sambhavi brought out a razor blade from her pouch. She sliced it into the flesh of her big finger and as blood dripped from it, she showed it to Rajaswamy. 'What's that?' he asked. She smiled and handed the blade to him. 'Cut out blood,' she demanded. 'We will have an oath.' He widened his eyes in surprise and asked, 'Why?'

'So you don't have to leave me,' she said and tears flowed down her cheeks.

'I can't,' he swore.

'You hate me,' she presumed. 'You hate me, that's why you can't.'

'No honey,' Rajaswamy said, indignantly puzzled. 'I love you.'

For fear of loss, he sliced the blade through his finger to produce blood. Deeply engrossed in his eyes, Sambhavi brought her finger to his and their blood mixed. She smiled, but Rajaswamy was in no mood to smile. He raised his eyebrows in utter surprise as their fingers clutched together. 'Swear!' she commanded and he repeated as she said, 'By the power of Agni, I swear to love you. In the light of our love, we share blood and swear that nobody will leave each other. If we do, let unhappiness rule over us.'

After that night, Rajaswamy grew really afraid of her. He began to distance himself from her. When they finally got back to Delhi, Rajaswamy became a free-lance journalist and Vimala was the Nigeria High Commission's lawyer.

It was in October of 1994 that Rajaswamy met Eunice and the two thought that it would be alright to be *one*.

First, they fell in love.

Second, they fell in bed.

Swathi was feeling uneasy as she looked at Sambhavi.

'Oh!' she said. 'I remember you!'

Mr. Choudhury stretched out his hand to Sambhavi. 'You are beautiful.'

Swathi quickly rose from her sofa, took Chaudhury by his hands, dragged him towards the door and slapped him across the face: 'Choudhury, get out!'

Choudhury buttoned his shirt. He made for the door and shrieked. Sambhavi froze. Fear cuddled her. She hadn't seen such a woman. Why did she have to slap him? Because he dared touching her? Or was she just jealous? Choudhury cleared his throat and was out of the room. Swathi stood in front of Sambhavi. 'So?' she said, looking stern and horrible. 'Rajaswamy couldn't have waited for ten years to marry you.'

Sambhavi felt repulsed.

'Or are you married?' Swathi finally asked.

'No!' she said, trapped in the sofa. 'I couldn't when we had taken an oath.'

Swathi's heart leapt. Oath? Why did Rajaswamy do that? She must have forced him into doing it, she thought.

Vimala was boiling some ribs of lamb in milk, when Rajaram appeared from nowhere wearing a Bermuda short and was bare bodied. He held her from the behind and kissed her cheek. She looked out through the window watching as the snow coated the street in West End. She turned and held his face in her palms.

'I deceived you, honey,' Rajaram said. 'I still love you.'

'I love you too,' she confessed. 'You are my life.'

'That means you have accepted me?'

'I didn't reject you, sweetie,' she said, holding him across his shoulder. 'You are the father of my son and the first man to…'

Vimala realized that she was dreaming after all. She got up from the bed and headed for the door. Sweat trickled down her face. Swathi's voice had woken her up. She stepped through the corridor, her hand on the banister as she walked to the parlour. She was behind Swathi now and saw her, staring at the door. Sambhavi was gone.

'What's wrong, mama?' she asked.

Swathi turned and exhaled. 'It was Sambhavi.'

'Who's Sambhavi?'

'The girl Rajaswamy wanted to marry.'

'Oh,' she sighed. 'What does she want?'

'Rajaswamy.'

'Is that what she wants?'

'Yes.'

'She can't be serious,' she said. 'After…'

'Ten years.'

'And she wants him?'

'Yes,' Swathi mumbled. 'She said they had taken an oath.'

'Oath?'

'That none would desert each other.'

Vimala hissed. 'She's an idiot,' she said and slumped into the seat. 'I think such ladies need some sense put in them.'

'Where's Raghu?' Swathi asked.

'He's having a nap,' she said.

'Umm!' her voice gabbled. 'Raghu is really missing David. Why can't he go and play cricket with Picard?'

'No, mama,' Vimala objected. 'Raghu can't be a cricketer. And he shouldn't be stupid. Why this sudden surge of feeling for

David?'

'Don't know,' Swathi said and picked up a newspaper from the couch she had just slumped into. 'Look at it.' She gave it to Vimala, indicating the page she wanted her look into. Vimala was quick at seeing her name: VIMALA RAJAGOPALAN, 28, HINDU BRAHMIN, BA,LLB (LONDON), SEEKS AN EDUCATED HUSBAND FROM A BRAHMIN HOME. She angrily threw it away. The smile on Swathi's face disappeared.

'What's wrong, Vimala?'

'I never asked you to do that for me.'

'You never, yes,' she said. 'But I want you to be happy.'

'Go to hell, mama!' she spat. 'I hate you.'

She walked out of the parlour, ran her hand through the banister and walked into her room. Swathi shook and mumbled curses.

Picard sat on the lawn of their house with his head bent between his legs. He looked up to the sky and it was grey-blue. He stood up and walked into his house. His mother was eating soufflé and paused when he saw how angry he was. Picard looked at her and turned back to the lawn. He sat there cross-legged. His taffeta glistened under the svelte evening sun that splattered all over the street. Bleary-eyed, he looked up to the Rajagopalan house and through Raghu's window, their eyes met. Raghu was in there crying. Picard called for him to come down, so they could play cricket. Raghu said that he couldn't. That his mother would beat him. Picard frowned.

'I'm eating brazil,' Picard lied. 'Come!'

Raghu shook his head.

'Have you gotten a reply from David?'

'No.'

'Umm,' he sighed. 'Africa is too far.'

'Yes,' Raghu mumbled. 'Their snail mail is stupid.'

12

Selected Envelopes

BEFORE RAJASWAMY and Eunice returned, a mail carrier who rode on a bicycle brought some envelopes. He handed them to Hatsu who in turn handed them to David. David scurried through them and found the ones that were meant for him. He shuffled them, tore them open and began to read them. When he finished reading them, he borrowed a pen from Hatsu and wrote replies. One by one.

Benjamin took him to the post office and they had the mails posted to India. He was very glad to have received the letters and the more he re-read them, the more he felt glad. Benjamin wanted to see the mails, but he said mails like that were to be kept confidential and completely sealed.

3/6 Rani Jhansi Road
New Delhi-55
20th December

Dear David,

How are you? It is now a long time since we saw each other last. I know you are having fun. But that Africa is not a country where people have fun. Do you have grocery shops there? Do you have McDonald's in Africa? Do you watch CNN? Nothing, I think?

How are Uncle Rajaswamy and Aunt Eunice? I think they are good? Yesterday, mom told me a Nigerian died at Tihar Jail, because of AIDS. You do not see AIDS people there, huh? You see, I know. Don't you want to come back to India? You see, India is more beautiful than Africa. Anyway, Kavitha was crying I miss David, I miss David everyday. She spoke to me yesterday and said that if you do not come back, she will die.

When are you returning to India? Week after week? Grandma smokes bidi in the cottage everyday. She does not make jam any more. She is not happy witout you. Mr. Choudhury came to speak to grandma and was asking her to join him for lunch. She flatly refused. I laugh the way grandma says Choudhury, get out! My mom is also smoking too much cigarette now. She is also drinking, only vodka. She doesn't want me to play cricket again.

I am sitting here with Picard. He is eating gulab jamun, sarai ki biryani, tomato chilli rasam, vegetable upma and burrito. You eat that? No, because there it is not good. Have you seen monkeys there? Mosquitoes? Oh, Farida cries where my David. Basanti and Pankaj are busy with themselves.

Mom is driving us to Aunt Helen's house. It's Sunny's birthday today. Talk to you later.

As ever,

Raghu

Gopalakrishnan House
Rani Jhansi Road,
New Delhi-55

Hello Dave,
　　I miss you so much. Ek zara si bhool khata ban gayi and you know I love you. Main hamesha tumhara chinta mein khoyi rahati hoon. Hamesha tumhara,

　　Kavitha

Frazier House
Rani Jhansi Road
New Delhi-55

Dear David,
　　Happy Xmas and a prosperous New Year in advance! I guess you are having real fun there? How is everyone in Africa? Anyway, I have been travelling with my parents around India since you left. We travelled to Manali then Simla. We just returned from Kashmir. The sleeting is waning. I really loved that. Dad was quick at returning to Delhi. But I'm not mad at him.
　　Now, I'm back to Delhi. Raghu and I watched a little of the European League match. We didn't like it much. Then Sahara played host to Sachin for cricket. It was marvellous. The bowlers were tough. And it was such that made me remember my stay in Dharamshala. We have been having some lull period in Delhi (REAL COFFEE!!) enjoying the city's more Western aspects (coffee!) with the snowy weather.
　　Yesterday, mom, dad and I went to Imperial Cinema and watched an entire Bollywood film without subtitles! It was Ashoka, with Kareena Kapoor

and *Shah Rukh Khan. You know my mom wants to speak Hindi like Sonia Gandhi. We really didn't understand it, but it was some fun.*

Last two weeks, we were off to Amristar, the Sikh holy city in the north of Punjab. It was really far too humid to plume around, but we managed to see the magnificent Golden Temple (750 kg of gold on top of white marble inlaid with semi-precious stones sitting in the middle of a huge part). Of all the temples we have visited, it was the best kept and serene. Later on, we escaped the brewing cold by heading for Dharamshala on a rickety bus with hard bench seats, a serious lack of toilet shops and a door that was never shut. Eight hours later, we made it to McLeod Ganj, home of the Dalai Lama in the Himalayan foothills. We managed to score a fantastic room with great views from the balcony and numerous windows overlooking a mountain range and valley. Occasional monkeys and sparrows visited us and Nick's Italian kitchen below us served great homemade pasta and fresh salads.

The town is a funky, tightly knit place of trinkets and travellers and there were heaps to do meditation, cookery, music and martial arts classes as well as treks in the mountains. We pottered around, walking to nearby villages and lakes, glimpsing the Dalai Lama (teaching, but in Tibetan…) and we ate lots of food. We then left for Kashmir and returned to Delhi through Balal Express.

Give my regards to your dad and mom. Even to everyone in Africa and keep in touch.

Picard.

Onwubiko House
Ezeoke Village
23rd December.

Dear Raghu,
    I am doing really fine and Nigeria is fine. Yeah, it has been long we saw each other. How are you? Yeah, we are having fun here. Africa is a

Continent and people have fun here. There are grocery shops here. There's Mr. Bigg's in Nigeria. We watch CNN and MTV too. We drink palm wine here, but in India we don't.

Dad and mom are fine. They go to spider café to check e-mails. In Nigeria, the Senate want to tell the Indians to go back to India because of how black people are treated in India. I have not seen people with AIDS here. I will come back to India. I will not say this place is better than that place, ok? Tell Kavitha not to cry, ok?

I don't know when we will return to India. Tell grandma to stop smoking bidi. When I come back to India, she will make jams again. You know Mr. Choudhury is half mad.

Picard has sent me a letter. I do not eat Indian food here because this is Nigeria. We eat akpu, foo-foo and melon soup. You see that? Africa is good. I do not see monkeys here. Tell Farida not to cry. Leave Pankaj and Basanti alone.

Wish happy birthday to Sunny.
As ever,
David.

Hello Kaavy,

I miss you too. You know I think about you and you are the only one in my heart. I love you too. Hamesha mere saath rehna.

Love, David

Dear Picard,

Happy Xmas and a prosperous New Year in advance too! Yeah, we are having real fun here. Well, I don't know everyone in Africa. Ugh! I do not even know everyone in this village, talk Africa? Cool that you travel around with your parents. How were Manali and Simla? Kashmir, was good eh?

Raghu also wrote to me. He did not tell me about the European League match. I watched here too. Nigerian people are good football people. They play well. You had coffee! Excellent. You should start taking beer then.

Today, one boy Benjamin told us a story. To my half-cousins, Yvonne and Jeri and me. He took me around and one man with one hand shouted at me: 'Shut up brown pig!' I do not know why he called me brown pig. He says that Indian people live on trees. But I forgave him. Benjamin told me his son died in India.

You have really, really toured India. That's good. Today, Benjamin says he will take us to a stream when I finish writing letters.

Picard, your letter was long.

I will give your regards to dad and mom. I don't know everyone in Africa. Do you know everyone in America? Haha. You don't.

David.

*

Now, Mama-Nkeukwu and the Bishop sat on the sofas in the verandah. The Bishop was a fat man with bulging stomach; tall and huge. His eyes looked as though they were protruding out. In his fingers, there were series of rings and at the top of his head, his red skull-cap glued. He was in a long-flowing red cassock that shone all through the verandah. On the smaller sofas sat two priests in white cassock. And Mgborie placed a tray of Schnapps with shots on the coffee table before the Bishop. She disappeared through the door that led into the hallway, smiling.

'What about your husband?' the Bishop asked Mama-Nkeukwu caressing his beardless jaw.

'He will soon be out,' she muttered.

'Good,' he said, beckoning on one of the priests to pour him a shot of the Schnapps. 'For how long has your daughter being married to that idol-worshipper?'

'Nine years precisely, for Christ's sake!'

'Damn,' he said, taking the shot from the priest and took a sip. 'That is too tough.' He coughed and added, 'But you couldn't have allowed her marry him?'

'She wanted him by all means!'

There was a long silence. Mama-Nkeukwu told the Bishop, 'My Lord, I asked the maids to prepare a hot dish of cauliflower cooked and served in cheese sauce for you. You will like that, huh!'

'Yes,' he smiled and smouldered in his cassock.

Mama-Nkeukwu chortled and disappeared through the door where Mgborie had gone through. One of the priests pulled out a bottle from the thick sack he had and poured the Schnapps into it, while the Bishop gulped the one poured out to him. From behind, a cock crowed cock-a-doodle-doo. The Bishop looked at his gold wrist watch and smiled. His small glasses stood on the tip of his nose, firm.

'D'you think her daughter can reconvert?' the Bishop asked the priests.

'Never know, my Lord,' the one with the bottle said.

'Unlikely, my Lord,' the second mumbled.

'Umm,' he groaned.

It was rare for any household in Ezeoke get a visit from the Bishop. But it was something the Onwubiko house had thrived upon for many years. They played host to all kinds of people and the Bishop (as a human, you know) was always fascinated whenever he was invited to that house because they prepared foreign dishes for them. And he would go on empty stomach so he wouldn't be bellyful at first take. He needed the whole thing to pack in his bulging belly.

'But my Lord,' the first resumed, 'if she fails to reconvert, what shall we do?'

He looked at him and shrugged. 'Then I stand to loose my prestige.'

'But it's unlikely that she would, my Lord,' the second

added.

'God is on my side,' he said. 'The only way for me to …'

Mama-Nkeukwu reappeared through the door, carrying a large silver tray. She laid the tray on the coffee table and handed two plates to the priests who began to spoon them hurriedly into their mouth. The Bishop started to eat, while Mama-Nkeukwu slumped into the sofa again.

'My Lord,' Mama-Nkeukwu began as she leafed through the Bible she had. 'I'm sure the Lord is doing great things in the church?'

'Yeah!' he said between mouthfuls. 'Great great things. But the only problem I have with the people of Ezeoke is the belief they have that we are embezzling the church fund.'

She looked at him. 'But you aren't!'

'We don't!' the Bishop grinned. 'Why should we?'

'No one has an idea,' she said sarcastically.

'You know,' he said. 'It takes really long for people to understand. I can't embezzle God's money. It's unthinkable.'

'And the church treasury wouldn't allow such an act.'

Mama-Nkeukwu paused. 'My Lord,' she called, 'I'm yet to know what you have decided to do about Reverend Paschal.'

'Nothing more.'

'Nothing more?'

'Yes,' he said. 'Since you've intervened.'

Reverend Paschal was a priest at the Cathedral. He was caught by the church catechist kissing a female churchwarden in the vestry. The case was reported to the Bishop who suspended the Priest. Inadvertently, the priest ran to Mama-Nkeukwu and pleaded for her to come to his rescue. And she did.

Some minutes after they had finished eating, Dada Felicia wheeled Papa-Nkeukwu out in his wheelchair to the verandah. The Bishop greeted him, as well as the priests. He had a newspaper with him and he began to read. Dada Felicia crouched near Mama-Nkeukwu. 'But you also asked Dibia Anyanzu to come?' she whispered to her. 'Yes,' she replied. 'Let me know which one works better.'

Dibia Anyanzu was a witch doctor. He lived on the outskirts of Ezeoke and there was this strong belief that he never failed in his magic. He was always seen wearing a loincloth with a bamboo stick to support him.

'The Senate is finally coming up with a decision,' Papa-Nkeukwu said, still engrossed in the paper.

'Really?' the Bishop asked.

'Yes,' he said. 'Tomorrow, they would declare what will stand out to be the fate of the Indians in Nigeria.'

'I think the first thing the government needs to think about is those Hindu temples in Lagos,' the Bishop continued. 'And then take some actions.'

'But what lemains the fate of Chief Mobutu's son in-law?' Dada Felicia asked.

'Chief Mobutu protects him,' Papa-Nkeukwu said.

The Hausa gate man opened the gate and Labata drove in. As Rajaswamy and Eunice stepped out of the car, the Bishop rose and made the sign of the cross. 'Let's pray,' he said, while everyone in the verandah rose in pensive mood. Eunice looked astonished. Papa-Nkeukwu felt really repulsed. 'It is written in Matthew chapter ten verse thirty-two that: those who declare publicly that they belong to me, I will do the same for them before my Father in heaven. But those who reject me publicly, I will reject before my Father in heaven.'

Everyone turned as there was a crash at the gate. That was the Hausa gate man struggling with Dibia Anyanzu. 'Some feofle are here!' the Hausa man said, pronouncing 'people' as 'feofle.' Mama-Nkeukwu shouted at him to allow *him* enter. The

Bishop looked on puzzled as the witch doctor stepped through the German floor to reveal himself.

'I bind you in the name of Jesus Christ!' the Bishop screamed at the top of his voice.

'No, my Lord,' Mama-Nkeukwu said. 'I sent for him, for Christ's sake!'

'You sent for him?' the Bishop was bewildered as well as the priests. 'Jesus Christ forbids such!'

'You should have known better,' Dibia Anyanzu said. 'Your church is no good. You take from the poor, when you should give to them.'

The Bishop wailed. 'By the power of the Holy Ghost, I bind you!'

Dibia Anyanzu coughed and lowered himself to the ground, (Rajaswamy thought it was a great spectacle) then he opened his raffia-bag and brought out a white chalk, with which he drew four lines and then a circle round line. In the Igbo tradition, the four lines indicate the four market days. Eke, orie, afor, nkwo. His eyes were closely fixed on the lines, then he cast four cowries shells and said, 'The land is evil, because of church people. And no matter what the eyes see, it cannot shed blood. When the cockerel farts, the earth goes after her. *O kirikiri ka anagba ukwu ose, anaghi ari ya elu.*' He hung his bag and headed for the gate.

'Wait, Dibia,' Mama-Nkeukwu shouted walking down from the verandah. 'Where to?'

'Come to the Gods!' he said. 'Amadioha is a jealous God. You can't serve another God before him.'

Everyone stared at each other. The Bishop laughed, as well as the priests.

Udunna, Kezie and Rajaswamy were sitting in the verandah, when Labata brought in a letter for Rajaswamy. He said it was from Chief Mobutu. He was inviting him for a dinner at Bossman Hotels. He and Eunice. So, when Labata left, Rajaswamy told Udunna and Kezie that while he had gone to check his mail box that day, he saw how an angry mob burned a young man.

'It happens everyday,' Udunna said. 'Nigerians are good when it comes to that.'

'Yeah,' Kezie cut in. 'I don't know why it keeps happening.'

Rajaswamy looked on, surprised. 'That's strange.'

'To you!' Udunna said. 'I think the government is so indolent. They don't want to look into this. They are stupid!'

'At times, you find those burning the so-called criminals to be real criminals themselves,' Kezie added.

'That's true,' nodded an astonished Rajaswamy.

That night, the dinner was extravagant. Eunice and Hatsu, even Dada Felicia had all gone into the kitchen and come out with their sumptuous pots. On the long table, all types of food were tastefully laid: boiled pumpkin leaves, sliced cassava, yam porridge, beans in a tomato sauce; jollof rice and spaghetti; bowl of white rice with a breakable plate of avocado stew, bowls of boiled and fried eggs. Pounded yam, eba and okra soup. But Papa-Nkeukwu paid more attention to the vegetable enchiladas sprawled on the table.

Everyone was eating to his or her satisfaction. Rajaswamy watched to see if David was eating and he was.

'Aagh!' Papa-Nkeukwu said as he ate a spoonful of the white rice, garnished with the avocado stew. 'Felly,' he called Dada Felicia, fondly.

'Yes?' she said, looking up, while everyone listened.

'How do you do this avocado stew?' Papa-Nkeukwu asked.

'It's vely simple,' she began, while they watched and listened. 'Anyway, the first day I learnt it, it was like, "How can I eat this tlash?"'

They laughed, except David and Jerry.

'When?' Udunna asked.

'While in London,' she said. 'It was my Chinese loom mate that taught me how to do it. She said, "Get that avocado peal". And when I got two of it, she asked me to peel off the body and I did.'

'Ripe ones?' Kezie asked.

'Yes,' she explained. 'She got about ten tomato fluits and mashed, got a small cup of buttel and evelyothel thing that stew needs. Then specially plepaled chicken meat. So soft. Allight, she pouled a small quantity of gloundnut oil into the pan on fire, added the avocado pears and began to stir it. After a few seconds, she poured in the buttel and it melted, then tomatoes and ingliedients. She waited for a few minutes, after putting the chicken and the stew was done.'

'Wow!' Yvonne exclaimed. 'That's interesting.'

'Yeah, it's intelesting,' Dada Felicia nodded.

David and Jerry looked at each other and laughed out loud.

Dada Felicia tip-toed towards the toilet and heard the thrashing sound of one's urine dripping into the water-closet. She peeked through the keyhole and saw that it was Hatsu. She arranged her night gown and looking around to see if anyone was staring at her, she gently pulled the toilet-door open and came face to face with Hatsu. She shuddered. 'What?' she asked. 'Oh, solly,' Dada Felicia said in pretense and made way for her to pass. Hatsu ran out quickly. Dada Felicia shrugged.

David was in a long dream now, traveling through an island in a caravan with Nfanfa. He only saw dwarves and elves. There was a woman dwarf performing magic in the centre of the market place. David liked the whole place. He smiled and Nfanfa smiled. 'Do you know we are in my grave now?' Nfanfa asked him. 'No,' he said. 'You don't?' 'Yes.' But he knew. Jolly naughty boy, he knew. As they got down the caravan, to cross the road and join the people watching the sorceress, a cab squealed to their front.

'Hens,' the dwarf cab driver shouted to them. 'Ain't you gonna take me cab?'

'None!' Nfanfa said. 'Your cab isn't what us need, ok?'

'You gotta need 'em, you know!' the driver mottled. 'You trek, trek to this place, no! You move with 'em two legs and they pain you '

'Us don't need that cab!'

'Crazy!' the driver shouted bitterly. 'You need 'em legs, huh? You blatter! Fool man!'

'Fool man!' Nfanfa screamed back and looked at David. 'He said I'm a foolish man.'

David felt the pangs of hunger and told Nfanfa, who took him to a restaurant where the waiters and waitresses were dwarves. He bought beef and mutton. David ate them, while they walked back to the caravan. They didn't go to see the sorceress again.

When David woke up, he saw Mama-Nkeukwu sitting by his side. He found his mouth was moving.

'What are you eating?' Mama-Nkeukwu asked him, feeling feverish.

'Meat.'

'In the dream?'

And he nodded.

13

The Blackbees

ON THE next morning, Saturday, there was a thorough cleaning of the house. That year, Christmas fell on a Sunday. Eunice walked through the corridor and entered David's room. She found him shivering under the woolly blanket that covered him. She lowered her posterior to the bed and felt his body. It was hot. Oh, he's sick, Eunice muttered. David opened his eyes and smiled at his mother.

'You're alright, honey?' she said.

And he nodded. But she knew that he wasn't. She felt him again. On the forehead. Round the neck. Like a woman kneading the buttocks of her child with olive oil.

'Your body is hot, honey,' she said. 'Can I get you some pills?'

'No, mom,' he grinned. 'I'm alright.'

Eunice walked back into their room and told Rajaswamy how their son was feeling. He was depressed. He picked up the desk phone on the bed head and dialed some numbers. He was trying to reach Ranganatha, instead a nurse answered who promised to let the doctor know that he called to have him go down to his house.

'But he has a mobile phone?' Eunice asked.

'I don't have the number,' Rajaswamy said.

'Oh!' she exclaimed and disappeared through the door.

Papa-Nkeukwu was sitting in the verandah, in his wheelchair reading a copy of Harvey Spencer Lewis' *The Secret Doctrines of Jesus*. His eyes moved slowly from one word to another. When he finally looked up, he saw the bearded Rommy B. standing there, ragged as ever. He smiled up to him and Rommy B. tried peeking into the house through the door. 'Ha-ha!' Papa-Nkeukwu laughed. 'You heard of one here?' He was referring to anything *white*. 'Yes,' Rommy B. said. 'I heard that Udunna's wife came?'

'Who told you?' Papa-Nkeukwu smiled.

'I heard,' he said. 'But South Korea never liked Russia.'

Papa-Nkeukwu laughed. 'You are funny.'

'No, give me a bottle of beer,' Rommy B. said. 'Her name is Chiang Yee, yes? She doesn't know that I played host to Mao in Venice.'

'You...'

'Mussolini was adamant,' he muttered. 'But a bottle of beer would do.'

Papa-Nkeukwu called Mgborie to get him a bottle of Star beer. She uncorked the chilled drink and he began to drink.

Dr. Ranganatha arrived in his Honda Civic with a nurse who was carrying a box. They ran through the corridor, while Rajaswamy led them into David's room. Papa-Nkeukwu was astonished and he began asking what was happening. But the doctor said that only Rajaswamy and Eunice were allowed into the room. When they were finally in, the doctor placed the stethoscope on David's chest and listened.

'Funny,' he said and nodded.

'*Kya*?' Eunice asked in Hindi. 'What?'

Ranganatha felt David by the forehead. 'How are you?' He asked.

'Mom,' David said, instead to Eunice. 'I couldn't sleep last night. Instead I was dreaming. I don't know '

Eunice sat beside him. 'What was the dream, honey?'

'I've forgotten,' he said. 'I'm confused. Who's that? Where's daddy? I can't see very well.'

Eunice turned to Rajaswamy and shuddered. He came near and touched him by the left hand. 'Dad,' he smiled. 'You are too lean.' But he wasn't lean. David was having a problem with his memory and sight. Throughout the night, he couldn't sleep.

'Raj,' the doctor said to Rajaswamy. 'The two of us need to talk, ok?'

'You can't do anything?' Eunice asked.

'It's minor, Eunny,' the doctor lied. 'Just let me have some words with Raj.'

Tears trickled down Eunice's cheeks. She gently rose and began to walk out. 'No!' the doctor objected. 'Stay behind with the nurse. Let me go and have the words outside, ok?'

'Alright,' she said and walked back to the bed.

Quickly, because they had to be fast, Ranganatha and Rajaswamy were out and walked to the drawing room. They sat on long stools, facing each other.

'Raj,' the doctor began in Tamil (so eavesdroppers would not understand) 'Something's wrong. We've got to act fast.'

'Ok,' Rajaswamy said.

'Have you heard of VCJD?'

'Creutzfeldt-Jakob disease?'

'Yes,' he muttered. 'And do you know if any of your relatives or Eunice's has died of it before?'

'I have no idea.'

'Good,' he said. 'The things your son mentioned that are coming to him are the symptoms of Variant Creutzfeldt-Jakob disease. But I'm kind of skeptical about this. He is just nine, na?'

'Yes.'

The doctor stopped, looked around the room, quite confused, like an actor who had forgotten his lines on stage, and resumed: 'This disease is a deadly illness and has no cure. If it eventually comes to be CJD, then be ready for cremation.'

'I rebuke that!' Rajaswamy swore.

'My advice is,' he said, 'take David back to India. I think there are better equipment and hospitals there. Nigerian hospitals are mere clinics. And for you to save David's life, a travel back to India will be worth it.'

'Why not cure it here?'

'No, Raj,' he said. 'There is nothing like that. This disease is rare. People who suffer this also suffer bipolar disorder .'

'Our therapist in India said he suffers from that,' a weary-eyed Rajaswamy confessed.

'Good,' he coughed. 'Alzheimer's or Huntington disease. We can't conduct any test because we have no way to detect it.'

When the doctor was gone with the nurse, Rajaswamy closed himself in the library, browsing through the books. There was no book on Creutzfeldt-Jakob disease. He got the large thick *Oxford Advanced Learner's Dictionary* and found the word.

It read:

A brain disease that causes gradual loss of control of the mind and body and, finally, death. It is believed to be caused by PRIONS *and is linked to* BSE *in cows.*

He looked up PRION: *A very small unit of* PROTEIN *that is believed to be the cause of brain disease such as* BSE, CJD *and* SCRAPIE. He quickly leafed through the pages and stumbled on BSE: *The abbreviation for 'bovine spongiform encephalopathy' (a brain disease of cows that causes death)* That's for cows, he assumed and put the book back into the shelf and walked out of the room.

The walls of the corridor were very cool and as soon as Rajaswamy stepped in through the shadowy archway, he met with Dada Felicia.

'Is David ok?' she asked.

'Somewhat,' he tiredly said.

'What do you mean by somewhat?' she asked. 'Is he ok? What's wrong?'

'He's ok.'

'You Indians!' Dada Felicia shouted. 'This is the way you use people to do voodoo. Let me just tell you that if anything happens to David, we will hold you and your fellow Indians responsible.'

Rajaswamy was taken aback. 'David is my son, woman!' He screamed back and anger pelted over his face. 'He's my son and I'm more concerned than you are.'

Mama-Nkeukwu emerged through the next door. 'You are insane!' She screamed at Rajaswamy and slapped him. 'You idol-worshipping Hindus have ruined the fate of my daughter. You charmed her, impregnated her and now you've brought your ill-luck into my home. You!' She snapped and walked away to the sitting room.

'Better get going back to India, mongol!' Dada Felicia shouted and as she raised her hand to hit Rajaswamy, Eunice pushed her and she crashed violently on the floor. She screamed and staggered up.

'You dare not touch my husband!' she shouted at her. 'Don't you feel ashamed being a spinster at this age?'

'Get lost!' she said and walked out.

Eunice held Rajaswamy in tears and fear surrounded them. She held his face closer and said, 'David is alright' and then kissed him softly.

There was this long grudge and silence that hung around the Onwubiko house. Papa-Nkeukwu was still in the verandah, largely reading *The Secret Doctrines of Jesus*. Rajaswamy, Udunna and Kezie gathered around and stuck to talking about things that riveled over the Senate's debate.

'Papa,' said Udunna, 'do you think being a member of AMORC is the ultimate?'

'Somehow,' he muttered. 'Because AMORC is not a religion. It has got to do with philosophy and finding yourself.' He read: "No doubt most Christians will be surprised as the intimation that Jesus taught secretly any divine principles, or praticised any divine art that He did not reveal to all the world.'

David, who was now sitting on Eunice's lap, said he knew something like that. They were coolly surprised, but it didn't matter. Dada Felicia asked him how he knew and he said his friend Nfanfa told him.

Dada Felicia choked. 'Nfanfa?' she said, turning to Rajaswamy. 'Lajaswamy, I'm sule youl son's not well!'

'I'm well,' David said disdainfully.

'Hooligan, you are not well,' she retaliated.

'Don't call my son names,' Eunice heard herself saying.

'Don't be silly, Eunice,' she shouted. 'Your son is being visited by a ghost.'

'No,' David screamed. 'Don't call my friend ghost. Nfanfa is no ghost.'

Mama-Nkeukwu quickly rose and held him by the shoulder. 'Yes, I know that Indians don't fear. They are magicians. But you must get this into your Jantar Mantar head now! Nfanfa died many years ago. His grave is behind this house. He was my husband's father's maid.' That was how Papa-Nkeukwu had detailed the whole thing to them. But that wasn't true. It was a different thing altogether.

And Rajaswamy who had been reading a newspaper gasped, while the paper fell from his hand. Still, David didn't understand what his grandmother was talking about. It made no sense to him. What was the whole thing? He couldn't say. As everyone stared, he rose and held the railing. His eyes were fixed at the gate. He startled. There was Nfanfa and some other dwarves. They were bare-bodied except that Nfanfa dressed as a Sikh, turbaned. The dwarves were about eight. They smiled. Barefooted. Gap-toothed.

'You see!' David pointed at Nfanfa for everyone to see.

'What's wrong with you, David?' Rajaswamy wanted to know. 'Are you ok?'

'Yes!' he replied, smiling. 'Can't you see Nfanfa?'

'I can't see anyone.'

Everyone stood (as though they were remote-controlled) and they walked to the railing.

'Nfanfa is here,' Papa-Nkeukwu, still trapped in his wheel-chair, said. 'He's here. But no one can see him.'

'David,' Nfanfa said, walking into the verandah. 'Go get your bag and let's travel.'

'To?' he said, heading for the door, into the house (while everyone turned and followed him)

'Into the grave.'

'Again?'

They stopped and were marvelled. Mama-Nkeukwu wanted to grab him by the cloth and slap him, but she couldn't.

'Yes,' Nfanfa answered. 'And if you don't mind, I'd want you to come and live with us forever.'

'No, Nfanfa,' he said. 'You know that I love Ma, daddy and mummy, even Raghu that I can't leave them and come to live in your grave.'

When Rajaswamy heard this, he felt he had been robbed of something. For his son to be speaking to an invisible spirit meant that he was one of them. Quickly, Mama-Nkeukwu and Dada Felicia sneaked into the kitchen.

'I told you, didn't I?'

'You did.' But Dada Felicia didn't know what Mama-Nkeukwu claimed she'd told her.

'That boy is ogbanje,' she assumed. 'No human being evel talks like that. I've told Eunice a numbel of times that we should consult Dibia Anyanzu to come and do something. But she wouldn't aglee. Why she mallied out of Aflica, heaven knows!'

'I'll take an exception to that,' she scolded her. 'She's still my daughter.'

'*Gbaghalam!*' she pleaded. 'Folgive me. Anyway, I think they should lealn flom what David is doing now.'

Later on that afternoon, Dibia Anyanzu arrived and after casting his cowries said that a generational curse had been laid upon the household for a crime none of them present committed. But Mama-Nkeukwu spat into his face and called him a fraud.

Nevertheless, Papa-Nkeukwu knew the truth.
But he couldn't tell it.

Chief Mobutu had called Rajaswamy over the phone that evening asking him to attend the gala night he was organizing at Bossman Hotels. By all means. That was the way he said it. By all means. As though it had something to do with 'biotics.' But didn't. So he told Eunice that they had to go. At the initial stage, Eunice said that their son's ill health was a hindrance. 'You know Chief Mobutu is politics himself,' Kezie explained to them. 'So you must honour his invitation.'

On the balcony of the White House, Rommy B. was reading a newspaper. His mind drifted and swept back to his days in Italy. He was a die-hard tourist then and his wife Rebecca, as Italian, almost knew everywhere. First on their honeymoon, they had lodged at Hotel Diplomatic Roma on Via Vittoria Colonna, and then on the next morning, they strolled through V.D Scrofa, Ripetta, Navona and down Gianicolo, then walked through Via Aurella and stopped at Citta del Vaticano. They took photographs of P.za S. Pietro and smiled at the people watching them.

When their twin sons were born, Rommy B. took a tour of the whole city, from Monte Mario, F. Tevere, Villa Borghese, Villa Ada, Villa Doria-Pamphili, and Campo Verano and to P.del Popolo.

A car screeched to the front of the gate. Rommy B. rose

from the seat he was sitting in and walked to the railing, he saw a white woman step out of the car. He began to remember their wedding at a church far away in Viale Regina Margherita. He widened his eyes and something tickled him in the inside. He choked and within some few minutes, the reality struck him that the white woman was Rebecca and the two boys emerging from the taxi were Benito and Carlito.

There were two half-Italian boys named Benito and Carlito, they rocked around the streets, down V. Satrico.

They had a father, who was mad and who answered Rommy B.

They loved their mother, Rebecca like they loved the restaurants on Tuscolana.

He squealed and felt dizzy. His eyes broadened as she took out their luggage from the car. Then Benito and Carlito carried the bags up the staircase as Rommy B. watched them. When they got up and saw him, they shrieked. Rommy B. looked at them sensuously and tears rolled down his eyes.. Seeing their father's bearded face, they felt it was something different. The bags they were carrying slowly fell from their hands and they began to sob quietly. When Rebecca finally came up to the balcony, almost bewildered by her husband's sudden shabby appearance, she broke down into tears. Rommy B. felt repulsed by himself and the newspaper in his hand fell off. He opened his arms and Rebecca fell in. They embraced. Oh, Rebecca perceived his odd smells. The fungus sweet smells. Then Benito looked at Carlito and they moved forth to embrace him. And they did.

There were two half-Nigerian boys named Benito and Carlito, they were good night-clubbers down the street of Via

Cipro.

Their friends were too eager to know their father,
And their girlfriends scurried around Aurelia Antica.

Benito and Carlito were twenty. And had blurry colours that matched with their curly black hairs that hung smoothly on the surface of their forehead. Mr. Cold cleaned two rooms in the White House and put their luggage in them. Rebecca ordered him to have her husband's beard shaved off. And the process began. When it was finally over, Rebecca looked at him and discovered her real husband. It wasn't Rommy B. anymore. She hugged him, hugged him, and squeezed him softly. She kissed him, but he burst into tears. He didn't kiss back because he knew he was dirty. His tongue. His lip. His everything. He kept on weeping and weeping.

Later on in the evening, she took him into the bath and had him cleaned. There was Eva soap and a hard sponge to scrub his body. She manicured and pedicured him and having found that her husband no more had clothes, Rebecca took out one of her son's Italian suits and had him clad in it. Still, he kept on crying, weeping, sobbing, lamenting. His eyes suddenly turned dark blue.

Benito and Carlito looked at him and smiled.

It was 7.30 pm. Labata had scrubbed off the mist on the windshield of the Volvo car and drove Eunice and Rajaswamy to Bossman Hotels.

The hall was filled with people. As soon as Chief Mobutu spotted Rajaswamy and Eunice, he rose to his feet and shook hands with them. He led them to the round table with four chairs where Ranganatha and Priscilia sat. They shook hands and took the remaining two seats. Chief Mobutu excused them and walked back to where he was sitting with a huge bearded man with a swarthy stomach.

'Hey!' Priscilia said to Eunice, pointing at the man. 'You remember him?"

'Not at all!' Eunice said looking towards the direction. 'Who's he?'

'Pete Edochie,' she replied.

'Oh!' It occurred to her. 'The man who played the role of Okonkwo in the film adaptation of Achebe's *Things Fall Apart?*'

'Yeah.'

Eunice held Rajaswamy's hand and pointed to the same man. 'Honey, look at him,' she told him. 'That's Nigeria's Amitabh Bachchan.'

And they laughed.

'Anyway,' Ranganatha said. 'How's David?'

Eunice sighed. 'He wasn't well when we left,' she said. 'We had to leave him with Benjamin, the cleaner's son.'

'Aagh!' he exclaimed. 'Your trip to Nigeria is important to you, but it's becoming unimportant day-by-day. If you think your son needs to live, you must go back to India quickly.'

'I know,' Rajaswamy said. 'We've planned to go by Monday.'

'Have you confirmed your ticket?' Priscilia asked.

'Yes,' Rajaswamy blurted out. 'By Monday, we would be off to India.'

'Nice.'

There was a large stage and a group of cultural artistes called the Blackbees scrambled on the stage and sang and drummed. When they were finally through, the audience applauded them awesomely. Then waiters and waitresses began to serve glasses of different sorts of wine on trays, as the musician, Onyeka Onwenu mounted the stage.

You and I will live as one
You and I will live as one
You and I, You and I
You and I will live as one.

Eunice told Rajaswamy that she was Nigeria's Celine Dion. But he said that her comparison was lazy. That there was no way Onyeka Onwenu created any metaphor for anyone to link her work to that of Celine Dion's. She said she had to compare them because she was the best female singer in Nigeria.

Muna gi ga-ebi n'udo
Muna gi ga-ebi n'udo
Muna gi, muna gi
Muna gi ga-ebi n'udo

For Priscilia, she thought Eunice was not saying the truth. She listed names of female singers who could beat Onyeka Onwenu in her heart. But there was no way she could print them. She had to hold them in there and that was all. She couldn't.

Eunice looked towards the large doorway and saw a blowsy woman emerging through the door with Mama-Nkeukwu. She knew her. That was her mother's younger sister, but she was so fat and untidy to the extent that one could be tempted to say she was Mama-Nkeukwu's elder sister. And to Eunice, she was just a bundle of crap altogether. So undiplomatic.

One day, Eunice and Rajaswamy visited her (because Mama-Nkeukwu swore that Eunice must go) in her zinced house at Ndiama, with Labata taking them there. And when they were seated, she brought out a breakable bowl of boiled stockfish, garnished with pepper, onions, little palm oil and salt. Then a keg of palm wine. But Eunice and Rajaswamy declined almost at the same time. She frowned and calling upon the maid to clear the 'nonsense,' howled: 'But you were eating that Indian nonsense, Eunice?' She spoke audibly in English for Rajaswamy to hear. Eunice felt ashamed.

'What nonsense, aunty?' she asked.

'Weren't you eating vegetables cooked with cow-dungs?' she said.

Rajaswamy looked disappointed. 'I never knew Nigerians think of us in this way?' He whispered.

The woman ignored him. 'Eunice,' she said, 'I have been waiting for this moment, so I'd ask you why you chose to marry an Indian.'

'Ugh?' she made a so-what face.

'You lived in India for a long time,' she continued, stressing her point. 'You know exactly the whole primitive tradition they practice. Women are strongly belittled and only recently are their women coming out.'

Rajaswamy had to cut in. 'You are wrong,' he said.

But she still ignored him. 'And you didn't even marry a Christian Indian,' she lounged in her seat. 'You are just a housewife.'

The situation changed. Rajaswamy had to be fast to talk.

The woman was loquacious. He spoke. They howled on top of their voices arguing, while Eunice listened in pure amazement.

'A woman has always been given a much higher status and position in Hinduism than in any other religion,' Rajaswamy said, for the woman to understand.

And the woman was saying something else for Eunice to understand: 'If I knew I'd ask you to abort the pregnancy that led you into the snare!'

'In the ancient times, Gargi, wife of Mandanamishra,' Rajaswamy argued, 'was appointed as judge because of her superior erudition and spiritual attainments ...'

'And how dare you go to bed with him?' she asked Eunice, looking at Rajaswamy.

He stopped and said, 'It was the foreign invasion and the rigidity of the caste system that led to the loss of independence of the Hindu woman.'

'You can do something,' she suggested.

But Eunice wasn't interested in her suggestion. She and Rajaswamy walked out on her and she cursed them.

Eunice watched her as she settled into a seat with Mama-Nkeukwu and Dada Felicia at the table where Chief Mobutu's wife was sitting. They were served drinks by a waiter and then food by a waitress. In few minutes, Chief Mobutu mounted the stage after Onyeka Onwenu had finished a second number.

Ladies and gentlemen, Chief Mobutu thought as he held the microphone to his mouth.

They clapped for him.

'Good evening, Ladies and Gentlemen,' he finally began in English. 'From the deepest part of my heart, I sincerely welcome you to this gala night of which I have generously plotted out so I could treat you to a delicious set of things.'

They clapped.

'…and,' he stammered. 'There is always a way to make the world yearn for a better ruler, a man who can change the world. Not the likes of our past military dictators who are so intent on getting on board home with the funds meant for development.'

They cheered him profoundly.

'Finally,' he said, 'I use this rare opportunity to canvass for your support to represent Ehime Mbano Constituency in the State House of Assembly. And on my behalf, I pledge to redefine the future of the youth of this blessed town and in realization of this, I'm instituting an essay competition with the sum of five million naira for students in the tertiary institutions.'

Before he even concluded, a thunderous cheer exploded within the hall. As he made to step down from the stage, everybody in the auditorium rose to his or her feet and applauded him. He waved his hand in response and smiled.

'Let me go to the toilet,' Rajaswamy whispered to Eunice.

'Alright,' she said.

He stepped through the tables and entered the hallway that led to the toilets and bath. Dada Felicia got up from her seat and walked through the archway. She closed a door behind her.

Rajaswamy opened the door to a toilet and entered. After he finished what he came for and turned the door open, he came face to face with a beautiful girl in a mini-skirt and spaghetti-lined top, with the upper parts of her breasts showing seductively.

'What?' Rajaswamy asked as the girl blocked his way out. 'What do you want?'

'You!' she said, smiling and then using her tall finger nails to touch his long nose.

'Why?'

'Can't you see you are handsome?' she asked, then

222

pushed him back into the toilet and banged the door. The two of them were in there now.

Back in the hall, Dada Felicia walked to Eunice and whispered to her: 'Why not go and see if Rajaswamy is alright, since he hasn't come back.' Eunice said she was right and then walked towards the toilets. At one of the rooms, she heard Rajaswamy's voice. He was saying: 'Please, please.' She slid the door open and met with the shock of her life: the girl bending over her husband. 'Raj!' she called out, afraid. And the girl turned. 'What do you want?' she asked Eunice. Rajaswamy was most astonished when Eunice disappeared through the door that he pushed the girl to the wall and she yelled bitterly.

When he was in the cool corridor, he saw Eunice racing through it. 'Honey,' he called out, weakly, 'I didn't do anything. Please.'

But she wasn't interested in what he was saying. She ran out and got to the parking lounge where she found Labata sipping on a bottle of Gulder beer.

'Take me home,' she demanded of him.

'Where oga dey, madam?' he asked.

'Get me home, idiot!' she shouted on him and got into the car.

Labata, not in any mood to irritate Eunice, dropped the Gulder beer bottle on the lawn, and accelerated the car out of the building, as the uniformed man at the gate waved at them. He held the steering-wheel firmly as his eyes were fixed on the fuel gauge. There was enough fuel, he said. From the rear-view mirror, his eyes met with those of Eunice.

'What's your own?' she asked him, leaning on the headrest.

Labata began to stammer. 'You are troubled.'

'Who told you that?' she was surprised.

'You look too troubled.'

She was silent.

'I could be of help.'

'Get lost!' she snapped. 'You can never be of help to me, commoner!'

But Labata wasn't demoralized. He had to know what was troubling her and he was determined to find out.

'I'm sorry,' he was apologetic. 'But...'

'Stop that, beast!'

'What you call me doesn't matter,' he said.

She sighed. 'Why are you so interested in me, suddenly?'

'Not in you,' he said. 'I seriously know that something is wrong and that's why you are going without him. I haven't seen the two of you separately before.'

She was stunned. What was he talking about? How on earth could he simply presume such nonsense? She retched and summoned the courage to tell him something. 'Yeah,' she said, now submissive, 'I met Rajaswamy in the hotel's toilet with a prostitute.'

'Were they doing anything?'

'Nothing.'

'That's funny,' he said and smiled. 'He's innocent I can tell you that.'

'Shut up!' she shouted. 'He cheated on me!'

Labata thought deeply and wheeled the car home smoothly.

Eunice was in the drawing room, sitting beside David who was sleeping on a straw mat. She caressed the body of her son, as tears filled her eyes. But she was going to hold the tears back. The room looked larger to her and what surprised her was that her husband was cheating on her. Her mind shuttled as the radio on the table in the room blared that it was 9.00 pm.

'Welcome to the network news of the NTA,' a female voice the newscaster said. 'The President has urged the African Union leaders to strengthen their hands to quell violence in war-torn African countries today, after the AU Summit in Abuja. A Nigerian writer gets shortlisted for Britain's most prestigious prize for women writing. The Senate has finally decided on the fate of the Indians in Nigeria.'

Eunice quickly got up in shock, scrambled to the desk phone, and held it up to her ear as the newscaster read on.

'… the Senate has finally decided, that since the Indian government is adamant in coming for diplomatic talks with Nigeria, that the Indians in Nigeria are ordered to leave the country in an organized manner or get violent exodus. This follows the murder of a Nigerian in India by two Indian police officers at the Old Delhi Railway Station. Speaking on behalf of the adhoc committee set up to look into the matter, Senator Taiwo Akin instructed Nigerians to take drastic actions if they found any Indian still lurking behind. The Minister of Foreign Affairs, in an interview with NTA noted that the Ministry would not waste time in bringing home as many Nigerians as they are in contact with and severe the diplomatic ties with the subcontinent. The minister added that Indians are to leave the country with no property, except the clothes they would be in to be flown back to their home country by flights mapped out by the Federal Government …'

She switched off the radio and shivered. Her hands were feeling shaky and quickly she ran the staircase, no more feeling the coolness of the banisters. She met with Labata sitting in the verandah.

'I heard the news,' Labata rose to his feet.

'Yes,' she shrieked. 'You have to take me back.'

'To Bossman Hotels?'

'Yes,' she said. 'I need to get Raj.'

He asked the Hausa gate man to open the gate and he sped into the darkness blaring his horns as he drove down to Bossman Hotels. Eunice ran inside and began to scurry her eyes around to find Rajaswamy. She couldn't. She ran out to the parking lounge, and there Rajaswamy was, talking with Labata. She ran to him and embraced him warmly. Rajaswamy apologized, but she said there was no need for that. She said the most important thing was that they get out of the country. He was surprised. She told him that the Senate had decided to have the Indians deported. He shook. They hopped into the car and Labata sped away.

'Dada Felicia planned it,' Labata confessed.

'Planned what?' Eunice asked.

'She and mama,' he said. 'I overheard them saying that they would trap oga in there, so you'd not go back to India with him.'

She knew. But what troubled her was what the press had written in India that Rajaswamy married her Nigerian wife to research for his first book. No, Labata was right. Was that why Dada Felicia had come up to her and asked her to go and see what was keeping her husband long in the toilet? How did she know he was going to the toilet? And what were they doing this for?

As the car got to the okada junction, they saw a group of young people screaming, 'Finally we can get jobs without these Indians standing against us.' They were jubilating over the decision of the Senate. That was the thing that shocked Rajaswamy.

'You will get a bus,' Labata said to Eunice.

She was asking if they would be able to get a bus to Lagos, after she had packed their things together. It was 9.53pm. Benjamin wasn't comfortable with what was happening. He thought that the Senate was a group of idiots. He and Labata took their bags into the boot. Mgborie and Babiana stood on the verandah staring into the emptiness of the night.

As Labata started the car, Eunice asked Benjamin to sit in the front seat, so he could accompany Labata back. She carried David in her arms, into the backseat. Rajaswamy entered the car and Labata drove out. It was night, the streetlights shone brightly.

After about forty-five minutes, they got to Owerri. And Labata drove into Mbaise Road, stopping as soon as he came to the ABC Transport terminal before Fire Service. He parked the car and then Eunice opened her purse and gave him and Benjamin some naira notes as they helped them carry in their luggage into the checking lounge.

They left Labata and Benjamin.

Eunice bought two tickets and paid the woman at the counter, while Rajaswamy cuddled David in his arms, sitting in the waiting lounge. 'Departure time is eleven sharp,' the woman at the counter told Eunice. She nodded. And made a phone call to Nduka.

When it was 11.00 hours, the bus left the departure terminal.

IT WAS 9.00 am. Mr. Choudhury had arrived earlier to the Rajagopalan house and Swathi offered him a cup of milk tea and a plate of Hide and Seek biscuits. They sat in the verandah and Swathi sat loosely in the chaise longue. She had just brushed her teeth, taken a bath and was waiting for the newspaper vendor who always came on bicycle. The birds chirped and her eyes roamed the whole place. Her mind was tracing Nigeria, trying to figure out what was happening to her son. She blushed, when she heard Choudhury speak.

'What, Choudhury?' Swathi was furious.

'Sorry for disturbing,' he apologized. 'But I still want to have lunch with you.'

'Stop, Choudhury,' she cautioned. 'I have told you that I'm too old for you.'

'No,' he said. 'I love you and you don't need to complain.'

Vimala stepped out into the verandah. She had overheard what Choudhury was telling her mother. 'Come on,' she said. 'Mr. Choudhury or whatever your name is, it is high time you stop coming to this house.'

'Why you talk like that?' He rose to his feet. 'Your mother I love. Why you '

Vimala raised her hand and slapped him. 'Get out!' she screamed.

The horn of a car blared before the small red gate. They turned towards it and as the gate flung open, an old and weary Anantha stepped in, with the same suitcase he had run away with nine years ago. Vimala was stunned. Anger swarmed Swathi's face. Choudhury looked on, completely flabbergasted. Anantha stopped half-way into the verandah.

'Are you back for good, Anantha?' Swathi asked. 'Anyway, this is your house. Come in!'

He walked into the verandah and Vimala took the suitcase from him. 'Welcome,' Swathi said, admiring his aging face. 'Thank God that you are finally back. Hale and hearty.'

'I'm sorry,' he pleaded. 'I was insane.'

She smiled and asked him: 'Are you sane, now?'

They embraced, while Choudhury silently walked out and almost walked into the newspaper vendor, who had newspaper dailies in his hand. Then disappeared totally. He had finally realized that Swathi's husband existed. He despised that morning, for the ill-luck it had brought to him. He hissed and walked out of the gated Rani Jhansi Road. And knowing that a black woman did live in that house, the vendor broke into their discussion and asked them to read the headline. It was: NIGERIA DEPORTS ALL THE INDIANS.

Anantha took the paper from him and read the detail. There were goosebumps on his skin. He shivered. Swathi shook. Vimala stood still and looked up to the sky. It was bluegreyblue.

'Raj!' she muttered to herself, not knowing what might have befallen him over there.

'What do we do now?' Anantha said.

'It's out of our reach,' Swathi said and slumped into the chaise longue.

Her heart began to jump up and down. Oh, these Nigerians are bestials, Swathi concluded. She looked up to the sky and thoughts raced through her head. She grumbled, rose and walked into the house, leaving Vimala and Anantha in the verandah. She walked past Farida, who was washing in the kitchen, with black velvet sprawled over her head, down through her shoulders. Basanti was wiping the dinning table, with a neat rag. And as she saw Swathi, she paused to greet her. She didn't reply, because one half of her was there and one was in Nigeria; there was no way one part could answer her. Basanti sighed and continued with her cleaning. She entered the puja room and knelt before the shrine. She prayed fervently and then left.

Swathi could possibly be described as a Hindu fanatic. But Vimala and every other person who knew her very well were surprised when she consented to the marriage of her son to Eunice. Vimala thought it was something that had to do with making her realize what had happened. 'Mama, that girl is a Christian,' Vimala had told her. She replied: 'And your AIDS husband too.' That was the way the whole thing pummeled through and she blessed the marriage. As confused as ever, Anantha left the house, went to Sarovar Hotels and Resorts to ponder over what his wife and son had discussed. He called in a friend over some shots of whisky, told him some parts of his dilemma.

'You get rid of that *kala*,' his friend had advised.

'*Nahin*,' he objected.

'So, what do you do?'

'I don't know,' he confessed. 'I should offer her money to

leave my son.'

'*Kitna paisa?*'

'*Paanch crore rupiah.*' He meant five crores rupees.

'That's stupid of you.'

'What do I do?'

'Kill her.'

'No.' And his no became a capital NO. Being unable to stand the gossips in the circus of his friends, he decided it was better to go and live in Mumbai. And he did so. But now, he was back and had been confronted with a reality that was sticking out its teeth to bite him. He shivered, entered the house, grabbed a desk phone, and quickly, with his shaky hands, dialed some numbers.

14

The Shraadh for the Little Man

IT WAS 5.00 am in Nigeria. Nduka drove speedily through the street, as mist covered the windscreen of his car. Lagos was engulfed by church bells tolling for Sunday masses. He muttered things to himself. Thank God that he didn't go to the village. Who would have done this? But not going to that village was wholly his decision, because of his mother. He despised her so much, for her constant pleads for him to get married. He decided to stay in Lagos on exile. Never to go back. Fast enough, he got to the ABC Transport terminal at Jibowu and parked his car.

Last night, a group of boys after hearing the news on TVs and radios, converged on Palm Grove Estate and began to loot the properties of the Indians living there. Nduka had heard the screams, yells from the Indians, and came out to watch, when he saw how one of the boys kicked an Indian man, pushed to the ground, in the face. And then shot him in the forehead. Then the boys advanced to his house and before they could arrive, he opened the gate for them to see him.

'Wetin you want?' Nduka had asked them in Pidgin.

The boys stopped. 'Na you?' one of them said, as if they knew him well enough.

'Ugh?' he hissed.

'Why you allow make we do your job for you?' a second boy asked.

'What?'

'You no hear wetin de government talk?' a third asked.

'I did,' Nduka leaned on his gate. 'But they never asked you to kill them. They just announced their decision so that the Indians would start going. Not for you to kill them.'

'Wetin be drastic action, jew-man?' a fourth said.

'They said that you should take action on anyone who stays behind,' he said. 'And they haven't even started going.'

'Dat one na your business,' a fifth sniggered. 'And we hear say you get one for inside your house?'

'No, he's Lebanese.'

'Na de same people,' they concluded.

Nduka said they were not going to enter his compound. He brought out his mobile. 'I'll call the police,' he told them and they laughed. He was amazed. He made a call to a police friend of his. And within some few minutes, a police man in a black uniform arrived, with a black baton. It was the policeman who spoke to the boys in a mellowed voice and they deserted his house. Nduka gave him some naira notes.

As he walked into the Arrivals Lounge of ABC Transport, he waited impatiently for Eunice to appear with Rajaswamy and David. From a distance, he saw them and rushed to them.

'Raj!' he said. 'No time for courtesies. You have to get into the boot while I drive you to the airport.'

'Why?' Eunice asked, shivering.

'These miscreants are killing any Indian, any Asian,' he explained. 'And I wouldn't want anything to happen to

Rajaswamy. He has to get into that boot, so I could smuggle him to the airport or he dies. You understand?'

She nodded and quickly they ran to the car. Nduka opened the boot, a huge Rajaswamy folded himself into it, and he slammed it closed. Eunice lowered David in the backseat of the car and sat with him. Nduka started the engine.

They got to the airport safely. Rajaswamy got out of the boot. They left their luggage in the car, and Eunice carried David as Nduka joined them racing into the Check-in Lounge. 'I got Bellview tickets for you all,' he told them. 'The flight number is B3 270.' He handed some bluewhite coloured tickets to Rajaswamy. He looked at it. It was a Lagos-Bombay-Delhi flight.

He watched as they were checked in. Then Rajaswamy was cuddling David in his arm. When Rajaswamy was checked in, a customs officer turned the back of the page where his Nigerian visa was stamped and wrote: *OBSERVATIONS. The holder of this passport has been ordered by the Federal Government and the Immigration to leave Nigeria immediately under order No. 2646.* She stamped and signed it. Then Eunice shoved her passport to the officer, who glared at her. Eunice looked away with her tearful eyes.

'You are Nigerian, woman,' the customs officer said.

'Yes,' she answered.

'An order has been given for us not to allow Nigerians travel to India.'

'I'm married to an Indian,' she said pointing at Rajaswamy over the counter. 'And that's my child.'

'Sorry.'

'You can't be only sorry,' she said. 'My son is sick and he needs to be looked after.'

The customs officer excused her and went to call a superior officer. When the superior officer arrived, Nduka crossed a barricade and came to the counter. In an almost crying voice, he explained to the superior officer that his sister needed to go and take care of her son who was sick. The officer said no. Nduka pleaded. He said no. Nduka pleaded and tears rolled down his cheeks.

'Alright,' the superior officer said. 'If she wan go, make she go. But if anything happen to am, make she no come begin to dey blame us.'

Her passport was stamped a departure stamp, but wasn't signed. She passed and they bade farewell to Nduka, who quickly disappeared from the place.

The plane went up into the air. David crouched on his mother's lap, looking straight into the eyes of a Sikh gentleman who was sitting near him. He wasn't afraid of the Sikh anymore. At a time, Eunice felt dizzy. She looked around and saw how the Indians in the aircraft stared at her. Rajaswamy bent over, wrapped his hand around her and kissed her. She exhaled.

Eleven hours passed.

They got to the C.S.I airport, Mumbai and the Sikh gentleman who had been sitting with them in the plane, followed behind them as they walked to the Domestic Lounge of the airport. They had gone to Nigeria with some things, but had left with nothing. They got to the Checking Lounge and it was the same Sikh gentleman who showed them to the Air Deccan counter and they got checked in and a bus took them to the plane. 'I'm Navjot Singh,' the Sikh told them. 'I'm Rajaswamy,' he said. The Sikh gentleman pitifully said that Eunice should allow him carry David for her because he found that she was tired. And David who had suddenly fallen asleep was heaped like a woodcock onto the shoulder of the well-turbaned man. They got into the plane and after two hours, they were at the domestic lounge of the Indira Gandhi International airport.

Eunice noticed something about David. She asked the Sikh gentleman to stop. And he did. She felt his body. It was cold. His eyes were milk-coloured and half-open. He was not breathing. She held her heart. She screamed to Rajaswamy as they got to the car park, 'David is dead!!!.' Rajaswamy choked. There were goose bumps on his skin. He became too fragile and sobbed, like a child who had just lost his mother. He couldn't say anything. 'Why?' he soliloquized. 'Why did this have to happen to me?' He coughed and asked the Sikh to just put him at the backseat of a taxi they had booked at the airport. He did. Eunice threw herself into the car and Rajaswamy sat with the breathless body of his son at the back. Then the taxi driver drove out.

Past Vasant Vihar.
Past Ring Road.
Past Chandra Marg.
Past Chandni Chowk.
Past Chowri Bazaar.
Past Civil Lines.
Past Kashmiri Gate.
To Panchkuia Road...

...And drove into Rani Jhansi Road. They passed the Gopalakrishnan house, past the Frazier's and Jashim's, which is now being occupied by a new neighbour, this time around a Vietnamese, who had come to India to learn spoken English. Mr. Naif who was strolling towards them, waved. They didn't reply. He sighed and continued going. As soon as the driver halted in front of the Rajagopalan house, Rajaswamy brought out some rupee notes from his wallet. '*Kitna hua*?' he asked the driver. 'Five hundred rupee.' He paid him and was out of the car. Eunice carried David out. The driver reversed and drove out.

Rajaswamy gently pulled the gate open and walked ahead of Eunice. They stopped as they saw Swathi and Anantha sitting in the verandah. When Swathi saw them, she rose and Anantha did the same.

'*Chalo*!' Rajaswamy told Eunice. 'Go!'

Eunice stopped to greet Swathi and Anantha, but Rajaswamy grabbed her and took her into the house. Swathi and Anantha followed them. Rajaswamy carried David and laid him on a straw bed in the drawing room. Eunice bent beside him. And when they turned, they saw faces: Swathi, Anantha, Vimala, Farida, Basanti, Pankaj, Raghu.

'Anything?' Rajaswamy asked, too confused. But the question wasn't meant for anyone.

'What's wrong with David?' Vimala said, coming nearer.

Eunice gave a tired smile. 'He's dead.'

There was silence.

Vimala quickly turned to Raghu. 'Get out!' she screamed

and Raghu ran out of the room, ran upstairs and as he entered his room, he locked the door from inside and lowered himself to the floor crying. He wept. Oh, he had told David that Nigeria wasn't a good place, still he was adamant. So, what Picard said about their birthday party being the last supper was true? He cried. He could visualize David being bitten by black mosquitoes. He looked at the four walls of the room and cursed the birds that chirped. He buried his head between his legs and drops of tears fell to the floor. *Ram nam satya hai*, Raghu said to himself.

David was cremated on the next day. Pankaj drove Rajaswamy for six hours to Haridwar, to dispose of his ashes. Since Rajaswamy arrived India, he hadn't spoken to Anantha, even while Anantha begged, going down on his knees. When they returned from Haridwar, Rajaswamy instructed that the sitting room be kept bare. Its furniture and tables were removed.

Relatives from Chennai and Delhi came to mourn the death of David. Helen came alone. For nothing went up, without coming down. If there was nothing that really moved Eunice, it was her son's death. She visualized him sitting and eating a peach; how he would smile. Now, he was nowhere to be found. The fishes in River Ganges had fed on his ashes, Eunice thought and streaks of tears rolled down her face. She couldn't hold herself. She believed that her pride, her happiness had gone.

'Don't worry.'

'Everything is going to be alright.'

'He's still coming back.'

'Only god knows the best.'

These words kept ringing in her ears. The relatives prayed and prayed. For the soul of the departed. Swathi couldn't be consoled. She wanted to cry her heart out. She couldn't hold herself because she had lost one of her fingers. If Rajaswamy knew that his son was going to die just like that, he'd have done something. But he knew that things could simply change in one day. That God Himself didn't even know when any man would die.

Vimala entered her car and drove through Main Bazaar to Connaught Place, and stopped at Little Venice. She got down from her car and made way into Little Venice, where she sat down on one of the seats and picked up a menu. She ordered for a bottle of Maaza and pizza. She was served. Her mind raced back to Raghu, who had finally locked himself in the room. With no food. No water. And didn't want to open the door for anyone. She knew that David's death was going to traumatize him. If she knew earlier, she'd have done anything possible to break the chord that held the two of them together. Her mind twisted over the fact that there was nothing so sparing that could have caused this tremor. She felt a bit shaky and her eyes turned red. She slipped out a pack of cigarette from the breast pocket of her coat and lit a stick to smoke. A Little Venice waitress politely walked up to her and said, 'Sorry madam, you can't smoke here.' She was startled and then in a few minutes, began to think deeply, stuffing the cigarette in an ashtray. For all her life, she had never seen a child die like this. She knew how children died and she knew when a child was dying.

A lady walked up to her, wearing a tight blouse and short skirt. Vimala looked up at her. 'Anu!' Vimala screamed and they embraced. 'How are you?' Anu asked in Hindi.

'I'm alright, dear,' she said.

'What's being happening?' Anu excitedly said. 'When did you come back from London?'

Vimala cheered up. 'It was this month,' she cheered.

'Where do you stay now?'

'Still in our house.'

'On Rani Jhansi Road?'

'Yes.'

'By the way, ain't you married?'

'Oh come on!' she squealed, sitting on the seat opposite her. 'I'm no nun and now live with my husband in Mauritius.'

'He's African?'

'*Nahin*,' she sniggered. 'I couldn't have. It's against the Hindu tradition and to be honest with you, I don't like them.'

'So who's he?'

'Bihari.'

'Really?'

'Yes,' she smiled.

'That must have been a tough decision?'

'Not at all,' she said. 'I was off to New York and one day, my father called on the phone and told me that they found an eligible groom for me. We arranged the dowry.'

'You love this man?'

'Yeah, I do,' she leaned on the chair. 'But it was a tough battle anyway. He had this moustache that I didn't like. His Bihari accent was confusing. His eating habit was primitive. You know I had to bring him over to the US. He kept on eating with bare hands even in front of my white friends.'

Vimala laughed.

'And I threatened him with a divorce.'

She shrugged. 'That was funny.'

'You think so?'

'Sure.'

'No,' Anu muttered. 'But I never made myself a fool. I became the groom after paying the dowry. I tried really.'

'Tell me more,' Vimala demanded.

Anu smiled. 'You know,' she continued, 'I helped him get a job at an internet shop. He worked for a short period, before his employer complained that he sneaked out and returned chewing gutka and betel nut. And he was sacked. And you just can't imagine how this man eats. Ah!'

Vimala laughed and people in the restaurant turned to her. She hadn't even touched any of the things she had ordered for. She couldn't have, when she had seen her long lost friend, she had thought. But even as she was almost laughing her ribs out, her mind raced back to where Raghu was.

'So tell me,' Anu demanded, 'where are your husband and son now?'

'My husband is in London and my son is here with me.'

'Good,' she sighed. 'I hope things are working out fine between the two of you?'

Vimala went down. She had been trapped. She wasn't used to lying, so why should she keep on lying to someone with whom she had been close enough for a long time? She was troubled. Did Anu know of her husband and was trying to get the gist from her? Could she gather the courage to tell her? No, she couldn't.

'Oh!' she exclaimed, looked at her wristwatch and got up. 'I have to be on my way home now, Anu. This is my card.' She slipped out a business card into Anu's hand.

'I'll call you, ok?'

'*No problema,*' she said in a fake Spanish accent and briskly walked out of the restaurant, while Anu smiled as she left.

RAJASWAMY WENT INTO THE STUDY and tapped on the computer keyboards. He punched out two pages of a long article and sent to a newspaper company. That evening, he got a reply from the editor that his article had been accepted and published. As he re-read what he'd written, he realized he only blamed the Indian government for the mass deportation of its citizens from Nigeria. He argued that if India had adhered to the diplomatic talks with Nigeria that what happened would not have happened. He came out of the study into the parlour where his parents, Vimala, Eunice were having discussions on various issues.

'I'm proud of you, son,' Anantha said suddenly.

'Thanks,' Rajaswamy finally said.

Swathi said, 'I wonder if your father was proud of you, Anantha. I think you were more of an idiot.'

'Yes, I was,' he confessed. 'I treated my own son with spite and hatred. I made him feel I hated him. Even my daughter in-law.'

'Have you changed finally?' Vimala asked.

'Yes,' he said and tears trickled down his cheeks. 'I realized it was of no use being hostile to the same man who will burn the pyre when I die. My pride.'

They watched him in silence as he talked. He was such a great orator. His days at the Delhi High Court were summed up as the days of a 'judicial tyrant.' Whenever he was to preside over cases then, lawyers who couldn't speak English quietly told their clients, 'No English.' And that was it. Of course, he never spared any lawyer who came to court and spoke Hindi. He would not listen to such trash. He said that if the Indian lawyers were to dress like British lawyers, that they should be prepared to speak English in courts. Unless they dressed in dhoti kurta, they could speak Hindi. His dismissal of lawyers who couldn't speak English became rampant and the media began to criticize him. He didn't change. Oh, Anantha was an Indian who stuck to his decisions. But as he sat in the rocking chair, he realized he had not kept to his decision to not to return to this house he left nine years ago.

'It seems Nigerians have one heart?' Vimala asked Eunice.

She yawned. 'I can't concentrate, Vee,' she complained.

They understood her. She couldn't concentrate on anything because her pride had gone and there was nothing left for her in this world. She was going crazy.

Vimala remembered Raghu. 'Where's Raghu?' she asked them.

'He hasn't yet come down?' Rajaswamy asked.

'No,' Anantha said.

Vimala rushed upstairs and when she got to Raghu's door, she kicked on it, screaming: 'Come out, idiot!' No one answered. 'Raghu! Raghu!' She shouted. But no answer. She ran down to the parlour and told them that Raghu had refused to answer her. Swathi, for fear of another loss, suggested that Pankaj break the door open. Pankaj went up for the job, while they followed him. When the door finally tore open, they saw Raghu's body sprawled in a pool of blood beside the leg of his bed, with the sharp edge of a knife thrust into his smooth flesh. Vimala shouted. She squealed; Swathi fainted, and falling backwards, Pankaj caught her and made her sit in a chair. For Eunice, she stood like a rock and was looking at Raghu in horror.

'We need to leave this country to the UK,' Rajaswamy whispered to her.

But she wouldn't say anything, with the heavy drops of tears rolling down her eyes. Then like Lady Macbeth, sleep-walking, she stepped out of the corridor, shivering. Her hands shook. Goose-bumps gathered on her body. She shivered. Shook. Shivered. And tears rolled down her cheeks ceaselessly.

TWO WEEKS HAD passed then. Labata had been sacked for taking Eunice and Rajaswamy to Owerri, for their escape to India. Udunna and Hatsu had left with their children. And Chief Mobutu won the primary elections against Professor Machiavelli, who for one day never organized any party for his supporters. He lost completely and went on to criticize the Chief Mobutu's party.

Nduka returned to Ezeoke finally. But he lodged at Bossman Hotels and vowed not to set his eyes on his mother. He wasn't someone who kept to his decisions but now he was keeping to it. He watched as youths queued up at companies, formerly controlled by the Indians, for job interviews. He realized that the whole place was busy. He came to the road and on the other side of the road, there was a pub. He went there and sat for some drinks and also to listen to the news of the mass deportation.

'Dis decision wey de government take na de best,' one of the three boys sitting round a table, drinking palmwine said.

'Na true,' the second added.

'I mean am,' the first continued. 'E be like say something touch dis government.'

'Dem no say the youth dey suffer,' the third said. 'You no know say wen dem Indians dey here, na so-so slavery dem dey do us?'

'You talk true,' the second sneered. 'I swear if I get that one wey Chief Mobutu dey hide for him house, kai, I go kill am.'

Last week, an angry mob consisting of youths from Ezeoke had protested in front of Chief Mobutu's house and demanded that Ranganantha be handed over to them. When he said no, the mob began to throw stones at his house, breaking his louvers and glasses. Having stationed armed soldiers around his house, he ordered them to disperse the mob. The soldiers tried, but the mob advanced more and more. He, Chief Mobutu, grabbed a gun from one of the soldiers and fired at the mob. Someone fell down. The mob scattered. It happened to be Benjamin. What Mama-Nkeukwu said was that he had killed his son with his own hands and so should not answer any questions. There was no case registered against him.

As Nduka listened to the three boys, he discovered that there was a strong hatred in their minds.

'Next are the Chinese!' a boy shouted from within.

'Yes,' another added. 'Those ying-wing-chong people.'

As long as Nduka could recollect, he read news of the murder of a Chinese family at China Town in Lagos. The whole thing was depressing to him. And the way Uncle Kezie spoke about the Indians the first time they met in the US, while he was still at Harvard, he understood that the Indians didn't like black people. But he, Nduka, was just being hypocritical. While in Harvard, to say the truth, he had spat into the face of an Indian who talked to his girlfriend, a white. To his amazement, the

Indian didn't do anything. He just walked away, smiling. Nduka
thought that the smile meant vengeance. For weeks, he saw the
Indian who would pass him and in a friendly manner wave to
him. Even without his white girlfriend telling him, Nduka made
up his mind and as the young Indian was passing, he stopped
him and apologized. They became very close friends.

Papa-Nkeukwu bore something in mind, even as he was in the
verandah, reading *The Secret Doctrines of Jesus*. Mama-Nkeukwu
had no idea why he was so much drawn to that book. She
complained that the cat be taken out of the house. Papa-
Nkeukwu said she must be mad. She said the cat must be killed.
He told her that if that cat was killed, that she wasn't going to be
spared.

Dada Felicia was seriously sagging in weeks. She came
out to the verandah and sat on one of the sofas.

'Stop reading that book!' she suggested to Papa-
Nkeukwu while they were alone.

'Shut up!' he shouted at her. 'Stop being a lesbian.'

'Huh?' she was astonished.

'Each and every one of us has a secret we are afraid of,' he
said. 'You think I didn't catch you?'

'When?' Dada Felicia shook. Was he referring to the one
she did yesterday with Mama Benji, who was feeling reluctant to
go to court over her son's death? She had been told that you can't
win the government in courts.

'You think I don't know?'

'How did you know?'

He laughed and said, 'Since your husband threw you
out!'

15

The Revelation

THE WIND of death blew through her ribs. Eunice felt the pangs of loneliness trying to bewilder her. She was surprised, for the death of her son, for the death of her husband's sister's son and for the sudden return of her husband's father. It would be better to return to Nigeria, she told herself. She knew it would be a right decision if she did go back to Nigeria. Of course, she would, but for Christ's sake, why did this happen to her? She realized quickly that she had just left her husband and the others in the corridor and began to walk down to the verandah.

She lowered herself to one of the chairs in the verandah and tears rolled down her cheeks mercilessly. She looked up to the sky and walked as the moon walked out, piling an angry smile on her. She looked away and began to move *nwayoly* into the garden, where her son had played cricket with Raghu and Picard. It made no sense to her. Why was she going there? She wept.

'God!' she confessed. 'Whatever my ancestors have done

that had laid this curse on me, quell it. I'm young but nervous. I don't know anything about this.'

She remembered something that moved deep in her. But she couldn't tell it. In her dream, she had seen that same albino dwarf who took her up to a hill and showed her a village. 'This is nineteen thirty-six,' the dwarf had explained to her.

In that village, there was a man called Akajiegbe. He complained seriously in the mornings when his child, Onwubiko was young, how the church bell disturbed him a lot when the Christians went for their morning devotion. He complained and complained, and, oh, nobody listened to him. Then one early morning, he rushed to the church (before the sexton would reach) and waited for him. When he finally arrived, he got hold of him and hacked him to death. Then buried him in the garden along with the bell.

The village of Ezeoke was saddened by the sexton's disappearance and so, the elders gathered in the obiama and deliberated on it. They resolved to do ozanmanya, a ritual that has to do with pouring the dregs of wine at the centre of the village to the Gods, in a bid of asking for their vengeance. Two elders performed the ritual while others watched. And tradition demanded that no woman should ever be present as that ritual went on. Clear that there was no woman in sight, they began. As they proceeded, the two elders begged the Gods to inflict untouchability on the family of anyone who had committed that crime: the sudden disappearance of the sexton and church bell. That the sexton should reincarnate into the family and wipe away their happiness, their joy and any chord that held them together. Done, they poured the dregs and chorused in unison: 'Ka ome!'

The dwarf was the sexton, he had told Eunice. And explained to her that was the curse that made the Onwubiko house a string of ume, a caste that could be counted more toxic and lethal than the osu. And when it began to manifest, Papa-Nkeukwu had no option than to keep the secret, for he believed he had little days on earth. He was wide-eyed as to why the customs of the pagans fought for the church. Of course, he learnt people were scorning the act and that Christians were shouting: 'May God forgive those who committed such crime.' And Amadioha was somewhere venting His anger on some people that had ruined the life of a Church Child. He stuck to keeping the secret. Yes, he held the secret, but kept going to soothsayers. They told him that the family of anyone who committed such act would weep tears, without knowing that it was his own family. That even if their children were married off, no matter what continent, that they would still bring unhappiness into that family. Yet, he kept to the secret, trapped with him in the wheelchair.

So, the dwarf had told Eunice everything and had concluded that he was taking David into his grave because he was him and he was *him*. Eunice had laughed it off.

Now, as she walked in the garden and tears flowed down her cheeks, she understood the harm she had done to the Rajagopalan's, for getting married to their son. All the dwarf said was true, she told herself. If it were not true, why was she so unhappy? She began to cry aloud and she looked down, she met with the shadow of a man. Not the dwarf again! She turned in fear and it was Rajaswamy, her husband. She embraced him. Then they kissed passionately, for the death of their son.

Partly (*on Eunice's side*) for the curse and on Rajaswamy's side, for the oath he had taken with the Aishwarya Rai-face shaped girl.

She thought of the photograph of David which hung in the empty sitting room and streaks of tears fell down her cheeks.

The picture had been taken by Rajaswamy during that year's Holi, which they had celebrated in Kerala. David had painted his face and head with red colours and garlanded himself with colourful flowers, which Raghu thought was fascinating. His spotless teeth stood out a bit while he looked on with a winsome smile, which troubled Eunice a lot and something crashed in her inside. Her eyes moved slowly and she found the copy of Salman Rushdie's *Midnight's Children* she had been reading, sprawled dirtily on the grass before the verandah. David must be reading it now, she thought. Only Abyssinian children read *Midnight's Children*. The moon had begun to walk into the cloud, frowning.

Acknowledgments

Abha Iyengar treated me like her own son, while I lived in her mother's home in New Delhi. She worked so hard for me and even though I had nothing to offer, her mother, Mrs Kusum Arya made me feel at home, instilling in me the fact that I was like her grandson. While living in that serene and quiet home, Abha's husband, Vinod and daughter, Radhika made sure I felt comfortable. Her sister led me into the *real* world of the Indians and made me relaxed, while correcting my misconceptions about the Indians. This family remains a great inspiration to me and I remain ever more grateful for everything, for being there for me always.

It was during the 2nd International Writers' Festival in India that I met Abha. I thank Dev Bhardwaj and the India Inter-Continental Cultural Association (IICCA), for inviting me to India and for making my stay memorable, taking us, the participants, to several 'holy temples' and exposing us to India's greatest places.

JD never left me in the dark as others did. He stood there for me, even in the darkest moments. For the financial assistance which kept me alive in India and for those countless mails and calls that tend towards making me a better writer.

Jahman Anikulapo, for introducing me to the world, for shouting my name before anyone else. I'm indebted to Molara Wood, for her honesty and tenderness.

Uzodinma Iweala, for making out time to read through my manuscript and for returning those mails. Teri Sillo, for the phone calls, mails and bunch of suggestions.

Tidolis Snaitang, my angel, my heavens, for being there and for never letting me down. For sitting with me in the gurdwara to talk about my stories.

Sir Innocent Ebere-Njoku, for never hesitating to tell people that *we* are also his children. For being a father to us as he is *to his* own children.

Ayodele Arigbabu, agent extraordinaire, best friend and supporter and all at DADA Books, for understanding me and my messy tale. Jumoke Verissimo, for nursing my baby as though it was hers. For the brilliant notes and suggestions.

Osondu Awaraka spent most of his time reading and editing the manuscript of this novel line-by-line. He made very delicate and intelligent notes and I'm humbled by his sincerity and honesty. I'm indebted to him and Eromo Egbejule, who was also ready to cross-check and make some brilliant suggestions. Thank you, for never being *too* busy for me.

Toyin Akinosho, Deji Toye, Minima Laloo, Lipipuspa Nayak, Tolu Ogunlesi, Chris Ihidero, Ugo Stevenson, Folu Agoi, Akeem Lasisi, Okechukwu Nwelue, William Dalrymple, Rana Dasgupta, Luke Dale-Harris, James Micklem, Ritesh Kumar, Obododinma Oha, Victor Rajkumar, Ugwunna Nnadum, Archana Borthakur, Juliet Bumah, Olly Anosike, Ifediora Okiche, Uche Nworah, the late Ikenna Egerue, 'Aunty' Nkechi Obiora, 'Uncle' Azubuike Nwelue, Sam Uwaleke, Venerable Collins Igwe, 'Uncles' Ossy and Ambrose for turning the pages of the life of *this* writer. And for putting them together again.

Francis Ushie, for standing behind me, financially and morally. For never letting go. Russell Hawkey, for gifting those CDs of the Beatles to me and for finding time to read through this book.

Sir Bright Nwelue, for burning the candles, so others can get the light.

Professors Femi Osofisan, Rafique Ullah Khan and Kanchana Ugbabe, for being mine. For believing in me.

Dr (Mrs) Shambhavi V.M Gopalkrishna, the first Indian I ever met, who showered me with motherly advices. For being so bold to say her mind.

Jacqueline McLellan, a Briton I met in India showered her motherly advice on me, while we sat together in a local restaurant in Pahar Ganj, sipping from our tea-cups. Tim Motz, best critic, close friend, English-master, after spending those days in the Tibetan monastery came out to teach me English. For not being arrogant. For replying to those mails.

Dr. Paschal Egerue, for everything.

Aditya, for cross-checking the Hindi words and Lauriel Moulin, for laughing at my French and for the invitation to Paris.

Professor Leslye Obiora and the Institute for Research on African Women, Children and Culture (IRAWCC) for that 'grant' to stay in school. Without you, I wouldn't think of *making* it in life.

Aditya Mani Jha and Debasish, my fellow bloggers, who never stopped commenting.

Stuart, a young Briton who was so keen to help me with my manuscript, read and offered additional editing help, after we met in a music-bookshop in Delhi.

Elder and Mrs Segun Adegoke treated me like their own son.

And without the support of Mr. Nicolas Ella and Mrs Monica Egonechi of the Nigeria High Commission in New Delhi, I would have been telling a different story altogether.

Professor and Dr (Mrs) A.C Anyanwu, for being dear to me. For giving me that Nsukka shelter that I needed the most. For being mine.

Nze Christopher Nnadum, for his fatherly and financial help. For letting me sneak into his parlour to devour some of the books in his bookcase. For trusting me to the extent that he let me stay in his house while he was away. I will never let you down.

Chief Chidebem Nwaebube, for all the support.

With her supernatural insightfulness, thanks to Sangeeta Sinha, a wonderful friend, an amazing guide and a committed editor, for working so hard.

Chukky, Chizzy, Gogo and Kaka, wonderful cousins, for 'sticking' with us no matter what.

Lizzy, for everything you've done for me. For those days that I called on you for help. For your forgiving heart. Alex, for being the big brother and Urch, for being mine.

Aunt Irene Ojini spent that November evening while eating her oranges to talk about her experience as a young girl during the war in Ezeoke. Her honesty keeps her closer to my heart. I love you as much as I love my parents.

Mr. Ifeanyi "Perry" Nwachukwu, for being supportive, Dr. Agabus Nwachukwu, for listening with rapt attention while I read out some passages of this book. For his moral support, which I cherish the most.

Barristers Okechukwu Nwelue and Chukwuma Nwachukwu for growing me up. For making me 'over-believe' in myself. For making me think more 'ambitiously' than Macbeth.

My god-father, the late Nze Henry Onyeukwe and his family, for all the assistance.

Sir Chibuzo Nwadigo, who unknowingly to him, has played the role of a father.

I wouldn't be spared if I don't mention these guys:

Chukwudi Nwadike, Chimaobi Nwokoro, Chiga Emezu Ofoduru, Ikechukwu Mbonu, Ndubuisi Igwe and loads of my friends.

Rita Dahl for, for influencing me without knowing, Aderemi Adegbite, for giving me that 'space' to dream in, sleep in, eat and read. For all. and Haresh Keswani, for the information.

For those I didn't mention, my friends, relatives, schoolmates and teachers, especially Mrs Elizabeth Nwadigo, for pushing me to the extreme, for shaping my future.
Shukriyah! Unu emela o!

ALTHOUGH THE CHARACTERS in this novel are my inventions and bear no resemblance to real persons, dead or alive, I've taken so much liberty to describe some structures as they still stand in Delhi. The Rajagopalan House, though situated on Rani Jhansi Road in the book, doesn't exist.
-O.N.

ONYEKA NWELUE was born in 1988 in Nigeria. After graduating from High School, he traveled extensively to Asia, particularly to India. He has received a grant from the Institute for Research on African Women, Children and Culture (IRAWCC) and contributes reviews to Farafina magazine and other online and print publications. In 2004, he was described in the Guardian as a 'teenager with a steaming pen'. His writings have appeared in The Sun, Wild Goose Poetry Review, Kafla Inter-Continental and the Guardian. He is presently a student at the University of Nigeria.

The Abyssinian Boy is his first novel.